Silent Danger

Writing Career Coach Press (a division of Writing Career Coach, 14665 Fike Rd., Riga, MI 49276)
functions only as book publisher. As such, the ultimate design, content, editorial accuracy, and
views expressed or implied in this work are those of the author.

Cover design by Zakr Studio www.zakrstudio.com

ISBN-10: 1938283058

ISBN-13: 978-1-938283-05-5

Table of Contents

Lesson 1: Getting ready to write

Welcome to a new way to learn writing. This is actually a book like none you've ever seen before. This book is designed to teach you how to write by critiquing another person's writing. This is the BEST way I've ever used to learn how to write.

Why is that? Because you'll recognize flaws in another person's writing that you're totally blinded to in your own. I learned this when I started judging writing contests. I began to see annoying traits in the writers who were ALMOST ready to be published. There was always something a little...underdeveloped. It is like soup that is missing something. It just doesn't quite grab you.

Normally, I found the issue was a pet phrase or a clichéd character. It got to the point that I could spot these things almost before they happened. I could FEEL the writer building up to some great REVEAL that I'd spotted 30 pages ago.

It wasn't until after serving as a judge for 20 entries of unpubbed writers and a dozend pubbed writers contests that I stepped out to being paid to edit. These were people who were one step below the entries many times. These were RAW manuscripts. I could see the great stories hidden beneath the stone of slow pacing or bad dialog. I chipped away at these and studied ways to help my clients write better. After months of doing this I finally had time to get back to my books.

What I saw STUNNED me and birthed the idea for this book.

My writing was just as bad, or worse, than the writing I'd been judging. How could I have such HORRIFIC craft? Was it always so hideous?

No, I was just able to recognize the errors now. It wasn't that it was junk, it just wasn't as good as I'd thought. I'd learned how to quickly spot errors. And now I knew how to fix them.

And that is the learning I now want to give to you.

In this book you'll have lots of space to edit my writing. Please, get a pencil. Scratch out sentences. Rewrite scenes. Move words around. That is the purpose of this. I want you to feel at liberty to edit this and learn from it.

This writing isn't horrible. It just isn't quite there. I want you to work to find what makes great writing by editing good writing.

What makes this book unique is that it was not written for a person to learn from. This book was twice a requested full by royalty publishers. This book was viewed by 3 different agents (requested manuscripts). This book was almost there, but not quite.

That is where your writing might be stuck. Now you can try to figure out why.

What are the fundamentals of great writing?

First, you have to grab the reader. You can do that with a car chase scene or

with something else dramatic, but underlying all of that is introducing a question. That

question may carry the reader for a page, a chapter, or for the entire book, but without

that question or sense of something to be discovered, you'll lose the reader.

You also need to create someone that the reader will want to know. That means

that they need to be flawed but still sympathetic. I need to care about them, but not feel

they're so perfect as to be unlikable or hard to relate to.

Throughout the course of this book you'll be learning and applying the

principles of good writing by editing another person's writing.

What are the traits of someone you like and respect?

_____
_____
_____
_____
_____
_____
_____
_____
_____
_____
_____
_____

Without using those actual words, demonstrate those traits by writing a very small scene or piece of dialog. [This is called showing]

_____
_____
_____
_____
_____
_____
_____
_____
_____

Now, create a small scenario where you [or the character you created] has to violate this most fundamental trait. Make sure we feel the conflict.

_____
_____
_____
_____

_____

_____

_____

_____

_____

_____

That is called prewriting. It gets your brain juices flowing. For more lessons on how to do that you can go to my website or buy my Writing Ideas Workbook.

_____

_____

_____

_____

_____

_____

_____

_____

_____

Chapter 1

"Much talking is the cause of danger. Silence is the means of avoiding misfortune. The talkative parrot is shut up in a cage. Other birds, without speech, fly freely about."

Saskya PANDITA

(1182-1251)

"Lying is done with words and also with silence."

Adrienne RICH

American poet (1929-)

"Therefore I will not keep silent; I will speak out in the anguish of my spirit, I will complain in the bitterness of my soul.

Job 7:11 (NIV)

Jake leaned against a large Oak tree and faced the direction of the house. The demons of mistakes past whispered their accusations, reminding him that the truth had never left; it had only been hidden. There would be an accounting, soon. Muffled sobs racked his body and his insides churned with the fear, both of what was happening in the house and what would come after. The air became thick as if the blue sky above were suddenly turning to liquid and lowering down on him to drown him even as he stood.

Above him was the tree house his dad had built for Bridget shortly after they moved here ten years ago. Now the white shutters against the pink paint was covered with smears of brown. Animals, likely squirrels, had taken up residence and he listened as they scampered about above him. Their light hearted chatter was soothing. It reminded him of the joy he'd felt with the hammer in his hand, and his sins behind him. Now they stood directly ahead as if each one were a sign post on the pathway to Hell.

All the prayers and all of the running had been nothing more than a diversion, a giant maze on a spinning floor where you ran to exhaustion only to find you were right back where you'd started. It was a fun house where the smiling faces laughed at your failings and the mirror showed you who you truly were.

And it was back to that funhouse him mom had just decided to take him.

"Jake!"

A woman's voice, his sister Bridget's, broke in and snatched him to the present. The fear ahead was replaced with the fear of what was happening at this moment in their house.

He raced through trees in the fading light toward the sound of voices. Branches clawed at him as if wanting to hold him in their sinewy embrace. He ran hard dodging low branches and jumping over roots. The path had fallen in to disuse and nature had again reclaimed its territory. Coming in the woods he'd meandered about, but now the urgency in the call ahead forced him to push straight through the trees and shrubs.

His throat burned with exertion. The dried tears of frustration from a few moments ago were now rehydrated with sweat. They completed their path down his cheeks and dripped off of his chin.

Why had he gone in the woods?

He wondered if they'd first tried to call him on his cell. The phone's signal never worked out there. He hadn't told them where he was going. How long had they looked for him before going behind the house and yelling his name?

He should have been closer to the house. He had let his emotions take hold of him again and thrust him out here, far from what was unfolding in the house. Already his promise to protect them was being challenged. These last thirty minutes spent alone could never again be recaptured.

The icy hands of death could be closing in on the house while Jake had been thinking of squirrels in tree houses. He needed to control his anger, stop getting so worked up every time his mom made one of her off-hand comments.

He whispered a prayer that all was in the house as he'd left it.

"Jake, hurry." His mother's voice had taken on the shrill tone of panic and the backdoor slammed as if replacing the period of her call with an exclamation mark. The sound echoed off of the trees and stopped the drone of cicadas momentarily.

Jake ran harder, sucking in large gulps of air. It burned his lungs like liquid fire and came out in punctuated wheezes. He grabbed his side to fight the cramp that tightened with vice grip force. He promised himself that he'd spend more time in the gym and cursed at his weakness. His feet no longer thumped on the hard ground but now made a sloshing sound through the underbrush.

He pushed his body harder, promising every muscle that they were nearly there. His toe caught on a root sticking above the dirt. He stumbled to maintain his balance and crashed hard against a trunk. Rough bark tore in to the side of his right arm. There, leaning against the tree, wheezing Jake looked through the rows of thin trees for a moment. The white house, badly in need of paint, was less than twenty yards from the edge of the woods. He could see the dark rectangles against the white background and knew he only needed to push a bit harder.

He drew in a deep breath and let it out as he used his left palm to push away from the tree. He focused his eyes on the house and ignored everything around him. His run was again strengthened and he pushed with all the force that the adrenaline in his body would give him. His breath came in and out in quick bursts with each foot plant.

In-out-in-out.

He repeated the cadence in his head to push himself. Don't give up.

In-out-in-out

The tree line was now less than five feet ahead.

In-out-in-out

He broke through the final row of trees and through the tall grass that lined the

woods.

"Jake!" Less than twenty feet ahead he now saw his little sister standing on

the back steps yelling in the direction of the path he had entered on. She weaved and

bobbed as if searching for him then turned when she heard him slosh through the tall

grass.

"Bridget. What's wrong?" Jake panted between broken breaths.

In-out-in-out

"The nurse said his breathing is changing."

Jake reached the bottom of the cement steps that led in to the back of the

house. He folded himself in half, bracing his hands on his thighs. "What does that

mean?"

Bridget didn't answer but turned quickly back in the house. Jake dusted away the dried leaves that clung to his shirt and stepped in the back door. The darkness of the room, in contrast to the light outside, plunged Jake into momentary blindness. Slowly a familiar image began to lift through the haze. The kitchen was littered with half eaten sandwiches and cans of flat pop. The metallic taste of effort coated his tongue.

He steadied his breathing by pulling in deep breaths, holding them for a moment and then releasing them in a noisy gush. The sound of blood sloshing through his veins was replaced by the ticking of the kitchen clock. Each second urged him on the last few fee to his father's side, but Jake needed to regain himself first. He had to be strong for mom and Bridget. He would have many more moments to secretly release his anguish but for now he had to be a pillar of strength, completely at peace.

He pulled a paper towel off the roll and wiped his face then walked to the fridge and pulled out a bottle of water.

He guzzled half the bottle in a few deep swallows then grabbed his forehead in response to the pain that surged in his brain.

"Ice cream headache." He muttered. Bridget laughed and Jake looked up, startled. "I didn't realize you were there." He said, then twisted the white plastic cap back on the bottle.

"I was seeing if you were coming." She said. Her face began to pale and the fleeting moment of brightness in her eyes was replaced with the dull, cataract of grief.

He followed her out of the small kitchen in to the smaller living room. The effort to slow time by slowing his pace had failed. Things were reaching a conclusion that Jake was helpless to prevent.

In the living room Bridget had taken her position at the foot of dad's bed. There was a smell Jake couldn't identify in the room. He'd smelled it before in hospitals, and once in a nursing home when he'd visited an elderly relative. He'd always attributed the odor to some kind of cleaning supply or detergent. Now Jake was certain it was the smell of impending death.

His dad was resting on the bed as he had been before Jake had gone in the woods. Mom was perched beside him back straight and fingers twisting a cloth handkerchief. She ran her fingertips around the lacy edge as if repeating the rosary on each stitch but her lips never moved. Dark circles of worry were painted under her eyes and lines of dread etched in her face.

His mom had stood vigil at his father's side, seeing to his every physical need but was even now planning to deny the man's last wish. Jake anger momentarily flared but then softened. He reminded himself of all the times his mom has issued one ultimatum or another only to withdraw without explanation or comment. Certainly her

decision to return to Blue Hollow would be the same thing. She loved the life she had

in Columbus and the friends she'd made. Returning to Blue Hollow would be like a

battered wife escaping her abuser, only to go back a decade later. With that settled, Jake

relaxed a bit and turned his focus to his dad.

His dad pulled in a shallow breath. His eyes were closed, as they had been

since last night when things turned bad. Six months of battling this cancer recurrence

had drained his dad of all color and energy. Once strong arms were now flesh draped

loosely on a bony frame. His skin leathered from days spent tending his garden was now

thin and pale.

Jake held his own breath waiting for his dad to exhale. His chest ached with

exertion from the run and he wanted to release his breath. But not until dad did.

The nurse holding his dad's wrist stared at her watch. Her face gave no

indication of her thoughts. Jakes eyes moved from her eyes to his father's chest. The

cramp in his side was now letting up to allow for a deeper ache inside.

The nurse looked from her watch, to the clock on the wall, then back to her

watch. He saw his dad's chest fall slowly and Jake released his own breath. Dad's breath

had become increasingly shallow throughout the day and more than once Jake had strained to see any movement.

He felt a hand on his arm where he'd hit the tree. It had to be Bridget, but he wouldn't turn to confirm it. His eyes were fixed on dad.

The nurse gently laid his dad's hand down and nodded.

The crashing of blood in his ears nearly drowned out the muffled whimper of his mom. He felt a hunk of his chest being ripped out.

It was over.

Jake groped for some emotion but none came. He felt utterly alone in the world. At 26 Jake was now fatherless.

Setting Up Your Opening

What questions did this opening chapter set up?

_____
_____
_____
_____
_____
_____
_____
_____
_____
_____
_____
_____

Who are the main characters? What do you know about them? What is your opinion of them?

_____
_____
_____
_____
_____
_____
_____
_____
_____
_____
_____
_____
_____
_____
_____
_____
_____
_____

How does the setting integrate with the characters and the plot? Do they work together or could this story just as easily have taken place someplace else? Why? Is that good or bad?

_____
_____
_____
_____
_____
_____
_____
_____
_____
_____
_____
_____
_____
_____
_____
_____

The illusion of Blue Hollow was not unlike many towns built primarily by

seasonal tourists. To arrive at this particular town a person would drive on I-77 in

Ohio to exit 28. Heading west they'd pick up the state designated scenic route near

Hoskinsville and meander up and down the hills and Mountains that formed that part

of the state. It was a place that more resembled Virginia and the Carolinas than the flat

farmlands that most thought of when they heard Ohio.

After an hour of driving past old homes with rotting porches that overlooked

breathtaking valleys, a green sign pointed to Blue Hollow. As the name implied, the

town lived deep in a valley along the river. Pines pointed high in to the heavens and

seemed to stretch on for miles. The ocean of green formed by pines, maples and oaks

rippled in the wind, like a single quilt covering the region.

The trees of the area were not unlike the town itself, a seeming monolithic

harmony that woke up every spring to greet the summer residents. The broad smiles

and welcoming gestures invited the city-worn vacationers to slow down, sit for a bit

along the river. A place where there was always a smile and a bit of wisdom delivered with down home charm and a slow southern drawl.

It wasn't until the cool air of fall swept in that the real nature of the inhabitants was revealed. Just as the cool air distinguished the deciduous with their flashes of red, orange, and yellow, from the conifers who held their color, the fall also exposed the presence of a few evergreen townspeople. Always true, they were plain folks.

But for others when the summer illusion faded the colors transformed from cool green to blood red, burnt oranges, and pale yellows. For those who lived there year round it was a place where the sins of the past remained as indelible as the happy memories in the minds of the summer visitors. Not only did the town remember who you were, but they never allowed you to forget.

Renny knew this as well as anyone. She had weathered the roughest winter since before she left the Hollow ten years ago. This time, she was facing the town and its people alone. Dale had died and here she was sitting in a Blue Hollow church.

She stood as the pastors walked up the center aisle to the front of the sanctuary. The wooden alter was covered by heavy fabrics. Ornamental tassels hung from the corners. She was two thirds the way back in the immense sanctuary and the air was as heavy as those fabrics.

Sunlight burned through stained glass window and splashed reds and purples on the heads of the people in front of her. The brighter colors seemed to highlight the person they fell on, as if in a heavenly glow. The darker colors shrouded the individual in condemnation. She looked down at the streaks of red and deep blue washing across her buttercup yellow dress.

Condemnation and sorrow.

The next chord sounded a familiar tune. It was just as ominous as the dark blue and red splattering on the people around her.

She sang the song in robotic fashion aware that she was making little more than a whisper.

"Glory be to the Fa-ther. And to the Son. And to the Holy Ghost."

Her daughter, Bridget, sat eight rows back with a group of friends. At least she'd come to church with Renny this week.

"World with out end. A-men. A-a-a-men." The final sound stretched on until the organist lifted her hands with a jerk. It made Renny think of what Beethoven would have looked like at the end of a piece. With wild hair flying, his fingers running up and down the keys. The notes completely unheard by the composer himself. In that soundless flailing dance, he would have ended with arms raised and head back.

But the organist did it after playing nothing more impressive than a quarter note.

For a moment nothing happened, then the pastor rose and walked to the center of the elevated area in the front of the sanctuary. His flowing black robe hanging down to just above his black polished shoes. He looked out at the congregation, taking note that all of his flock were present, and turned to face the cross. His back was now to the congregation.

"Join me in reciting the Apostle's Creed." His voice boomed over the invisible speakers all around the sanctuary. It was a trick that was done to convince the faithful that this man truly spoke for God.

"I believe in God the Father almighty..."

Renny continued her mechanical recitation. It was the same routine each week. Same responsive songs. Same creeds. Nearly an identical message. A loving God was sending nearly everyone to hell. The only way we could hope to avoid His wrath was to obey his every whim.

Well Renny had known people like that. Not someone she'd ever want to spend an afternoon with, let alone an eternity.

What do you think of this character?

_____

_____

_____

_____

_____

_____

_____

_____

_____

_____

Some writers seek to turn the setting in to a character too. Is this setting a character?

_____

_____

_____

_____

_____

_____

_____

_____

_____

_____

Why or why not?

_____

_____

_____

_____

_____

_____

_____

_____

_____

"So Renny, if you hate going to church so much, why do you keep at it?" Bill set down his coffee to cut in to his omelet. Since moving back to the Hollow Renny had met with her brother Sunday after church at Hank's diner to talk. He was the only man, other than Dale, who'd known all about her but had never rejected her. In fact, her brother knew even more about her because he alone knew of her doubts about church.

"It would kill Dale to think of his wife as lost Bill. I just couldn't miss."

"Dale's passed on eight months ago Renny."

"All the same." She said, barely tasting her pancakes.

Bill took a scoop of his omelet and grimaced as he chewed. "Hank's food is really sliding."

"Mine is fine." Renny said.

Bill shrugged his shoulders at her and drank a bit more of his coffee.

"Warm you up, Bill?" Midge's voice came from behind Renny.

"That'd be good of you Midge. Thanks." He lifted his white ceramic cup to her. She filled it then dug out a handful of creamers and put them on the small white saucer on the table.

"More water, Renny?" Midge said, friendly but without the sing-song lilt reserved for Bill. Midge was a kind woman, at least to those who liked her, with wisps of grey streaking her formerly auburn hair. She was nice to Renny, for Bill's sake, but her eyes were ever probing a person's soul seeking out their deepest shame so that it could be turned in to the fodder of conversation over a malt or mingled in to the fantasy of a truck driver rolling through town. Renny had given very little to Midge and it caused her to probe all the more.

"No, thanks Midge." Renny answered without looking up. The raw emotion of their conversation was far more than Renny could hide and it would be Midge's pleasure to probe and dig until Bill would blurt it out. Renny was powerless in this moment-but Bill was fully under Midge's spell.

Midge went back behind the counter of the old diner and Renny allowed herself to exhale. Renny had been in high school when Hank had opened the place. At that time it was the only restaurant in the Hollow. Midge was a local and had attended school with Bill. They'd even dated for a while in school but then Hank came to vacation with his grandparents and Midge found her "Beau for Life". Midge, the local, married Hank and his restaurant became a part of the fabric of Blue Hollow. Now, nearly thirty years later, it was the only one locals went to.

Bill ate another bite of his food then pushed his plate away. "Tastes like Hank rolled the thing in salt." He pulled his coffee in front of him and leaned over to Renny.

"You did all that church stuff when he was alive. If it's not your thing, just stop going."

Renny stared down at her plate, unable to make eye contact. Church was a piece of Dale. For nearly thirty years of marriage they'd attended the services, served on the boards, organized the potlucks, played on the softball teams and gone to witness to the lost. Dale came alive in church and robotic text had life in his eyes. The church calisthenics- up/down, up/down-never annoyed him like it did Renny. She'd loved Dale with everything that was in her, so she never would have hurt him by rejecting this faith he held so dear.

She'd thought the familiar would soothe her. Sitting in the sanctuary, listening to a new variation on "We're the only ones not going to Hell." But she was no longer sure it had anything for her.

"Why do you go to church?" Bill's voice was more demanding now. His tone reminded her of the one her dad always used with her and Renny struggled against the shudder of fear that rode those memories. She focused on the words rather than the tone. She studied them like an art critic might examine a statue in an exhibit. In her mind she walked around each side of her argument and the reasoning that supported it and considered its composition and style.

What was the difference between those people and the people they'd condemned to Hell? There was none. Renny knew the parishioners of the small church she now attended. They were like nearly every other Christian she'd ever met-other than Dale. They did all the same things as everyone one else, the only difference was they hid their hatred behind stained glass eyes and hypocritical smiles.

"Can we talk about something else?" She said finally. She couldn't think about all these things right now. She needed to push the 'whys' out of her mind. Otherwise she'd go back to the one big why that stole sleep from her every night.

Applying Character Lessons to your Story

What do you learn about the character by examining their relationship with others?

_____
_____
_____
_____
_____
_____
_____
_____
_____
_____
_____
_____
_____
_____
_____
_____
_____
_____

How can you work that in to your stories?

_____

_____

_____

_____

_____

_____

"So technically, I'm deaf." Dreama said. It was more a statement than a

question. Without her hearing aid in she wouldn't hear the answer anyway. In the

distance there were indistinguishable sounds but she couldn't identify them. They

were similar to figures behind a translucent shower curtain-nothing more than moving

shapes and patterns.

She held the results of her most recent hearing test in front of her, the circles,

squares, lines and Xs sealing her fate. Each ear was equally bad, registering below the

forty decibel range in almost every frequency. The changes from the last test weren't

dramatic unless they were looked at in light of the last ten years then the tests became

dramatic and unmistakable.

Push it away. Don't allow yourself to feel it.

She reached for her hearing aids sitting to her right. Over these years these

little computers had held open the door to the hearing world. She'd lived and walked

in that world and, through aggressive speech therapy, lip reading classes and her own stubbornness, hidden her deafness from everyone else.

She walked in her parent's world and denied the pull of the deaf and hard of hearing world that beckoned her with its silent symphony of movement and expression. It wasn't that she disliked hearing, it was that she didn't feel crippled because she couldn't hear. She pulled back from that path of introspection and back to the waiting world. She held on to the silence for a moment longer then reached up and clicked on her right hearing aid.

Sounds erupted in her head with the force of a sudden thunderstorm. What had been a low droning of background noise was now a jackhammer somewhere outside. The rapid fire sound was like a giant woodpecker pounding in to her skull. She hesitated momentarily before clicking on her second hearing aid and being fully immersed in the chaos. Seeing she had turned her aids on the audiologist smiled approvingly and began to speak.

"The next step, since you want to pursue surgery, would be referring you on to the surgeon. There are a few really great doctors locally who do the cochlear implant surgery."

She felt like correcting him and saying it was her parents, not her, who wanted the surgery. Eighteen may still be a teenager, but in the eyes of the law, she could make her own decisions. Instead she remained silent, only nodding at the directions and diagnosis.

"So how much different will things sound with the CI?" She'd heard it all before but it seemed that she should at least make some kind of meaningful statement at the moment. Rather than sitting there sniffling and trying to force back tears that insisted on coming.

"You will notice some difference but overall your hearing should be considerably improved." He continued. Dreama was too consumed with the thoughts screaming through her brain. She decided not to have that debate with herself at the moment.

She took the packet of papers the audiologist gave her, took the referral sheet from the woman at the check-out window and walked out to her car. The machine gun pelting of the jackhammer intensified as she opened the door. She pulled her hearing aids out and stuck them in her purse. Immediately the drumming quieted to a low hum. Like a movie where everything goes in slow motion, sound stops and all focus is on the heroine-Dreama was suddenly able to target the thoughts that reverberated in her head. She got in the car and looked again at the results.

It wasn't the loss of her hearing that bothered her at this moment. She'd known her whole like that this day was coming, and would soon be here. It was the progressive rejection of who she was by her family. As the X and O on the graph dropped down from one line to the next, each step showing her movement to deafness, her parents had sought to pull with greater fervor to keep her in the hearing world.

When she first dropped below the twenty decibel reading her parents had learned a little bit of sign language and took her to play groups with other deaf and hard-of-hearing children. English and ASL were mixed in a form of pidgin sign that everyone understood.

Then she dropped below the thirty decibel range and it became even more difficult to hear. She was fitted with hearing aids around this time and with them ASL all but disappeared. She was introduced to speech therapists and learned to lip-read-even though she could hear well with her hearing aids in.

She slid her finger down the page of the audiological report each line bringing in new memories until she stopped on today's readings. They told her that before long cochlear implants were going to be the last thread of hearing. Refusal to have the CI would effectively cut her connection.

The decision didn't need to be made today but the hearing was slipping away faster. She set the report aside and started the car. She turned down the road that surrounded the hearing center and eased the car in to traffic. Even without her hearing aids her mind recreated each sound so she heard everything around her. The chatter

on the radio would always stop to play her favorite song. She slowed at a stoplight only

to have it flash to green. Her mind amplified an indistinct sound in the direction of

the rusted Camaro to her left. She imagined the sharp squeal of pealing tires, a revving

engine and the whine of machinery.

At the four way stop her brakes would squeal slightly, not enough to get them

checked yet, but soon. She drove through a neighborhood that was being swarmed by

young children with backpacks leaving the elementary school around the corner. Their

paths were like an army of ants who just learned of a nearby picnic. They fanned from

the small road that led back to the school and filled every side road. Groups of girls

talked and giggled while pretending to ignore a group of boys showing off not far away.

The walkers must have been dismissed last because there was no sign of busses.

A couple of students looked her way nervously and Dreama smiled to assure

them she was safe. She caught the glimpse of a slicker from her side mirror and

instinctively looked. A row of cars had formed behind her and she realized they must

have been honking at her. Her face reddened and she took her foot off of the brake.

There was no logical reason for her to prefer her world of silence, and with a

CI it would still exist after she took off the gear. It would spare her the embarrassment like she'd just felt, but it was about more than sound waves on a piece of paper and the honk of a car horn.

Instead of going home she turned south east on to state route 33. She knew if she faced her parents now she would agree to the surgery. She needed to think it through first. For her whole life she'd stood with a foot in the hearing world and a foot in the deaf world. She had to decide which one she really was. And home was not where she'd find that answer. She had left her clothes in her trunk last night when she got in from school. She'd unloaded the dorm herself and couldn't imagine unloading the car.

Maybe she'd known deep inside that she'd need to get back to the Hollow.

False Friends:
Using POV to feed wrong information

Remember, our perception of the scene must be influenced by the point of view character. That means sometimes the way we see things will be wrong. That is how life is. That is how you can make your stories more realistic. What is the perception we are feeling through this character?

_____

_____

_____

_____

_____

Hank peered through the window separating the kitchen from the rest of the diner. His eyes were locked on the grey car pulling in the diner's parking lot. With a sigh he threw a patty of meat on the griddle and flipped the one he was already browning. He had set it aside knowing Bill would be in for his Tuesday burger and onion rings.

"Well Bill good to see you." Midge's voice was syrupy above the crackle of the fry vat. Hank threw on an extra few shakes of salt, as usual, then flipped the burger and did it to the other side.

"Burger will be ready in a few." Hank called through the hole. He managed to make his voice friendly and suppressed an urge to spit on the man's burger. Through the hole separating the kitchen from the serving area he could see Midge preparing Bill's special spot at the counter. She laid down a napkin and placed the silverware on top, poured a cup of coffee and pulled out a handful of cream from the back of the fridge. "Want to give the best to our best customer." She'd said when Hank had wondered aloud about Bill's special treatment.

How Bill had earned the title "Best Customer" had very little to do with the man's purchases and much more to do with Bill and Midge's history.

The sizzle blotted out the conversation except for Midge's occasional overly expressive laugh.

"Order up for table two." Hank hollered. "Bill, yours is next."

He nodded at Hank in reply and lifted his hand in a half salute, just as he had for more than a quarter century. That folksy charm endeared him to the River Rats, the summer residents. Bill had made a nice living as the kindly grandpa type who'd keep your lawn mowed and cut back branches.

Janice appeared suddenly in the window and began loading her tray with her order for table two. Her silent gesture to Bill and Midge was answered by Hank lifting the salt shaker with a smile. She nodded in approval and gave a warm greeting to Bill Colewick before taking her order to the river rats in the corner.

Janice had been the one to alert Hank to Bill and Midges oral indiscretions. That was the term she used. Hank called it love talk and they'd both done it less than a yard from where he was sweating over a greasy stove.

"Burger up for Colewick." Hank hollered.

"No need for all that noise, Hank. I'm right here." Midge scolded as she took down the plate and slid it in front of Bill.

Of course she was right there. She'd ignore the first four or five tables to stand there and chatter with her old Beau. The thought burned Hank's cheeks. He focused on his grill and left his wife to her mischief. The dinner rush would be coming in soon

and Hank dropped a vat of chicken patties in to the grease to be ready. He looked up

in time to see Bill slide his plate to the right at the same moment Midge handed him a

glass of water.

Used to be folks came in the diner to learn the town gossip, not to become the

town gossip. He'd allow Midge to think that she'd fooled her big old hubby but no

woman was going to make a cuckold of him.

A slice of conversation "get that checked Bill" floated in to the kitchen as Midge

sliced off a piece of pie and slid it before Bill.

Evaluating Dialog

Dialog is often one of the most difficult things for a writer to master. That is because
we need it to sound realistic, but it cannot model actual speech. When a writer
is skilled at writing dialog, however, there is a wealth of information that can be
conveyed by what is said, how it is said, and the non-verbal communication [tics] that
accompany the writing.

Evaluate the dialog in this book and identify what works in the dialog and what
doesn't work. Write notes here and in the manuscript itself.

***

Dreama slowed in to the final curve before Blue Hollow. During the two hour

drive she'd pushed the audiogram far from her mind. Instead she'd taken advantage of the silence to rehash her Freshman year of college. Smaller ripples of pain wiggled through her memory and she rode over each one in a boat of resignation. She comforted her wounded emotions with the balm of peace and solitude. The cabin would provide a refuge to work through the web of rejection that clung to her, even now. She soaked in the colors of flowers on tree limbs and birds fluttering from tree to tree. Safely within to cabin she could pull each decision, past and future, down and examine it from all sides, leaf through it like the pages of a book and return it to the shelf.

It would be three peaceful months before she'd need to venture back to the claustrophobic schedule and the lingering questions. She'd sent her parents a text half way in to her trip to let them know where she was going. The family had planned on coming out for the summer in about a month. She'd said she was going early to get things straightened up.

Less than a mile separated her from the solitude that her dorm room-battered body craved. The road straightened and in the valley below was a blanket of evergreens coating hidden cottages like a thick layer of green icing. The river cut a winding line down the north side of town in Blue Hollow. It meandered a few hundred feet from her family's summer cabin. When her brother and sister joined Dreama later this spring they'd sit on the bank and watch people canoe past. For the next three weeks, however, the cabin was hers alone.

She descended below the tree line along the edge of town. The car jolted as it dropped from the cement road and on to the asphalt roads that ran through the Hollow.

A canopy of maples and pines closed over her as she continued down the road in to Blue Hollow. The row of Elms that had grown with her through the years waved their leaves in welcome. As a child trees were as comforting as the quilt her mom tucked under Dreama's chin in the Hollow. Time stood still when a person was there as if the leaves of the various trees that lined the ridge of this deep valley would shield them from the truth waiting on the outside.

Reality grabbed at her insides and twisted hard. The push and pull of her mission here in the Hollow increased as she moved closer. She pushed back at the assault of lingering questions and future decisions. She felt the pull of happy memories and old friends held in this small town.

The battle to hold on to the moment surprised her. When she'd set out she knew the sanctuary of these trees and the memories that clung to them would make everything clear. Then why now this rehashing of forgotten offenses and broken promises?

Mr. Colewick's yard came in to view and with it the road back to the family's summer home. Determined to win this battle against her mind and fine the joy she craved she rolled down her window and waited for the wind to carry the scent of the river to her. It smelled of canoe trips followed by picnics on the beach. It smelled of secrets shared about boys with her sister in the firelight.

She turned on to the gravel lane that lined the edge of Mr. Colewick's property and led back to her parent's home. She stopped her car and looked over Mr. Colewick's yard. The house was situated in the center of a rectangular piece of property that was deeper than it was wide. The ranch house was surrounded by a well manicured lawn, perfect bushes and large shade trees. Despite her unexpected arrival he had already begun to clean up the underbrush along the driveway leading to her cabin.

Her eyes looked up the winding driveway went up a hill that twisted back in to the woods nearly half a mile. A small shutter rippled through her as she realized that she'd be alone in the house for the first time. The bending shadows coming through the trees held a sinister quality she'd never noticed before as if they were hiding an unseen danger.

Convinced she was overly paranoid from exercising caution while on campus

Dreama turned her focus back to Mr. Colewick's house. The smell of the river which caressed her with each breeze was only slightly tainted by the car's exhaust that mingled in. Around the side closest to her driveway Dreama saw Mr. Colewick. She honked the horn in two quick taps. Mr. Colewick set down the trimmers he was carrying and adjusted his cap. Suddenly recognition registered on his face and he began to walk to her in great strides. She climbed out of the car but left it running.

"H-I" he always greeted her by signing 'hi'. It was a small gesture that meant a great deal to Dreama. It brought him in to her world just a bit.

"How have you been Mr. Colewick?"

"It's been a good winter. You should have seen the snow up here." He held his hand to about the level of his knee. "It came in big batches. We'd have a whole pile of it then nothing for weeks." He pointed all around the yard. "It was so peaceful to look at. It was that fluffy stuff on account of the cold. Not that wet mess we're used to getting."

"We got the messy snow our way." She thought about tromping through the wet mush back and forth to classes. The idle chatter of weather, a filler to most people, was a passion to Mr. Colewick. Dreama was always amazed at how he could take something as mundane as a rainstorm and seemingly create a cast of characters-named wind, humidity, rain-and build an entire story. His back deck had various rain gauges and other instruments.

"Farmer's Almanac said we're in for a nice summer up here." He continued. "I'm trimming my bushes back now to get a jump on things. My garden back there is already getting run with weeds." He turned and motioned to the yard. When he turned the wind stole his words. She touched his arm.

He turned to face her. "I can't see your lips." she said.

He smiled and shook his head. "It'll take me a day or two to remember again." Something flashed in his eyes. It was only there a moment but the message tore at her once again. He pitied her.

Dreama had gotten quite good at masking her own emotions and without a pause he continued. "Said I had some nice peas. Got them in in time. I froze some of them, real good ones. Wanted to keep some to give your folks." He pulled a handkerchief out of his back pocket and wiped his neck then pushed the corner down in his pocket. "Now tell me. How was your first year at the university?"

"Tough but good." She smiled and leaned back on the door of her car. "College is nothing like high school."

"Ach" he swiped his hand at her "but you're a smart girl. Can't have been that tough. Keeping the boys away, now that had to be tougher."

"Well, unfortunately that was one challenge I didn't have to deal with." If she had done a better job of keeping one away. She tucked a wild strand of hair in the space between her hearing aid and the side of her head and wouldn't allow her mind to finish the though. She looked up the lane in the direction of her house. As soon as the car was unloaded she'd go for a walk by the water.

He pulled the worn rag from his back pocket again and wiped his head where there had once been hair. "So when your folks coming up?"

"Three weeks. They have to wait for Val and Avery to get done."

"Well, I won't keep you." He took two steps then continued. "My sister Renny and her kids just moved back to the Hollow and are coming over for a bit tonight. They're around your age. You're welcome to come and join us."

"Sure, that would be great. What time?"

"Well let me think now. You come on down any time after you're settled and visit for a bit. We'll be eating some time between 5:30 and 6."

"That will be fine. I'll call my parents and let them know I'm here and get unpacked then I'll come down."

"We'll see you then." He turned and raised his arm in the air to say goodbye then walked back to his hedges.

Dreama drove up the curved road past the maple and oak saplings that her brother had planted a few years back. The ginko that she'd put in was closer to the house. The fan shaped leaves had been what attracted her to the tree. She liked leaves. In early November her family always had one last family weekend at the Holler to enjoy the colors. The ground was carpeted with the remnants of last year's colors.

She knew she was rambling in her own mind about leaves to keep other thoughts about the woods away. As if thinking two thoughts at once would muddle the thoughts and prevent either from taking root. The driveway widened and the family cabin sat on two acres of well manicured lawn surrounded by large trees. She put the car in park and turned off the car. She was anxious to get back down to Mr. Colewicks and be with people. Despite the craving she'd had for solitude she wasn't ready for full isolation.

Backstory

Information that takes place before the actual events of the book is called back story. A common issue with writers is they want to insert large amounts of back story in their writing. This is a huge mistake. It distracts from the story, it is almost ALWAYS telling, and it really serves the writer more than the reader or the story.

As you're reading, look for times when it appears there is back story that is distracting because of the way it is shared or because of the amount given in a single place. Mark it here and identify it in your own story.

"What do we know on the Hillcrest property?" Janice asked, her eyes scanning the prospectus that her assistant had put together. Rows of numbers told her what the cash flow had been and what her expenses were. The numbers looked decent, but not stunning. The dropping market that had plagued many other investors and was now creeping in to her own portfolio.

"You can see the ROI is at your minimum." Walter moved close and pointed to a column of numbers. Despite having bathed in cologne that morning he smelled of day old alcohol and sweat. Janice pulled the paper away.

"Barely." The frustration in her voice was more out of her own stupidity at hiring him at this moment.

"The real estate market is bad overall." His bloodshot eyes pleaded with her. Weakness in men was unattractive. This kind of weakness in an employee was unacceptable.

"At this rate, Walter, I'm going to be living off those waitressing wages before too long."

"The Hillcrest property isn't your only property."

She raised her hand to still him before he could go any further. "But I'm seeing similar results with every file you show me."

"It's not my fault that the market-."

The chair squeaked as she leaned forward. "The key to success in any market is anticipating change and adjusting for it."

Or in life for that matter.

Walter had squandered the revenue from over a million dollars in assets in the last three years. She didn't think it was possible to be that incompetent. She had allowed herself to be dazzled by a resume full of networking groups and affiliation with various organizations. He'd even come to her with a very strong academic record. She'd made her classic mistake in selecting Walter to assist her by assuming such qualities meant he actually knew what he was doing. He'd spent all of his time learning the conventional wisdom that he was now using her portfolio of properties to practice on. And he was failing this class.

"As I told you last spring, the market has been slowing a great deal in rentals."

"Exactly, Walter, you told me as the markets were slowing. What options did you present?" He opened his mouth to reply and again she silenced him with her hand.

"You were hired to watch the market and give me input on options to prevent loss."

"And I-."

"And you did neither, Walter. I could have found the information you provided

for me by reading a blog." All muscles were now tense. It was his fault that she'd had to

go back to the Hollow. It was the only place she knew the people well enough to create

the deals that would save her business. And now that trip had brought her face to face

with Jake. She longed to release her full wrath for this entire situation on him.

"I"

"You." She finally yelled. Walter's face grew red and he raked manicured fingers

through his hair. She saw the yellow pit stains on his shirt darkening with new sweat.

"This is more than slow, Walter. I'm generating less than half of the positive cash flow I

pulled in a year ago."

"I could contact the investors out of Tennessee." His eyes were fixed on the

ceiling as he spoke.

"No." She said, her intellect once again overcoming her emotions. "I'm not

ready to sell, but what could we be building in to diversify? Precious metals have been

trending up."

Walter straightened again in his chair and began to blather about the value of

precious metals. Janice didn't let on how insulting his tone was to her; her thoughts were lost in Blue Hollow and her conversation with Charlie.

Janice sat up straight and began to rummage in her purse.

"What's wrong?" Walter stopped his monologue.

"What time is it?" She located her cell phone in her purse and checked the clock. "I need to call the diner."

"Need to check in with your boss?" Walter's mocked. She turned her back to him as the ring chirped in her ear

"Hi, it's Janice." She said. Over her shoulder Walter laughed at her sudden drawl.

"Things going well with your visit?" Midge asked, the clink of dishes nearly drowning out her voice.

"Yes, Auntie is doing much better than I'd thought she was." Janice stuck the files back in the case she'd brought in to the office then leaned back in her chair. "The both of them are doing real good, thanks much for your concern."

"If you'd like I can hold things down here so you can rest a bit longer with them."

"That would be wonderful, thanks so much Midge." She closed up her pen. Needles of guilt poked at her but she pushed them back. She'd be visiting her Aunt and

Uncle soon so it wasn't quite lying. Her stomach wasn't content with the justification

and tightened. The acidic taste of vomit crept up her throat. She sipped on her coffee

to hold back the next wave.

"Think nothing of it." Midge said. Janice quickly finished her call then ran to

the bathroom. By the second heave she'd regretted her breakfast choice and was silently

repenting for each thing she'd eaten that day.

"Are you alright in there?" Walter called through the door. She rinsed her

mouth quickly and pulled together what dignity she could muster before walking out

of the bathroom. Walter's face was twisted to that of someone who'd stepped in animal

waste.

Without a word Janice collected her things and turned to leave the office. The

outside air flooded in as she pushed the door open. Diesel fumes and tulips replaced

the smell of body odor and cologne from inside the small office. Janice sucked in the

air suddenly refreshed. She turned to Walter.

"You're fired." She said, and then walked out the door.

Info dumping—Back story, only WORSE!!

At the end of the last section we talked about back story. That is where you share information that is really outside of the story. When someone puts in a large amount of back story—or when they simply share a large amount of excess information— that is called an info dump. These are extremely common in the manuscripts I edit for clients. All of us have a tendency to want to make sure the writer 'gets it'. The problem is that an info dump is a lazy way of showing that information.

As you're reading, watch out for large sections of back story or information. Flag them and rework them.

By the time Dreama brought in the last load of clothes the cross breeze had nearly replaced the smell choking of dust with the cool smell of the river, moss and sweet flower blossoms. She was sweaty from her work and the damp air raised goose bumps on her arms.

She reached in the purple backpack leaning against the couch and pulled out a brown envelope stuffed with paper. Her parents had sent information to her at school about cochlear implant surgery. She had stuffed the information, unread, in this envelope. Now, one piece of paper at a time, she read about the surgery that her parents had determined would fix her.

Tears rolled freely down her cheeks. The fist of rejection once again squeezed her heart as she saw page after page of solutions to "Dreama's problem." Of course, it made no sense why she rejected the surgery. People with CIs were very happy.

But so were deaf people.

Again the irrational voice grabbed hold of her and welcomed her in its accepting embrace. When she surrendered to it the answer was always so clear. Why couldn't she simply articulate these feelings?

Because they were simply NOT rational. She had no reason to give her parents that satisfied their needs. Until she did she knew the packages would keep coming and she'd have to push back the culture she felt drawing her in, for the one that was rejecting her.

She checked the satellite connection on the wi-fi, the area was far too remote for DSL or cable, and logged on. She saw that her dad was still in the office on her instant message buddy list.

"You got there safe." An IM box suddenly popped in to say.

"Yes. I'm here." Her father asked her a bit about the trip out and the condition of the house and she assured him that everything was fine and that Mr. Colewick had done a great job of keeping the place up and doing the spring landscaping.

"Your mom will be jumping in soon. I just called her at home." Her dad said with an emoticon of a winking smile. She sent the winking smile back but wasn't interested in letting her mom "have her say" this time.

"I'm here." Her mom's greeting popped in on the IM box. She responded to all the same questions she'd answered for her dad about the trip and her mom asked a bit about the bulbs.

"I think the tulips are poking through already. They may bloom before you get up here." Dreama typed, hoping that her mom wouldn't decide to come in for the weekend so that she could be sure and see the flowers. To her relief her mom only asked her to photograph them if they opened before June. Her dad next asked about the doctor's appointment.

"I'm losing more hearing." Dreama typed. She chose her words very carefully and decided not to say that things were getting worse. She'd remembered some lecture in Fall semester that talked about how vocabulary choice affected perception of a situation. She needed every arrow in her quiver to prepare for the questions she knew she'd next have to defend.

There was a long pause and then her mom was the first to respond. "Did the audiologist make any recommendations?"

"Yes." Dreama typed, then clicked send.

Her dad responded next to the unspoken portion of her answer. "We really think you should consider this option, Dreama."

Of course he did. Dreama put her face in her hands, again trying to find words inside herself to help them understand something she couldn't even articulate fully. It was her decision to make, but she needed them to understand why. She typed slowly, "I don't want to." Then she deleted what she said and typed. "I'm not sold on it yet."

Her mom's response was immediate, "What is so bad about hearing?"

Dreama reached around the computer and ripped out the wi-fi card. She tossed it on the couch next to her then pulled out her hearing aids and tossed them in the same place. The tweet of birds was gone as was the humming of the fridge and the CD playing in her laptop. She watched the seconds tick by as the song continued to play.

"If a CD plays in a laptop and there is no one there to hear it, does it make a sound?" She signed to the computer.

***

Renny washed the last dish and set it in the drying rack. Outside a sparrow darted its beak in and out of the hole in the bird feeder while on the ground a squirrel grabbed the corn and seeds that dropped. Her back was tight and she rolled her neck from side to side trying to loosen the muscles. Before Dale died he'd come behind her in the chair and massage away every tension in her shoulders. Now her best relief was to stretch out on her bed and close her eyes for a few minutes.

She walked down the short hall admiring the empty walls and closed doors. She'd been careful not to make this place too comfortable or homey. To do so would violate Dale's memory in some way, as if her joy would call in to question the love she'd felt for him. Once again conforming to a set of rules she'd neither seen nor understood Renny walked, head hung low, in to her bedroom.

She pulled off her shoes and blue jeans then climbed in bed. She only needed a small nap before she got ready for the picnic. Bridget was down the hall studying and Jake was out for a drive. She'd thought this would be a homecoming. It was lonely. Sleep climbed over her and wrapped her up in the promise of escape. As she slid in to her subconscious a memory crept in of her teen years in the hollow. Instead of drifting to sleep she drifted back in time.

She dropped her towel at the edge of the grass and stepped onto the cool mud along the edge of the pond. The water was clearer on this edge, if a person called muddy brown water clear. Down along the far end of the pond under the train trestle the water was full of green pond scum and snapping turtles. She stepped down in the cool water. Teeny fish scattered at her feet while the water spiders surfed on the waves she stirred up. She walked until she was knee deep then dropped to her knees, lifted her feet and swam with long strokes to the cattails on the other edge.

The chirping of cicadas and croaking of frogs was broken only by her occasional splashes. She warmed up her muscles slowly and progressively sped up with longer arm strokes and harder kicks.

"Thought I'd fine you here."

Renny stopped and stood in the waist deep water. Her older brother Bill stood next to her towel on the shore.

"Had to get out the house a bit. Daddy's at it again." She walked up to the shore and picked up her towel.

"You think running off to the mud hole's gonna make him warm up?"

"No but least I ain't got to hear it for a bit." She dried her face and wrapped her towel around her body. Even though it was just Bill she didn't feel proper standing outside the water with nothing but a swimming suit for covering.

"Well, they sent me out to get you."

"Needing supper?"

"Probably." Bill stuck he fingers in the back pocket of his jeans and scanned the pond. "You really think swimming's going to get you out of the Hollow?"

She followed his gaze to the dragonfly buzzing around the cattails. "Don't know if it will or not. Ain't why I do it."

"But if it could..." He snapped off the train of thought and turned to her. "If you could get out, would you go?"

She shrugged her shoulders and turned back to the dragonfly. No need to fill her head with all that mess anyhow. Things in the hollow pretty much always the same, factory work, working in one of the five businesses that made up the downtown or raising babies. She planned on doing the last, and being darn good at it. Didn't want to ruin Bill's dreaming none though so she allowed him to imagine her escape.

"Ready to go back?" She said.

"Yes." His quiet tone told her he wasn't. He loved walking the woods at the edge of the pond much as she loved swimming in the pond.

"Want to walk the woods a bit first?"

He turned to her and smiled. "Not on your life. This time of day in late May. You're just asking to be dinner for every skeeter around here."

She bent down and dried off one foot then the other and slid them into her shoes. They were wore out and dirty but they were the only shoes she had except for the black ones. She saved them for church.

She led the way up the hill to the railroad tracks. They walked along the tracks for a long while with the only sound the crunching of their feet in the stones that lined the track.

"You're going to try out for the team, right?" Dale's voice startled her. She took a moment to form the answer.

"Been thinking on it." She tried to make the answer sound as if joining the swim team were a fleeting thought rather than the all consuming desire it actually was.

"You should." He kept his eyes straight ahead. "You're good."

She smiled and looked back at the train tracks. Some of her happiest and saddest moments were spent along this stretch with Bill. This was spring of Bill's senior year. In a couple weeks he'd be graduating and joining daddy over at the factory. She was only finishing up the tenth grade but she understood better than most that Bill was too big for the hollow. He could be one of them big important people she'd learned a bit about.

"Bill?"

He grunted in reply.

"You ever think of leaving the hollow?"

"Never." His words were quick, as they always were when they discussed him leaving. Overhead a bird screamed at them from behind the apple tree blooms. The two of them continued on in silence to the road. She stepped off the rocks and on to the dirt road.

"Aw, Renny." Bill said. She stopped and turned back to look at him. "I left my pocket knife back at the mud hole."

"Want me to go back with you to-."

"No, you best be getting on home before Mama gets turned inside out." He spun around and went back down the tracks. She watched him go the first few feet then tightened her towel around her and started up the dirt road to home. The tracks were elevated and she allowed her pace to quicken to build momentum up the big hill to her house. She'd heard about rich people living up on hills but here it was the poor ones living on the outskirts of the hollow up in these hills where winter ice and spring rains kept a person trapped half the year.

She reached her yard and before she could get to the back of the house her mom yelled through the screen window.

"Bout time you got back here. For your sake I hope you got something fast planned cause your daddy ain't gonna wait for supper."

"I do Mama." She said as she came in the house and scurried to the back of the house and her room. It was impeccably clean with her brush sitting on her small dresser and the faded scrap-patch quilt her grandma made pulled to cover most of her bed. She opened the bottom drawer of her two drawer dresser and pulled out her pair of jeans and a brown T-shirt.

"Renny." Her mom yelled from the other room. "Daddy's going to be here in an hour. Best be getting along in there."

She was going as quickly as she could. She picked up her small hand mirror and moved it around to see what she looked like. "Awful, but it'll do." She said then stripped off her suit and put on her clothes. No doubt her daddy would comment on her smell but that was preferable to him getting supper late. That was for sure.

There was no time to wash up the suit in the sink so she went out the back door and hung her suit and towel on the line to wash after she'd done the evening's dishes. Corn bread was fast enough. Thirty minutes and she could have that done but what else could she have done up quick.

"Where's your brother at?" Mama yelled from in front of the TV.

"He had to go back for something he dropped. He'll be along before supper."

She moved the quart of spoiled milk, if she had time she'd make a sour milk cake with it, and looked in the back. Nothing but mushrooms and a few greens but it'd have to do. She washed and cut the green up small so they'd cook quicker and put them in a pot with some water and bacon grease. She remembered that piece of meat from two days ago so she pulled it out of the fridge and fried it in some butter then added flour and milk.

"That about done?"

Renny turned and saw Bill sneaking in the back door. "Yeah, why?"

"Daddy's coming up the road now."

"Thanks. Mama wants you in the front room." He nodded and walked in the other room while Renny pulled out the large plate and heaped up greens, fried potatoes, creamed beef and corn bread and set it at Daddy's spot before putting the rest in serving dishes and setting them on the table.

The back door squeaked open and Daddy walked in. His shirt was grimy and his hair was matted back with sweat. He walked straight to Renny and put his arm around her.

"You know what I said earlier was for your own good, right?"

"Yes, Daddy." She nodded as she spoke but never looked up from the counter.

"I just don't want people filling your head with all sorts of foolishness is all."

"Yes, Daddy."

He pulled her against his chest. He reeked of body odor and gasoline. She tried to breathe only through her mouth to avoid some of the stench.

"Renny, darling, you stink like pond water." He said then walked to the sink and scrubbed grime off his hands. "Don't sit too close to me or you'll spoil my appetite." He winked at her.

"I'll go freshen up now." She went quickly down the hall and washed her daddy's sweat off of her cheek then wiped her body down and put on a bit more deodorant. The house was stuffy and there was no airflow in the kitchen. If anyone was going to smell up the kitchen it wouldn't be her. "Mama, Bill, supper's ready." She called into the living room on her way back through. She pulled the sour milk cake out of the oven and sprinkled it with powder sugar.

Daddy said the blessing and they started spooning food on their plates as Daddy dug into the food on the plate Renny had prepared for him.

Bill leaned over to Renny. "You pulled it off after all."

"Told you I would."

"Dad." Bill's voice was deep and forceful. The voice reserved for speaking with other men.

"Hmm?"

"You know Renny here's real fast in the water."

"I heard." He said then jammed a forkful of greens in his mouth.

"Word is she could be fastest in the county."

Daddy set down his fork and looked over at Mama before turning to Renny. "I suppose you're going ask about that swim team again."

"Daddy, I-." She stammered

"Renny we been through this." He bit off some cornbread and swallowed it down with sweet tea before continuing. "It ain't that I don't think you're good, but I don't see it is proper for a girl to be off sleeping in them hotels and doing God only knows what."

"Now, Dad." Bill jumped in. "Renny wouldn't never do that."

"Renny's a good girl." Mama came in. "But all them other people out there ain't so good. She's just impressionable."

"But Mama-." She tried again but it was the three of them now.

"True but I trust the coach." Bill leaned on his elbows as he spoke.

"Now a man spending all his time with girls in swimsuits." Daddy shook his head.

"I was thinking on that same thing." Mama pointed with her fork as she spoke.

"I personally will take responsibility." Bill said. Renny looked over at him. She wasn't quite sure how he'd be able to do that.

"You're willing to keep an eye on your sister and be sure she's not in trouble?" Daddy said then looked from Bill to Mama. Bill nodded. Suddenly all eyes were on Renny. Her cheeks burned with the focus of their stares.

"Well Renny." Daddy cleared his throat and continued. "You make the team and we'll let you go so long as you keep out of trouble and don't neglect your chores."

She jumped from her chair and ran around the table and threw her arms around Daddy. "Thank you Daddy." She squeezed him tight around his neck and looked up at Bill. He was chewing with a smile on his face. Thank you. She mouthed and Bill nodded in reply.

Preaching isn't for Books

How many times have you been reading a book and suddenly the story paused to force some political, social or religious view on you? Was it irritating? Distracting?

_____
_____
_____
_____
_____

While it is sometimes more common for a character in a Christian/inspirational book to preach, the fact is that I've seen NYT best selling writers of main stream suspense stop the entire action to give me a lecture on the environment or their thoughts on a political party. Readers read for entertainment, not to be lectured.

It is logical for a politician in a book to talk about a bill or a pastor to share scripture, stopping the story in order to lecture is poor craft.

The characters in this book are Christians and sometimes preachy. How could this be rewritten to be more organic without stripping that part of the character completely?

_____

_____

_____

_____

_____

_____

_____

Jake parked the car at the top of the hill and looked over the peak. He

allowed the wind to caress his cheeks and remind him of a time before life became so

complicated. To his right was a small picnic area with six wooden picnic tables and four

metal barbeques. It was a favorite spot of his dad's. A metal guardrail surrounded the

area. Behind him, to the north of the parking lot, there was a bathroom. When he lived

in The Hollow as a child there hadn't been any plumbing up here. Now there was a

drinking fountain, a few vending machines and flush toilets.

No one was at the park other than him. The variety of beer bottle caps and aluminum can tabs told him that it had become even more of a teen and young adult

hang out than it was when he'd moved away ten years ago. Even then it had already

begun to transition to a place that families rarely visited. The steep drop beyond the

guardrail and the blind turns the entire way up had made it less attractive to parents

with a van full of small children.

He turned to the south and the road that wound back down this hill, the one

he'd brought up here. He listened close for traffic. There was not a sound. The rocks

crunched under his loafers as he walked to the blacktop road. He turned to the right

and walked tight against the side of the hill. The layers of blasted stone rose on his right

as he rounded the first curve. There were only two feet between the painted yellow line

on his left and the wall of rock on his right.

As he came around the second curve his heart thudded fast. As if recognizing

their destination, his entire body began to fight. His palms were clammy with sweat and

his arms shook. A few steps further and his legs became weak and he battled the urge to

turn and run back up the hill.

He had to face it. He pushed hard. The scene more familiar.

He couldn't.

Cursing himself the whole way back up the hill he marched. The shaking stopped with each huff but his anger at his own fear and its power over him introduced a new tremble: a tremble of rage. In a few minutes he was back at the park. He walked to the bathrooms to splash water on his face and regain his nerve. He pushed the door open as was assaulted by the pungent smell of urine and standing water. He backed up and the door blew a final assaulting breath at him as it closed.

He walked to the edge of the rail and tried to look down to the spot. It was not quite visible from where he stood but he guessed the drop to be at least forty feet. He looked at the spot where the fear had been too great to go on. He'd been less than ten feet away.

He walked back to one of the picnic benches and sat down. He shuffled through the files of his memories to find a happy day with his dad in the Hollow. He'd remembered when he was fifteen and Bridget was only five or six the four of them had come to this place for a picnic after church. They ate cold fried chicken, potato salad, lemonade and grapes. They had laughed at the grapes as they rolled off Bridget's plate and placed a game of bocce ball in the parking lot.

And now he was back. His mom had ignored Dad's dying wish. Jake refused to forget his promise and so was sucked back to the Hollow.

***

Dreama stretched long on the sofa then looked at her watch. She must have dozed off. Her head was heavy and her tongue stuck to the roof of her mouth. Her hearing aids sat where she'd tossed them. She picked them up and put them back in. The first sound she heard was the chirp of her cell phone.

"Twelve missed calls?"

She slid the wi-fi card back in her computer and brought it out of sleep mode. Almost immediately a dialog box appeared.

"?????" Her dad had typed. Dreama thought for a minute before responding. She couldn't tell her parents that she'd essentially hung up on them by ripping out her internet connection. Her fingers hovered over the keys waiting for an answer. She flipped the cell phone open to confirm what she already knew: Mom.

She found the closest thing to the truth she felt comfortable saying. "I lost my connection." She typed.

There was nothing for a long time then her Dad replied. "And your phone????"

"My hearing aids were out."

She could feel his disapproval over the miles. Her mom popped up a few moments later. The pink letters of her IM read, "We'll talk later." And then her buddy list showed her mom had signed off the computer.

"See you in a few weeks. Will talk before that. Bye, dad."

She stood up and walked around the couch. This was her parent's house and every cushion and throw reminded her of that. She picked up her keys and put her IDs in her back pocked then walked out the door.

The wind blew her hair across her face as she walked down the wooden porch steps. The cool hint of evening scented the air with camp fire smoke. She tucked a few unruly strands of hair behind her ear and looked up at the leaves. When she was little her sister tried to describe the sound of rustling leaves. Dreama had only begun to lose her hearing then and Val was always amplifying the hearing world for her big sister.

"The leaves sound different in the summer when they're in the trees." Val had said. "Once they get dry and fall they scrape across the ground." To demonstrate Val pulled a large green Maple leaf off of their family's tree. Then she picked up a dry one that carpeted the floor of the woods that surrounded their summer cottage.

She'd covered her palm with the green leaf and held Dreama's cheek with it. It was cool and moist. Then she put the dry leaf in Dreama's palm and folded her fingers around it. As the leaf crunched it poked the tender part of her palm. Val had smiled and said "Now when you lose all of your hearing you'll be able to remember it by crunching the leaf in your hand."

Dreama pulled herself from the memory and pulled a leaf off the Maple and pressed the cool fingers to her cheek. Then she picked up a dry one and crunched it next to her ear. It made a crackle sound as she smashed it.

"I still hear it." She whispered.

***

Jake walked up and down the aisles of Charlie's boat rental shop. A man stood at the counter studying a black card of fishing lures while chatting endlessly about how eager he was to get on the water. Jake thought about the days in the water with his dad. Despite the river that divided the town most of the year-round residents of the Hollow didn't fish. There were a few places that only locals swam at, but he didn't share this town's obsession with fishing.

Charlie was the closest thing Jake had to an ally in Blue Hollow. The store dated back to the days when Blue Hollow began its transition from small town to summer retreat. The walls were covered with framed yellowing newspaper clippings of fishing festivals and Charlie teaching summer residents, the locals called them river rats, how to fish. The inside of the shop had wood floors and smelled like moss, mud and worms. It was a place for people to come and buy bait in the morning, then buy a malt and share their fishing tales in the afternoon.

"Jake, what can I do for you?" Charlie's voice snapped Jake back to the present and he turned from the clipping he'd been reading. Charlie stood with his arms folded tightly across his chest. Despite their mutual dislike of Bill Colewick and Janice, there was really very little love between Jake and Charlie.

"I was hoping you had thought more about my business proposition." Jake said taking a seat on one of the three barstools that lined the counter.

"I don't know Jake. I don't see how it could work around here. The town likes it quiet and trying to bring in tourists, other than the regulars who live in the cabins, doesn't seem like a way to make friends."

"I didn't ask if we'd make friends." Anger seeped in to Jake's voice but he caught it quickly. "I asked if we'd make money." Jake leaned forward and smiled. Charlie had never been a person to pass on an opportunity to earn a few extra dollars. Charlie's face softened a bit, almost to a smile, then he opened the door to a small dorm refrigerator below the counter. "Well, I don't know how much of that we'd get either." Charlie pulled something that resembled a box of dirt and began filling a Styrofoam cup with worms.

Jake leaned forward on his elbows. "Charlie, there's money to be had with the river and all that land. I'd do it myself but I don't have the credibility with the bank you've got."

"Or with Blue Hollow." Charlie held Jake's stare for a moment. The silence

hung between them. "Why don't you talk to your uncle about it?"

Jake sat up. "I'm barely on speaking terms at the moment."

"Jake I just don't think I can do it."

"How did they get to you Charlie?"

Charlie looked out the front window, then back at Jake. "You best be getting

along, Jake."

With nothing more to say Jake walked out of the shop and plopped in to his

car. Fingers of warning poked at him and he clicked the power lock on his car. The

plan to turn the Eastern edge of the river in to an indoor water park was worth more

than a few dollars. Jake looked through the trees to the slope on the opposite bank.

Charlie owned the ten acres on the opposite side. He stood to earn a small fortune by

developing it.

Uncle Bill wouldn't give Jake the money he needed to develop further down the

river. His uncle would claim it was out of principle but Jake had made a promise to his

dad to help his mom.

He let out a sigh and flipped on the radio. He needed to make an appearance at his uncle's cook-out. The only other person with the contacts and the cash like Charlie

was Uncle Bill. Once again the Haller had squeezed the dreams out of him.

Heavy-Handed Foreshadowing

Watch out for Heavy Handed foreshadowing. While this can be as obvious as the clichéd "Little did he know there was an axe murderer on the other side of the door", sometimes it is more subtle and shows up with the writer taking a clue one step too far.

As you read, look for places where the clues were well placed as well as places where they were overly obvious. Note them in the story and look for them in your own writing.

_____

_____

_____

_____

_____

_____

_____

_____

_____

_____

Dreama parked the car halfway up Mr. Colewick's driveway and lifted out her

picnic basket. The air was thicker than it usually was in May but a cool breeze carried on it the promise of an evening rain. Dreama walked to the front door and peeked in the large front window that ran nearly the length of the front of the house. A long couch that appeared to be dark beige was against the opposite wall and a recliner was to the left. The room was small, nearly a perfect rectangle, and she could see straight through to the backyard where Mr. Colewick was carrying an armful of split logs.

She walked to the edge of the porch to walk to the back when a shadow darted in to the bushes that separated Mr. Colewick's property from her family's driveway. She froze, searching her memory banks for a more detailed image of what had just been there. The icy breeze blew across the hairs standing on Dreama's arms and gave the sensation of tiny bugs crawling on her body. She tried to reassure herself that it had been a startled fawn but her conscious thought rejected the explanation.

She searched for the slightest indication of what she'd seen in the bushes but whatever it was had run quickly through the rows of brush or was silently waiting for her to pass. Again she repeated words of comfort in her mind. There was no reason to feel the stab of fear, but something deep within Dreama would not allow her to brush away instinct so quickly. There had been something in the bushes and whatever it had been had taken the path leading to her home as refuge.

Suddenly the terror that had held her ankles firm like quicksand released and she moved quickly around the house in search of the comfort that comes in groups. Mr. Colewick had dropped the pile of wood on the ground beside him and was studying his outdoor grill.

"Am I the first one here?" She called from the picnic table. The attempt at sounding casual for the lurking bush creature had come out forced. Mr. Colewick nodded without turning around. He was focused on adjusting a metal grate inside the makeshift outdoor barbeque.

***

Renny chopped a head of lettuce with trembling hands. Her conversation with Bill had churned up piles of slime from deep within her. Her pulse quickened and the safety of her bright kitchen was covered in sack cloth.

The choking smell of sweat filled her nostrils and she heard laughter. First one voice, then dozens laughed at her. Unseen hands groped her from every direction and tore at her clothes and hair. She didn't fight, she couldn't fight. The terror of the moment enveloped her in its suffocating embrace. Things that she'd thought were long buried now flashed in front of her like a macabre slide show. As if an unseen hand were clicking through snapshots of her life, images flashed on the screen.

"Mom?"

Renny spun around knife raised defensively. Bridget stood in the doorway

mouth open wide and terror burning in her deep brown eyes. Renny let out her breath

and lowered the knife, though not releasing it.

"I'm sorry darling." Her voice squeaked and she swallowed hard to clear it. "You

startled me."

"Sorry." Bridget's eyes were still fixed on the knife. Renny set it down and

folded her arms around her in an attempt to look natural and to protect her body from

the unseen hands she sensed were waiting to grab at her again.

"What time are we leaving for Uncle Bills?"

"As soon as I get the lettuce chopped up for the salad." Renny said, turning

again to the cutting board and taking up the knife. Bridget let her mom know what

she'd be wearing and offered to dig a few yard games out of the garage. Renny agreed

that each idea was good without fully considering anything her daughter was saying.

The laughter was again ringing in her ears, and with it, the memories.

***

Dreama scanned the length of trees that lined the long drive up to her parent's

summer home. She had never before considered the dangers in the woods. In fact,

she'd never had any sense of danger in Blue Hollow. This year was very different. It was as if a film of darkness was covering the tops of the trees, never fully letting the light in.

She glanced around seeking some bit of motion in the trees. Not even the breeze was blowing at the moment and every leaf was still as if in anticipation. She struck a long wooden match against the outside of the box. The flame flared then settled and she touched it to the paper. The flame climbed from the bottom of the paper and then in to the teepee of small sticks and split wood. She struck a second match and lit the other side, then walked back to the table to see what she could do to help Mr. Colewick.

She busied herself at setting up the table and stole glances across the yard to be sure the smoke was rising from the burning logs. The sense of freeing independence was giving way, if only slightly, to loneliness. She busied her mind by folding the paper napkins in to envelope shapes and stuffing them with silverware.

"You must be the young lady who lives up the drive?"

Dreama looked up to see a woman in her mid-forties holding a large wooden bowl. Her eyes were deep brown to match her hair and wisps of grey streaked past her pale skin. Although she smiled there was pain in her eyes and she seemed to curve the corners of her mouth up with considerable effort. Dreama wondered if it were possible that such a woman were Mr. Colewick's sister. She realized she was staring and replied

"Yes, I am." She extened her hand in greeting. "Dreama."

"Dreama? What an unusual name. I'm Renny." She shook Dreama's hand and turned to the right "Over that way is my daughter, Bridget, and my boy Jake should be along shortly." Despite the heat the woman's hand was like ice and Dreama had to stifle a shiver.

They continued to set the bowls around on the table and chat. Dreama joined in, one eye always focused on the grove of trees behind her.

***

Jake snaked his way through the center of town and thought of his dad.

Spring had been Dad's favorite time of year. An outdoorsman at heart, his dad would tell him stories of tent camping and waking to snow on the ground or other such 'roughing it' tales when Jake would complain about cold hardwood floors or drafty windows. His dad always had a tale to recount with a smile on his face and a wink at the end-in case you missed the humor.

This would be the first Memorial Day weekend Jake wouldn't go camping with his dad. In fact, he wouldn't go camping at all. His mom had sold the camper before moving back to the Hollow.

"They're'll be no place to store it and I'm not one for camping."

Jake wanted to buy it but he had no place to store it either. So it was one of the many things to be sold off quickly after Dad's death. She'd packed away his dad in cardboard boxes and shipped the memories to storage or Goodwill stores before Jake could grieve. Sometimes when she was gone Jake would sneak to the storage unit and grieve for just a bit.

When they set out to their return visit to Blue Hollow the one redeeming thing was he'd thought that the familiar roads, parks and people would bring back memories of his dad. Up until eleven years ago, Jake's whole life had been spent in the Hollow with his parents and sister. On these streets he'd skinned his knees learning to ride a bike, stole his first kiss from a girl in the eighth grade and learned to drive in the downtown parking lot.

But every memory in the place had been scrubbed clean of his Dad. Their old home had been demolished and a two story pre-fab had been built in its place. Most of the people here would have only vague recollections of who Dale had been, if they remembered him at all. Many of the kids Jake had gone to school with had realized the limited income potential of the town and struck out in search of their own futures. The year-round people who remembered his dad had their memory tainted by how his dad had defended Jake after the accident.

Driving through the town Jake was struck by the large number of trees compared to the city they'd moved here from. The town reminded him of a Venus flytrap. The plant opens wide and entices its victim with a sweet nectar. Inside there are numerous sensitive hairs that wait to sense the movement of prey so the jaw-like leaves can clamp shut around the fly. The pointy ends of the plant becoming prison bars as the carnivorous plant digests its prey. Then, after a few days, it slowly opens. The gentle breeze blows away any remains of the digested fly while at the same time carries out the sweet smell to the next victim.

Jake now spent each day waiting to hit the sensory hair within the Hollow that would close the trap around him. His dad had known the potential evil in this town which was why he'd insisted they not return.

But his mom had insisted that they should.

His mom had never fully left the Hollow, even though they'd only visited a few times since moving away-and then only to visit Uncle Bill. Something other than history tied her to this place and while Jake had promised his dad to help his mom adjust to widowhood, Jake was increasingly aware that to keep that promise could mean the surrendering the hopes he had for his own life. As well as the dreams his dad had left the Hollow to maintain.

Jake arrived at Uncle Bill's house shortly after 6pm. About three hours remained of daylight but the darker clouds to the west brought with them the promise of early nightfall and a spring storm.

He prepared for his mother's glare at his slightly tardy arrival but instead found her engrossed in a conversation with Uncle Bill. Bridget likewise was involved in a conversation, but with a girl about her age.

"Bridget, c'mere a second." Jake touched his sister's shoulder gently as he spoke. She turned to look at him, then excused herself from her current conversation. Jake smiled a silent greeting to the woman and stepped back far enough that the unknown guest couldn't hear what he said. Then he recounted to Bridget his conversation with Charlie.

"I wouldn't think too much of it." She said after he'd told her everything.

"Don't you find it the least bit threatening though?"

Bridget shrugged as if trying to reassure a madman that his tirade was justified then looked over her shoulder back to the woman she'd been speaking with. They walked together to the picnic bench and sat down.

"I'm Jake." He said extending his hand.

"Dreama." She said and smiled slightly.

Jake returned to his own thoughts as Dreama and Bridget occupied themselves

with their conversation. His mom was not making eye contact with Uncle Bill, instead

focusing on the toe of her shoe. She looked away and appeared to swipe a tear from her

cheek. What was it that could have her so upset? Jake bumped Bridget on the arm.

"What kind of mood is he in?" Jake motioned to Uncle Bill with a quick flick

of his finger.

"I don't know. I was talking to Dreama."

Jake nodded and focused again on his mom but was pulled out when he heard

his name.

"What?"

Dreama smiled at him from across the table. "Are you always so serious?"

"Oh, I'm sorry." He searched for an excuse for his rudeness that wouldn't

require an explanation. Finding none he took an old regular, "Rough day."

"Sorry to hear that." Dreama said. "What do you do? Mr. Colewick never talked

much about a family."

"I'm not surprised." His tone slipped out more negative than he'd intended.

She paused, as if unsure how to continue, "He preferred to talk about the local

lore, the river level and last year's snow." Dreama smiled.

"He has always been a huge fan of current events." Jake jumped headlong in to the excuse for Uncle Bill's oversight that Dreama had provided.

"When did you move here?" She said as if searching his face for some familiarity.

"Late last fall. We're actually from the Hollow. We moved a little over eleven years ago when my mom found a job up north of here."

"I wondered why I didn't remember you."

"We moved away when I was sixteen. I didn't visit Uncle Bill much in those days."

"I don't imagine you did." Dreama paused as if considering something. "That was about the time we got the cabin. I was nine then. I should have remembered you."

Jake heard his mom and uncle moving closer. He struggled to pick up some piece of their conversation. He looked suddenly at Dreama. "What? I'm sorry."

"It was nothing." She said and she seemed to retreat. The open smile faded slightly and her eyes. What was it about them? He tried to think of a way to pick the conversation back up. Then an idea broke loose in his mind. "Dreama, where does your family live when not in the Hollow?"

The last bit of sparkle drifted away. "Columbus." She said and immediately he knew he'd chosen the wrong subject to shift to. Rather than make another blunder on

this already messed up day Jake stood and walked in the house.

When you write dialog watch out for a few common issues.

- Ending every, single piece of dialog with 'Said' or some derivative [commented, sighed, yelled, screamed, etc.]
- Flipping the said. This is a recent thing I've seen and it is so irritating. It looks like this. "I was going to the store." Said Elliot. "Not without me." Whined Susie. It just feels awkward
- Writing like we talk [with lots of uh, or um]
- Writing long speeches or 'monologing' or phonetic writing [more on that in other sections].

Chapter 3

The trees thrashed beneath the security light outside as if distorted shadows of a ring of dancers. Dreama put her hand against the glass. The wind vibrated the windows. Dreama's hearing aids were on in a small saucer. She enjoyed experiencing storms unaided. The steady flashes of lightening followed closer and closer by rumbles that she could feel deep inside her bones. As the storm drew closer it would slowly enter her range of hearing.

When the hearing world heard loud crashed and bangs that sounded like every tree was being ripped from the earth and split in two, Dreama would hear faith echoes, more like rumbles and growls than full sounds.

Something, a figure, darted in to view and disappeared quickly. Dreama jumped back and screamed. The sheers fell softly against the lampshade allowing Dreama a closer look at the peeping intruder.

It was her reflection.

She was not fully convinced that the hollow eyes that stared at her from the glass was indeed the one she'd caught a glimpse of when the lightening outside flashed.

Just in case there was someone in the wilderness outside her home she put on an air of confidence and slowly lowered the sheers, pulled the drapes, picked up her hearing aids and put them in as she checked the locks on all the doors. The wonder of the oncoming storm now eclipsed by the suffocating isolation she'd felt earlier in the day.

She'd weathered storms here with her family. More likely than not, she'd soon lose power and rely on the candles she'd set out around the house. With the power would go her connection to the outside world. The only phone in the house was a cordless. While it had an amazing range that allowed them to sit in the back yard and talk on the phone, it was completely useless in a storm. Her cell phone would work but she'd forgotten to charge it and didn't want to risk plugging it in with the lightening.

She walked up the steps with a candle in her hand. The power wasn't out but she didn't want to be trapped upstairs without light if she lost power. She turned on the tub and let it begin to fill. No power meant no pump, and no pump meant no water.

She debated going to bed so she wouldn't know if she lost power. Fear of the dark couldn't grab her if the house was already dark. She looked at the clock. It was far too early for her to go to bed and have any hope of sleeping.

The afternoon at Mr. Colewick's replayed in her mind. The family was nice enough when Jake, Mr. Colewick and Renny were not exchanging cold glances at each other. In fact, she'd enjoyed talking to Bridget and Jake. Throughout the evening, however, she couldn't shake the feeling Jake was trying to see through her. It was as if he were probing her mind with his eyes. She broke his stare more than once but when she'd look at him again-

She shuddered and pushed the feeling away.

It was possible she was seeing too much in to the glances. He'd said very little to her or anyone else the whole evening. If he'd been a bit more personable he'd have been almost attractive but his dour expression and clear animosity stole whatever benefits he gained with deep brown eyes.

The tub was nearly half full so she turned off the water and picked up the book she had been reading. It wasn't so much reading. Really it was more looking at a page full of letters while thoughts of college and the afternoon vied for her attention. Her book opened with handsome man finding the dazzling woman on page five. By the end of the book they'd be in love. She wished things were as easy as the book she was trying to read. In real life, relationships were built over time with a great deal of work and effort. They took prayer and understanding and a bit of luck.

After reading the same sentence for the third time she stuck her bookmark in the book, set unlit candles in each room and started dusting and cleaning. For some reason concentrating on finding hidden grime or a spider web helped her clear her own thoughts. This trip alone to the Hollow was meant to clear her head not clutter it with new problems.

She moved her course schedule off the table. Her freshman year of college had been challenging. The questions she'd left college with, however, were far worse. She tossed the catalog in to the newspaper pile and went back to dusting.

A lightning flash outside brought her back to Blue Hollow. Thunder rumbled and growled then crashed in a violent burst of lightening. The storm was right on them.

Maybe writing in her journal would be a better way to occupy her mind. Rather than being exhilarating, this storm was conjuring up the fears of childhood. Doing a second pass around the house to be sure every door and window was locked she climbed the steps to her room. She changed quickly in to her pajamas praying the lights stayed on long enough for her to jump in the bed. She picked up her journal but decided instead to read her Bible for a little while.

She lit the oil lamp on her nightstand and turned out the light. She wouldn't know if the power went out.

She prayed for morning.

***

Janice pulled the raincoat tighter around herself. The rain ran down the slick plastic and formed a river that seemed to want to flow directly in to her oversized fishing boots. Jake's car was still in Bill Colewick's driveway and she hid herself in the trees that ran along the property line.

She'd returned to Blue Hollow after visiting her aunt and uncle. She still had two hours left to her shift, and Midge clearly needed the help. She'd stayed until the last trucker filled his stomach, and his thermos, and helped Midge lock up.

The winds were beginning to kick up and she knew the storm would shield her from the snooping of others. She put on her rain slicker, rubber boots and binoculars and made her way to Bill Colewick's house. She wasn't sure yet what she'd planned on doing when she got here, but she'd felt driven just the same.

Now, standing outside as the rain pelted against the hood making loud drumbeats she watched.

Jake paced back and forth in front of the large front window. She wasn't close enough to see his face. She looked to the driveway where Jake had parked. She could sneak across the yard and let the air out of his tires. That would force him to lay on the wet ground and change the tire in the pouring rain. Knowing what she did about Bill and Jake's relationship the boy'd be out there himself in the dark trying to do it.

But then she considered that he might have roadside assistance. He could sit dry inside his car and wait...then she'd be forced to stand in the rain.

The idea was no good.

It was too tame anyway. No high school prank or roll of toilet paper would fix what Jake had done to her.

She stood in the rain and let the hatred ferment.

***

"Uncle Bill, hear me out." Jake had waited until his mom and sister left before talking to his uncle about his business proposal. Before Jake had set out the papers Uncle Bill was already waving it off.

"Jake, I'm getting too old to get involved in some risky scheme to-"

"But it's not risky. The bank looked over my business plan and they said it makes good sense."

"Well, if it makes such good sense they can put their money behind it, not mine."

"They would if I could have someone like you to say you back me up."

"Which you don't have." His uncle tossed the paper.

Jake slammed his hands on the table frustration coursing through him. This is exactly how he'd expected the conversation would go. Jake already had an uphill battle trying to convince his uncle to support him without the deep tension buzzing between

Uncle Bill and his mom all night. He looked for calm words to persuade his uncle, not

the accusing ones that flew so readily from his mouth.

The wind howled through the trees that surrounded the house and the thunder

pounded. Had it been a clear night Jake would have likely stomped out the door and

out to his car. Instead the pounding rain on the roof held him in the house.

"You're just a bitter old man Uncle Bill." He finally blurted out when no other

words came.

"Oh am I now? Was I a bitter old man before you come looking to clean me out

or only now when I decide I want to protect what little I got." All small town charm left

and pure anger remained. Jake remembered the last time Uncle Bill looked like this. He

shuttered with remembrance but held firm.

"What little you got?" Jake stifled a yell through clenched teeth. "You've got

more money than most people in this town could hope to have."

"It is no concern of yours."

Jake knew where a good deal of the money came from and that only intensified

his frustration over the injustice of this situation. He came to build his own future,

however, and if he pushed back a little, Uncle Bill might concede. He pulled out a group of papers that were clipped together he handed then to Bill. "What would you change in this business plan to support it?"

Bill took the stack of papers and looked at them one page at a time. He stopped once or twice as if concentrating on a point or preparing to speak. Jake held his breath and waited. Uncle Bill pulled the clip off the papers, tapped them on the table then re-clipped them and handed them back to Jake.

"All of it."

"All of it?"

"Yep."

"There is nothing constructive you can give me except all of it?"

"Jake, you and I both know after what you did to that girl there's no one going to be interested in any business you start in the Hollow. The best thing for you would be to go out to the city where no one knows you and start fresh. That's what your folks tried to do for you after it happened."

"It wasn't my choice to come back."

His uncle smiled. Jake hated that smile. It wasn't the jovial kindness of a beloved uncle but a smirk born of contempt. "But you did. And now folks are back to talking, ain't they?"

Jake said leaning on the table towards his uncle in silent reply.

"Well, I ain't one to spread gossip so let's just leave it where it is." His uncle said, dusting invisible dirt from his hands. " I'm not giving you money unless you want to use it to start a life out of the holler and then I'm not giving you all that's in that paper." He motioned back to Jake's business plan as if waiving flies off of something rotten.

"But Blue Hollow is the only place this will work. I know this town and-"

"And this town knows you. Go on now and get yourself home to your mom before the storm gets any worse. She'll be worried about you."

"But I don't need the people from the Hollow to make it work. It is for tourists. It will bring new people to the Hollow."

"And see there's a chunk of your problem. You think you don't need anybody. You're just going to run off with your great ideas thinking nobody's smart as you. Then when the time comes you need some help, you'll be crawling on hands and knees to these people in the Holler and they ain't going to have nothing to do with you."

"I'll get this going. It's a good plan." His voice was more confident than he felt.

"No you won't and if you try it'll be the ruin of your mom." The statement hung in the air. Uncle Bill seemed confident in the force of his impact and strutted slowly to Jake. He folded his arms across his puffed out chest "One last thing before you go Jake."

Jake readied his tongue for Bill's next insult. "What's that?"

"We need to talk about your mom."

Jake faced him, "Okay, talk."

Monologues and Speeches

In the previous section I gave some common issues seen in writing dialog in a book. One common error I spot is Monologues and Speeches by characters. This is long sections of speaking by a single character without a break of any kind.

What do I mean by long? A few lines or more.
Think about it. If you stopped to read a paragraph of 4 or 5 sentences without stopping to take a breath, without touching your face, adjusting the paper or hearing someone in the room shifting, it isn't very natural. We gather information constantly. You can create the scene and the tone simply by breaking the dialog to let us in the mind and body of our POV character.

So, what if the POV character isn't talking? Interrupt the speech to let us hear how the point of view character perceives what is said or what they observe in their environment.

For more on this I strongly urge you to pick up a few books on dialog, read them and then study people as they talk. What do you notice when you're listening to others. Do you take notes? Look around? Notice the sun coming from behind the clouds? How do your own emotions skew the perception of what is going on around you? Write some notes here, note it as you edit this story and then look for it in your own writing.

_____

_____

_____

_____

_____

_____

_____

_____

_____

_____

_____

_____

_____

_____

Janice watched Jake walk out of the house. His movements were slow, far too slow for this kind of downpour. Under the security light she could see Jake stop and look back up at the house. She was nearly forty feet away and hiding behind branches but the twisted look of pain, or possibly confusion, was evident from even this distance.

The light from the large picture window brightened the raindrops as they dropped from the roof and pooled in the pebbles that surrounded his perfectly manicured bushes. The appearance of perfection for anyone who was that easily fooled.

Janice was not.

She turned away from the house and headed to the main road. The few houses that lined this part of town were either abandoned to the care of Bill Colewick by the river rats, or the few year round residents had closed their curtains and only slivers of light or glowing shades indicated that life existed on the other side of this wet world.

An engine rumbled from the direction Janice had come from. She turned and saw a car turn in to Bill Colewick's driveway. She was now nearly 20 yards away and the car was partially obscured by the hedges that lined the opposite side of the driveway. She could see a silhouette of the top. The car wasn't white, yellow or tan but other than that she couldn't tell what shade of dark it was.

Had Jake come back?

***

Jake didn't know what to think.

Ever since she started paying attention to grown up matters he'd known Uncle Bill to be a tough man to really know. That was part of his appeal in Blue Hollow. The summer people wanted to live an illusion-and Bill offered it. He offered just enough of himself for the people to think he was a plain-spoken man but no one ever got past that image. It was like the neighbor, Dreama, calling him her "Summer Grandpa". He was family to all the River Rats in the summer. Family without the dysfunction.

Tonight in just a few moments that had all been shattered.

"I'm worried about your mom." Uncle Bill had said. "She ain't here for the reasons she's telling you."

Jake had still been raw from his uncle's tirade on Jake's business plan so his response was think with anger and sarcasm. "Then why are we here." Jake looked up at

Uncle Bill and in that moment he saw behind the wall.

The lines of anger had softened from the old man's forehead, shoulders

drooped and his face went slack. Worry clouded his usually steel blue eyes. It was as if

the force of every emotion packed deep inside were a churning lake behind a retaining

wall. Every day the weight pushed hard against its cement cage looking for the single

crack that would cause the every layer of resistance to dissolve. Something happened

inside Uncle Bill in that moment that caused the whole wall to fall. In that instant Jake

felt his own wall fall and he felt tenderness toward his uncle for the first time since he

was a boy fishing with his dad and uncle near Charlie's boat shop.

"This town has a hold on her, Jake, and 'til she lets the past die, well." Uncle

Bill had pulled a white handkerchief out of his pocket and begun twisting it. Like

a hammer to the chest Jake was suddenly shot back in his own past. As his uncle

nervously fingered the square piece of cloth Jake remembered his mom doing the same

thing in the moments before his dad died.

"What is it about her past that has her held?" Jake said, his mind replaying the

film of his dad's death like a horror film he couldn't stop: the fight, the woods, the

nurse, the end. It wasn't the first time something had triggered Jakes memory but the sting remained just as painful.

His uncle stood silent as if considering his words-or regretting haven begun this subject. Then as if watching his own mental film his uncle spoke, his eyes focused across the room at nothing in particular. "Jake, you're mom ever tell you she had dreamed of being a swimmer in college?"

"No. She didn't go to college." Jake said as if Uncle Bill were thinking of someone else.

"I know that." He said, only slight agitation in his voice. "She dreamed of going to college and swimming when she was there." Again, a long pause followed. Jake began to think Uncle Bill was waiting for some kind of reply but then he continued. "She was good at it too, despite our parents objecting. Until them boys hurt her." Before Jake could ask the obvious question his uncle continued. He recounted all he'd known about the gang rape and its effects on Jake's mom. Unable to move, or even to breath, Jake imagined how he'd feel if Bridget had been brutalized in the way his uncle was describing.

"I couldn't do nothing for her then, Jake." Uncle Bill had said. "But I don't want her hurt again. And this town will hurt her, on account of you."

Jake snapped back to the present as he pulled in his mom's driveway. The small lamp by the front door was on. It illuminated the three diamond shaped windows that ascended from left to right. The front porch light blinked on and Bridget walked out to greet him.

"Mom's been worried about you." She said. Her voice was not accusing but he felt a stab of guilt at adding any kind of hurt to the pain his mom had already experienced. He looked at his sister, now only a year younger than his own mom had been when she was attacked, and his determination to get out of the Hollow intensified.

"Sorry about that." He scooped up the business plans he'd show his uncle and tossed them in the trashcan along the edge of the attached garage. He wasn't going to have any attachment to this town. Uncle Bill had managed to remain by throwing up a wall of secrecy around himself and living a solitary life. Jake wasn't that cold, or that strong. There'd been a deeper warning in what Uncle Bill had said. He'd been scared, really scared, of something.

"Jake? What was that?" Bridget said pointing to the trashcan.

"A bunch of junk from my bag." He said. Jake looked up and down the street, watching for anyone with evil intent. Everything around him made him think of the pain he'd experienced the first time he lived in the Hollow, and the pain his mom must have felt living here every day. As if a fog surrounded him like a giant projector screen

images flashed before him on every house, every tree and every street sign.

"Better get in. The rain will be over this way any time." Bridget turned to go

back in the house and Jake followed. He pulled out his cell phone to call Uncle Bill

and see if they could meet in the morning. If the two of them worked together his mom

might see the wisdom of leaving. He dialed the number in with his thumb and walked

in the front door.

"Did everything go okay with your uncle?" His mom said. Her voice startled him

and he spun to the left to see her in the doorway to the kitchen, a dishtowel still in her

hand. "Who you calling so late?" She said looking down at his phone.

"No one." Jake said and flipped the phone shut before the call could connect.

There was no way he could say he was calling Uncle Bill without raising some suspicion.

"I made up some shortcakes to go with the leftover strawberries. I didn't think

about them or I'd have taken them to the picnic." She walked back to the kitchen and

Jake followed. There were so many questions he wished he would have asked but the

most daunting was how they'd manage to get mom to leave before the town destroyed

her.

***

Four-thirty A.M. came much too early. Janice reached over and punched off the alarm clock. Her body begged to remain under the warm covers but her work ethic pushed her on. Downstairs the diner would open in ninety minutes to hungry truck-drivers and early risers.

She sat up and her back rebelled. Every muscle in her neck and shoulders was tight from crouching in the bushed on the edge of Bill's property. She stood slowly and pushed her heels in the floor to stretch her legs. Already she dreaded the next ten hours of her day with standing, bending and lifting to accommodate the diner's customers. It had taken a while to fall asleep when she got home. Too many unanswered questions bouncing in her mind. The last time she remembered looking at the clock it was 11:47 and must have drifted off shortly after that.

She finished dressing and by five-thirty was filling napkin dispensers while Hank pulled cartons of eggs from the industrial refrigerator. Wednesday nights Hank and Midge always went bowling so Janice would set up Thursday morning. Today, however, Hank was getting his grill ready wordlessly.

"Midge coming soon?" Janice said as she set up a pot of coffee.

"Should be around any time." Hank said, never once looking at her. Janice wasn't in a talking mood herself so she welcomed the silence while it was there.

Shortly before six a.m. Midge came in the diner, three regulars fast on her heels. "No use having you boys wait outside over five minutes. Hank and Janice surely have the place ready for you." Midge said taking off her light jacket and the scarf that protected her graying locks.

"Good to see you folks." Janice said as she set down white paper placemats.

"You feeling better?" Midge said quietly when she got in the kitchen. Janice continued to exchange pleasantries but her ears were tuned to the conversation in the kitchen.

"I'll make it." Hank's usually gruff voice was weak but not a weakness from illness. It wasn't that the voice was low, or even raspy. Just as earlier, Hank sounded distant.

"Let me get your pills." Midge's voice had concern Janice had never before heard directed at Hank.

Janice took the orders from the three men but didn't clip them to the metal wheel that would circle them in the kitchen. Instead, she dished out fruit in to white chipped bowls. "Food'll be up in a couple of minutes." She offered in explanation, then turned her direction back to the kitchen. Hank was a large man with a history of heart problems. The concerns that had kept her standing in the pouring rain last night now paled against the real possibility that something was really wrong with Hank.

She walked through the swinging door in to the kitchen. "Y'all okay in here?" Janice said trying to mix sincerity and concern but ending instead with quivering fear.

"Hank's just not feeling well is all." Midge patted Hank's arm and offered Janice a tearful smile. "He'll be just fine soon as I can get him his nitros."

"I done told you that I left'em at home." The mention of his heart pills only exacerbated Hank's agitation. He pulled himself loose of Midge's hand and reached out for Janice's order pad.

"You got orders for them three?" He said. His face was bright red and, despite the chill in the air, there were sweat marks growing under his arms. Janice tore off the order and gave it to Hank. "I'll be fine if I can get back to my routine."

He walked to the grill and cracked half a dozen eggs on the griddle before Janice realized she was staring.

Midge motioned to Janice and spoke to her in a hushed tone. "I'm going over to the pharmacy soon as it opens to get him a refill. In the meantime, I'm going back to the house and see if I can't locate them pills. He's been like this since bowling last night. I'm getting worried."

"You go ahead. I got the front." Janice looked at Hank then back at Midge.

"And the grill if I need to. Don't worry yourself one bit."

Midge went to the front of the diner and Janice followed. She chatted up the three regulars and thanked them for their combined one dollar tip. By seven in the morning Midge had not returned and Hank was looking worse.

"Should I get you to a doctor, hon?" Janice asked trying to mask the fear that gripped her.

"No one else can run the diner and I'm not going to lose a day's pay." His voice was no longer gruff. The worry must have been getting to him too.

The phone rang and Hank looked at it then back at the grill. Janice answered and Midge said she'd been unable to find the pills so she'd called the doctor. They wanted to bring Hank in to the hospital and would Janice be able to watch things. Janice agreed. She called a local high school girl down the street who sometimes helped out on weekends. Her mom told her there was school today but that the mom would come in for this emergency. As soon as the woman walked in the diner five minutes later Janice walked back to the grill and Hank went out the back door.

As she watched him go Janice knew someone she cared for was being snatched from her again.

Don't talk to the reader!! Unless this is a book written in 1ˢᵗ person or 2ⁿᵈ person, do NOT talk to the reader! That is just as bad as breaking the 4ᵗʰ wall in theater. Don't do it. It can be subtle when it is done, but watch out for it. If it doesn't seem a logical thing to say in a conversation, don't say it. NEVER say, "As you know, we've been friends for 12 years and our moms are cousins." That is talking to the reader [and doing it using an "As you know" statement. Double bad!

Watch out for places in this book and in your own writing.

Dreama raised the blind and shielded her eyes from the blinding glare of sunlight. Throughout the night she'd replayed the terrifying moment when she thought she saw someone watching her. She still wasn't sure if her mind was playing tricks on her or if there had been someone there.

Outside the twisted wreckage of the previous nights storm littered her yard. A few large branches were down along the back yard, one limb dangled and swayed a few feet from her power line and countless twigs were scattered about. It would take the better part of the morning to clean up but nothing looked damaged.

She clicked the light switch up and down and was happy to discover that the lights still worked. She got dressed and after breakfast got to work cleaning the branches. As Dreama drew closer to the woods the air came alive with hums and buzzes. The air was damp and each time the wind blew through the tree branches it shook rain held on the spring leaves down on her. For over an hour she drug branches and raked leaves. She gathered up sticks and took them to a small shed at the edge of woods at the back of her parent's property. It was about forty feet from the back porch to the shed. Each time Dreama walked from the back of the yard she'd glance to the figure stood.

She tossed a load of sticks in the shed and marched to the front of the house. The driveway was gravel covered but the person she'd seen appeared to be at the edge of the tree line. She'd found deer tracks and raccoon footprints, surely a person would leave something behind. If she found something, she'd have proof of a trespasser. If there was nothing, she could sleep sound.

She looked between the window and the woods a few times before deciding exactly where she'd seen the person. The embankment was fairly steep at the edge of the driveway so she grabbed a large sapling before stepping down. The hill was full of trails cut in the mud by last night's downpour. A couple of feet from where she stood a half circle cut in to the side of the hill, it looked like the toe of a boot.

No, her mind had to be playing tricks. She leaned closer.

SNAP

Dreama registered the source of the sound only a moment before she began to fall, the branch still clutched in her hand. She slid down the hill grabbing for anything to stop her fall. The sticks cut at her jeans and rocks dug in her hands. A tree appeared just ahead and she prepared for the impact. She closed her eyes and shielded her face with her arms. The tree crashed against her legs in a flash of pain.

And the world went silent.

***

By nine a.m. Jake had cleaned up the sticks and weeded the small garden in his mom's backyard. Uncle Bill was an early riser and Jake had considered calling him when Jake woke up but he didn't want to fend off the barrage of questions that would come from his mom.

"I'm going to the grocery." She called to him as he collected the discarded grass and dandelions.

"Okay." He called back, already dusting off his hands to make the phone call. He dialed the number but the phone rang busy. Uncle Bill's line was never busy so Jake dialed it a second time.

Still busy.

A shudder of worry crept in for a moment. What if Uncle Bill had left town? Could that late night confession have been a final goodbye? Could it have been Uncle Bill putting his affairs in order before escaping the Hollow forever?

He couldn't think that. There were too many questions that his uncle had planted in Jake's mind to think that they wouldn't be answered. Not the least of which was Uncle Bill's question on Jake's paternity.

**

Dreama looked up at the distance of her fall. She hadn't slid more than seven or eight feet but her arms were covered in thin red lines and mud. She dusted her arms delicately and looked around. Her hearing aids had come out just about the time she hit the tree. She checked her hair and her shirt hoping that they'd been tangled in the folds of cloth or in the strands of her hair but she didn't find them.

The ground was damp but not thick with mud. It was only bad luck mixed with gravity that had forced her down the hill in the first place. Of course, if the hearing aids tumbled the rest of the way down the hill they'd be in the river by now. She considered the idea a moment and for the first time confronted what it would really mean to be alone and deaf. The whole world was muted, but for the first time it wasn't by her choosing. It had been taken from her. Did she still welcome deafness? The idea both alarmed her and intrigued her. A small tingle of what she could only describe as rebellion raced through her. Suddenly the choice had been completely jerked from her parents' hands.

As quickly as the idea entered her mind it was followed by the badgering voice of guilt and its sister, reason. Her parents couldn't decide but neither could she. And was she embracing hearing loss as a twisted form of rebellion? She looked to her right and saw her hearing aids in a pile of dirt, twigs and leaves. She felt a bit of relief that she hadn't washed ten thousand dollars away in a single fall, but she also felt stupid. It was like a person panicking that they'd lost their wallet only to have someone point out that it is in their hand. In five seconds of uncertainty she'd faced more introspection than she had in months of college. And she was left with more questions that she didn't want to answer.

She scooped up the hearing aids and checked their condition. She had nice digital aids, and she wasn't sure what dirt could do to their mechanisms. As soon as she took a good look she realized the damage was already done. The top had snapped off exposing the microphone. It was now caked with mud and there was mud inside the battery compartment.

She put them in her front pocket and trudged up the hill. The spot she'd thought was a footprint was now clearly a ripple in the dirt and nothing more. She left her muddy tennis shoes on the front porch and walked in the house. This nagging question would be the death of her yet. Her plan to escape the confines of the city and come to a safe place to think was turning in to even more questions.

Like when did she go crazy?

She changed out of her muddy clothes. They were pretty stained up but they were work clothes anywaysshe was otherwise fine. Her hearing aids were another matter. There was mud caked up inside the units and around the buttons. She'd need to take them in to the audiologist for repair.

She tried to think of a way to contact her audiologist without involving her parents. This was an opportunity to prove that she could function fully even if her hearing were to continue to worsen. She couldn't use the phone when she couldn't hear.

She removed the batteries and left the hearing aids open to dry out, found her audiologists business card and walked down the driveway to Mr. Colewick's house. If she had him call early enough she might be able to have them back next week.

Dreama was actually proud of herself as she started down the long driveway. She had taken some initiative without relying on her parents. Being on her own felt pretty good, liberating, in a way college hadn't been. There things were still structured with the curfews and assignments. She could come and go but her student ID reported when she came and went. She had rules that dictated her movements and her meals were restricted to when the food court was open. Her mean plan even told her how much of each item she could eat.

At the cabin Dreama was responsible for running the house, buying the groceries, cooking the meals and then cleaning up. She could leave the house and no one would know. If she decided she wanted fast food at 3am she could jump in the car and find a drive-thru. The sudden realization of how free she was lifted all the cares off of her for a moment. Did everyone feel so light when they stepped out on their own? Was this adulthood?

As she reached the end of her driveway she noticed the branches that covered Mr. Colewick's yard. Not only was he a morning person but he was meticulous about his yard. His lawn resembled a golf course with the perfectly mowed lines, shaped hedges and weeded flower beds. The first inkling of danger whispered to her but she pushed it back. She had beaten that fear, and had the scratches to prove it. She wouldn't let it get her back that easily.

"Mr. Colewick" She called. Without her hearing aids she tried to judge her volume by the strength of the vibrations in her throat. She looked and yelled a second time.

How in the world would she hear him reply? She laughed at her own stupidity and walked close enough to the house to see inside.

Mr. Colewick's car was still in the driveway and the lamp was on in the living room. She looked in the window along the front porch but there was no sign of him. She rang the door bell and waited. The jarring memory of the motion in the woods at the picnic, and the figure in the storm, continued to wait for a moment of weakness. She could feel its influence even if she hadn't allowed the memory full reign of her mind.

Dreama ran off the porch and around the house seized with what she knew was an irrational need to be around another human. Only having another person with her could still the silent pounding in her heart. She came around to the back of the house resisting the urge to scream. She hadn't realized how much she relied on her ears in the past, without them she felt vulnerable. Alone.

"Shut up." She screamed although she couldn't hear her own voice. Something was clearly wrong and only finding Mr. Colewick would calm her. She walked to the back door just off the porch and peeked inside. The kitchen storm door was open a crack and relief washed over her. He has to be somewhere in the yard wondering why she was making such a fuss. She scanned the yard quickly then decided to go in the house. She didn't want to startle him so she tapped on the door

"Mr. Colewick? It's Dreama. Do you need help with-?"

Just in front of her she could see Mr. Colewick's fingers curled slightly on the floor. She came in the house, her heart trying to escape the confines of her chest. He was laying on the floor on his side, eyes wide and frozen straight ahead. She ran to him and stuck her fingers to his carotid artery. Her warm fingertips met ice cold flesh and she jumped back.

"No." She blurted out. "Please, God, no." She prayed.

Mr. Colewick's eyes continued to stare ahead.

She fumbled up from the floor and looked for a phone. Every horror film she'd ever seen flashed in her mind all at once and she considered running to a neighbor to call the police from there.

No. She couldn't abandon Mr. Colewick. It was wrong to leave him. An irrational voice assured her that if she stayed here and called an ambulance that everything would be alright.

"He's not dead." The voice promised. "But if you leave him, he will be." It turned from assurance to accusation. Dreama fumbled around searching for a phone while trying to watch Mr. Colewick for the slightest indication of movement.

"If you would have come this morning you might have saved him." The seething voice continued. "You were so worried about your yard that you didn't consider that

Mr. Colewick might have needed help after a storm."

Dreama was crying, praying hard to push the voices away but they wouldn't

stop.

"This is your fault."

She knew it wasn't. There was no way she could have known.

"What if the person in the woods did it?" The voice hissed in the instant

Dreama found the phone. It dangled from a long cord. Had he tried to call for help

when his assailant came?

"They came for you but got him when you saw them." The voice answered.

"They would have hurt you too."

Dreama pushed her finger on the connection button then released it. She held

the ear piece of the receiver against her cheek and turned the volume on maximum.

Thankfully Mr. Colewick had an older phone so she could feel the vibration of a dial

tone.

She turned the volume all the way up and held the earpiece against her cheek to

check for the vibration. Then she dialed 911.

There was a long pause. Two short vibrations. Then nothing.

With all the calm she could muster she spoke slowly. "I cannot hear you. This is

Dreama. I am at Mr. Colewick's house. Please send an ambulance quickly. I am at Mr.

Bill Colewick's house, please send an ambulance quickly."

She wasn't sure if the person on the other end was there or had her on hold so

she kept her voice as steady as possible and kept repeating

"This is Dreama. I am at Mr. Bill Colewick's house, please send an ambulance."

She stood with her back against the wall and scanned back and forth through

the house, ready for someone to sneak up behind her.

But she couldn't leave him. She had to be here. She willed him to live but knew

in her heart he was already gone.

Once she was confident that the person was there and heard her she choked

out.

"And send the police. I think he's dead."

How are your main characters developing?

_____
_____
_____
_____
_____
_____

We're solidly in the story now and it is time to evaluate the characters a bit. How are they developing?

_____
_____
_____
_____
_____
_____
_____
_____
_____

Are they changing as the story continues or are they staying pretty much the same?

_____
_____
_____
_____
_____
_____
_____
_____
_____

We may even see them get worse before they get better (personal development can be like that), so have we seen any of that movement yet?

_____
_____
_____
_____
_____
_____
_____

These are important questions to consider because the ideas, circumstances and

actions of a character must change during the course of a book in order for us to see movement in the story. It isn't just the plot that moves the story, but how the plot impacted the characters. Both of these things are important.

Take time now to evaluate the growth of the characters in this book and in your own story. Make adjustments as needed.

Chief Fogg spoke very slowly. Dreama tried to focus on his exaggerated lips but the sloshing black liquid in his mouth forced her eyes away. It had been a while since she'd been forced to rely solely on lip reading to communicate and she knew she wasn't catching most of what the officer was saying.

"I didn't touch anything but him and the phone." She said hoping that she was answering his question. His attention turned to something behind her and Dreama looked to see what it was. Jake stood at the edge of a group of police officers. His face was scrunched in something that looked like confusion and agitation. He was having a heated conversation with a younger officer near the door.

Dreama felt like an interloper on this family tragedy. She'd known Mr. Colewick for most of her life but she only knew him during the summer and the relationship never went past superficial chatter. Yet she was standing in the living room and it appeared that Jake was being asked to leave.

"Can I go now?" Dreama asked the Chief. He said something that she didn't understand then nodded his head.

Once outside she found Jake sitting on top of the picnic table they'd eaten at the night before.

"Jake?"

"Hi." He said. Tears were pooling in the corners of Jake's eyes.

"Where is your mom?" She looked around then back at Jake and realized he had answered her when she wasn't looking. She had to remember to pay better attention.

"I'm sorry, Jake. My hearing aids are broken so I couldn't hear you."

He was obviously surprised and for a moment looked at her skeptically. "She doesn't know yet." He replied. "I was coming over to talk to Uncle Bill about something he told me last night." He looked back at the house then turned to Dreama. "I can't be the one to tell her."

Dreama searched her mind looking for some word of comfort to give Jake but what more could she offer than greeting card sentiments. She barely knew him and had no idea how close Jake had been to Mr. Colewick.

"Is there anything I can do to help?"

Jake shook his head. She leaned forward and wrapped her arms around him in a hug. It was something she'd done countless times at youth group and when comforting friends. She'd done it without even thinking. Jake stiffened then wrapped hesitant arms around her. He squeezed her lightly and then moved back.

"Well, goodbye. Let me know when, well, you know." She said then she quickly walked around the house and to her driveway. Police cars as well as Mr. Colewick's and Jake's filled the driveway and the spectacle hadn't gone unnoticed by the few year round residents who lived here. They stood out on their lawns, arms folded observing the scene. One woman looked at Dreama as she rounded the end of Mr. Colewick's yard and started up the incline to her own house. For a brief moment she could see Jake through the branches. He was still sitting on the bench. Staring at the woods.

When Dreama reached the top of the hill she looked around. The yard was still cluttered with debris. She walked down the length of the back yard's grass bending to scoop up branches. She would clean the yard up and it would be as if nothing had changed.

When her arms were full she tossed the sticks in the shed and collected another bunch. As questions tiptoed in she began counting the sticks. She didn't want to hear the questions or think about the fear.

27-28-29-30 sticks.

She dropped them in the shed.

1-2-3-4

Her mind was overwhelmed with three new thoughts:

5-6-7 sticks

Could someone have killed Mr. Colewick?

8-9

Was it the person watching her last night?

10-11-12

And if so why?

Chapter 4

"Hey there Chuck."

Charlie stopped what he was doing. Thirty years had passed since she'd called him that and it still had the same effect on him.

"Janice." He replied, his voice, like his heart, cracked as he spoke. He turned to face her.

The two of them exchanged awkward glances for a moment. Ever since he'd heard she came back to town he'd stayed away from the diner. The ache that squeezed his chest and throat every time he pulled out their old photographs now squeezed him with such intense force that he wondered if he'd even be able to speak.

He still saw their baby every time he looked in her eyes. The giddy bliss of teenage love mixed with the bile of teenage ignorance. There'd been so many times over the last thirty years that he'd longed to be in this exact position-standing in front of her alone. He always envisioned an articulate apology from him followed by tear-stained forgiveness from her. They'd embrace and start over. Build the family that they'd lost that summer after graduation.

Never in any of those fantasies did she stand before him in blue jeans, a beige shirt that amplified every delicate curve, an expectant smirk dusting her face.

And a cat holding his tongue.

"Charlie." She continued softly. Her voice had the gentle depth of a star from the golden age of Hollywood where the screams were ear piercing and the lovers voice was sensual.

"It's good to see you." He managed to stammer out. Her smirk widened to a smile and she took two confident steps in his direction.

"I wanted to come sooner but-"

"I know." He cut her off before she could finish. They both understood the twisted unfairness of hate that tore them apart thirty years ago and he wanted to leave dead things dead.

"But I'm here now."

"Yes, you are." He replied. The lift in her voice awakened a long dead hope and he motioned for her to sit. When she did, he sat directly across from her.

Janice wouldn't look directly at him. She never did when she was waiting for something. Their first kiss started with just that look. That had been a fall night as seniors. They'd gone together to watch a football game. After meeting up with some friends they'd lingered at the park at the top of the hill. She'd looked past him, not saying a word. When he kissed her that night under the picnic shelter every inch of his body applauded his bravery. He'd held her there in his arms and couldn't imagine a better feeling.

Just a few months later he'd hold her in that same spot under the picnic shelter as sobs wracked her body. He'd promised her to stand by her side. He wouldn't abandon her in that delicate state like most boys would.

But he had at the worst possible moment.

Now she sat before him in his shop with the same beautiful innocence that had first cast the spell on him. And again she was waiting on something from him.

"Chuck." She looked up and blushed, "Sorry, I guess they call you Charlie now."

"Chuck." He said. He loved the way it sounded when she said it.

"This thing with Colewick has me thinking." She stopped long enough to scan his expression. "He just, well, he was alive...then...wasn't." She took a deep breath as if steadying herself. "Well, I've been angry long enough."

Charlie sat waiting for the implication of her words. What exactly was she saying to him? His voice caught in his throat. She slid off of the stool and took a few steps to him. She was directly in front of him and probing his eyes as if hoping to answer a yet to be spoken question. Charlie's effort was solely focused on steadying his breathing.

She reached up and gently touched his cheek with her finger tips. She traced the lines on his face that had been the path of so many tears since she ran away from him. When her fingers reached the edge of his mouth he could stand it no longer. He took her face in his hands and kissed her deeply.

The moment exploded as it had when they were teenagers under a picnic pavilion only this time it was better. This kiss had thirty years and countless memories behind it. The pavilion, the car, the woods, the campground, the...

No, he'd stop with the campground.

***

It was after dark when Dreama pulled in the driveway. The audiologist had no good news for her or her hearing aids. They'd have to be sent out and would take a week or more to get back. There was nothing he could loan her in the meantime.

The long ride back she continued to wonder how she could hide all of this from her parents, and if she should. They should at least know about Mr. Colewick's death so they could pay their respects. If she told them they'd come down, find out that her hearing aids were broken and insist that she come home with them.

With no radio to listen to Dreama had nothing to do but think. Was it possible that he'd had a heart attack? He was lying on the floor near the phone but it didn't look like anyone had been there. On the other hand, why would the back door have been open? Mr. Colewick was picky about letting flies in the house. It was unlikely that he would have left it open. There was the possibility that he'd left it open if the chest pains started outside and he stumbled in the house.

Back and forth the questions volleyed in her mind.

Then the most pressing question for her, had someone been watching her in the storm? That one question had nearly sent her running home when she was visiting the audiologist. If someone was watching her from the edge of the darkness, why were they? Who was she other than a summer resident? As she pulled in the driveway the questions had continued to mount with no more answers.

But time was running out on whether or not to let her parents know Mr. Colewick was dead. She only had until bed tonight to let them know in order to have time to come down for the funeral-if they wanted to.

Development of our Antagonist

Writing bad guys are the best part of writing! I love it!! You can do things with a bad guy that a person would NEVER let you do with a good character.

The problem with writing bad guys is people want to make them pure evil and that just doesn't work!! I'm not afraid of a burned up school janitor invading my dreams and killing me as I slept. I am afraid of the nice guy in town who turns out to be a serial rapist. It is because we trusted them. We let our guard down and they were evil. The key to writing a great bad guy is that crazy people do not think they're crazy. They find their desire to kill, maim, attack and control to be totally rational. When we can find the rationale in our antagonist we can create chilling and memorable characters.

Right now take some time to evaluate the rationale of the bad people in this book. Why is it logical and permissible to do the evil things they do [in their minds]? Now look in your own story and come up with a reason why it is okay to do all of the evil they do in your book.

Brainstorm here

_____

_____

_____

_____

_____

_____

_____

_____

_____

_____

_____

_____

_____

_____

_____

_____

_____

_____

_____

And now, while you're at it, find a weakness in your GOOD guys and let them rationalize why they don't need to change. Build that in to the character arc.

"Swimmers take your mark."

Renny stood on the block and shook her arms. The crowd quieted to a murmur and she breathed in the scent of Chlorine.

"Get set."

She crouched down, eyes fixed on the water. The yellow florescent lights above her hummed and she imagined it was her muscles buzzing, waiting to connect with the water.

The starting pistol fired and Renny dove in to the water. Cool water slid along her arms and she went as long as her lungs would let her before breaking the surface of the water and grabbing it by handfuls. She was no longer a sixteen year old girl from the hills. She was now a dolphin pushing through the water with smooth efficiency. Meters slid past her with every arm stroke. Nothing was happening around her, no competitors, and no crowds. There was only her and the wall on the other side of the pool.

Her hand smacked the wall.

"Time." She opened her eyes and wiped water from her face. The screams of the crowd echoed.

"You did it." Brenda screamed.

"I did it?"

"You did it."

She spun around and looked at the numbers clocking the top three times. There was hers, a full second before the runner-up.

Her team mates were swarming the side of the pool. She grabbed the ladder and climbed out of the pool.

"Congratulations Renny." Coach said, beaming. He held his clipboard out to the side and wrapped one arm around her dripping wet frame.

"Mama and daddy will have to let me swim now." She yelled in Brenda's ear. "They promised if I made the team I could swim."

"You made the team, alright Renny. Just look on up there at them numbers. I wouldn't be surprised none if you didn't go off and break some kind of county record with that time."

"Go on up there. They're giving out the medals." Coach's words sounded more like a single word gwon as opposed to go on. Something Renny found charming about coach. He and Brenda knew better than anyone else in that place what that gold medal meant to her.

Mama and daddy weren't much for young lady athletes. They said that almost every day. Only thing they found more ridiculous than being a lady athlete was being a lady academic. Renny had tried school route but that didn't work out when she got in to higher mathmatics.

But spending afternoons down at the pond by the train trestle, was Renny's safe place. She could dive down deep and bring up rocks and plants from the bottom or wait on the edge and catch a few frogs to fry up for supper.

"First Place, Renny Colewick." Renny stepped up on the wooden box that served as the podium. The crowd of forty or fifty people could just as well been a stadium at the Olympic Games.

She waved like she'd seen the athletes do on the TV then stepped down.

"Now let me get a good look at that medal." Brenda was the first one to reach Renny after the award ceremony. "Renny, I tell you this is your ticket out this place."

"Now why'd I ever want to go and leave the Hollow?"

"Renny, in this Hollow all you going to find is some man who'll keep you pregnant or keep you poor. Maybe even both." Brenda was something of a pessimist when it came to life here. Her eyes were always beyond the tree tops of the Hollow. She talked about going to New York or Nashville but everyone knew she'd be like the rest of them and settle down in the Hollow.

"I can't see me going off to the Olympics with my swimming."

"No but you could go to college."

"I ain't got the brains for all that. All I want's to be happy."

"Renny, Brenda we need to get on the bus to make it back in time for your girls to be home before dark." Coach said then walked on to the next group of socializers.

Brenda turned back and got real serious. "Renny, I know you don't want no fancy degree but we got opportunities opening to us right now that people ain't never seen fore. You ought to think on them before you go deciding that you don't want nothing more."

Renny walked over to the bench and picked up her towel and bag. There was plenty more than the hollow she'd like to have. She'd seen the sky scrapers on her parent's television. Even without color the lights twinkled on the mammoth structures and drew her to them. Thing was there wasn't no point hoping for things that weren't never going to happen. That only left a person unhappy all their days. Like those girls pining over the Beatles and the Monkeys. Why stick a boy on their wall that they'd never know let alone marry.

She'd left the beans and ham hock in the slow cooker when she'd left this morning but there was still corn bread to make and greens to wash and boil. She

needed to be home well before dark so she was sure to get all her chores done in time to

fix supper for Mama, Daddy and Bill.

***

Charlie watched her taillights driving away until even the red dots disappeared

in the distance. Had he really spent the last three hours with her or had it all been

a fantasy that he'd wake from in the morning? Would the sunrise bring with it that

eternal hole where his heart had been? Would he replay their final moments as kids or

was this the start of new and better memories?

They'd talked about their days in high school as well as what each of them had

done with their lives. She laughed as he told her about the various antics with the river

rats and he had listened with wonder as she talked about taking care of her elderly aunt

and uncle. And she spoke with obvious concern about Renny. Her husband had only

been gone a few months and now her brother was gone too.

Of course, Charlie had no sense of loss with Bill Colewick's passing. In fact,

when the estate was settled there was about $60,000 coming to Charlie from the lawsuit

he'd won against Colewick. Despite how much he needed that money it felt wrong to

get it from Renny. He walked to his room in the back of the bait store and switched on the TV.

"Salisbury steak or lasagna?" He said out loud as he scanned the microwave dinner selections in his freezer. Neither one sounded any good so he closed the freezer and opted to make a roast beef sandwich instead.

Who'd have figured that Bill Colewick dying would bring Janice back to him?

***

"Hank are you sure that you are up to this?" Midge spun the next table around to form a second row. The diner was respectfully done with black table cloths draping the pinball machine and a large picture of Bill in the corner.

"Midge, I told you I was. Now stop fussing over me. We'll be late if we don't get going." Hank had insisted on having the brunch after Bill's funeral here at the diner. Midge thought the church would have been more appropriate-given the circumstances.

"Should I get your pills?" She didn't wait for him to answer before scurrying to her purse.

"No." His voice was tight. Midge spun to Hank. His eyes were pale blue against his bright red face. "Now I told you we'll be late if we don't get going." He lifted his arm and slid it in the sleeve of his suit-the only suit he owned. He was sweating too much again.

"Why you got to be so darn stubborn?"

"Why can't you listen when I tell you no?"

She pulled her purse off of the hook with enough force that Hank would be sure to notice her anger. Seemed it was the only thing that man noticed about her at all anymore. He had once been the kind of man to leave her little gifts for no reason or to send a card to the diner where she'd find it when she brought in the mail.

She slid in the car next to Hank and now wondered when the magic had died. It seemed the only thing so could do for him was care for his health and wait tables at the diner.

"Did you remember to plug in the slow cookers? That shredded beef won't be-"

"Handled." Was his one word reply.

Of course he'd handled it. The tone in her voice made her feel stupid for even asking. It wasn't a far drive, at most five minutes, to the funeral home from the diner. As they curved through the streets Midge thought about the people who lived in those houses. How many of them would miss Bill? How many would miss her when she passed?

She glanced briefly at Hank. His hands were firm on the wheel and sweat beaded along his salt and pepper hairline. She remembered back to when they were dating. His hair was cropped much like it was now only then it was black like night.

He'd been mysterious, a boy from the city just out of the Army. She'd swooned over

his good looks and sharp green uniform. She was so smitten for this wild boy that she

dropped her boyfriend, Bill Colewick, and spent all of her time with Hank.

Since she heard of Bill's death she considered what it would be to be a widow.

If Hank hadn't moved to town Midge would likely have married Bill. Then she'd be

winding down this road in a family members car preparing to bury her husband. The

thought of is wrapped her body with impending doom like she had never felt.

When Hank had gone to the doctor a few days ago she'd been worried but her

quest for a cure kept her motivated-driven. What must it be like to helplessly watch

someone die as Renny had done? Renny had been so young when she lost her husband.

What did a person feel as they prayed for a miracle and prayed for an end to the

suffering at the same time?

She couldn't imagine. There is no way she thought she could watch someone

slowly slip away like that. The pain would just be too intense. The smell of cold fear

mingled with death each night as you closed your eyes, then to wake up each morning

with both hope and dread-wondering if they were gone.

Midge looked down the road ahead of them as Hank drove. A long line of cars was filling the funeral home parking lot. Renny had set aside a spot for them to be close to the door so they could also leave quickly to unlock the diner. Hank was breathing heavier but she wasn't going to be snapped at again so she simply ignored him.

She slipped again in her morbid ramblings. What would it be like to know you were going to die? To silently pack up each memory in a box to be sold off at auction for a dollar a box? She imagined packing up the remains of her life like a person packs for a long trip.

Then she considered Hank. Was she losing him too?

False Clues

When constructing your story don't forget that these characters are REAL PEOPLE. That means they don't have a perfectly developed sense of what to do in every situation. They'll do things wrong. They'll perceive things wrong. They'll act on those wrong assumptions.

In the spaces below brainstorm a few false clues you can use in your own writing.

_____

_____

_____

_____

_____

_____

_____

_____

_____

_____

_____

_____

Make sure you label false clues in this book after you've finished reading. And if you think you've found a false clue, label it and see if you're right.

Jake stood beside his mom as each well wisher came in the door. They all filed in and paid their proper respects but very few seemed phased at all by Uncle Bill's death. Who had truly known his Uncle Bill? Had anyone actually liked him?

The last sentence stuck in his brain and hurled accusations at Jake. It repeated over and over until it had twisted itself in to a new question. Who actually liked him, Jake? As each person walked in with their dutiful remorse and tearless eyes he wondered if half as many people would come to his own funeral from this town.

There was something else. The spirit in this town was dead. It was as if a stream of souless people were parading past him in a pale procession. The music inside was little more than whole note chords in the bass clef. The mood was somber and there was palpable tension. Despite his big grin and jovial nature with the river rats Uncle Bill had not had much time for the things of the spirit or the afterlife. This service was devoid of the celebration and expectation of the hereafter that he'd seen at his dad's funeral.

His mom was even paler against the black outfit she wore. When his dad died

months before mom had comforted herself that he was in the presence of Jesus. She'd

embraced every person graciously as they walked past. But the Hollow had taken

something from her.

"Get her out of the Holler. It will kill her." Uncle Bill had warned.

"Mom, do you need to rest?" He asked, suddenly aware that his mom was

swaying in her spot.

"No, honey, I'm doing just fine." She turned to him without the slightest light

in her eyes. All of her tears had been cried and now she looked at him confused and

alone in a town that hated her.

What grip did Blue Hollow have on her and why couldn't she let go?

"Hi Jake."

He looked at the person in front of him. "Dreama. I am glad you could come."

She gave her condolences and blotted at her eyes as she spoke. The sincere

sense of loss touched him greatly. Among the many she was one of the few who showed

honest emotion in this town.

"Dreama, sit with us." Jake said it before he realized he'd spoken. His mom

snapped her head in his direction.

"No, thank you." She said, her eyes focused on his mom and the sudden color in her cheeks.

"Are you sure?" He said unable to figure out his mom's sudden change.

"Really, it is fine. The front row is for family." Dreama said as she walked in the room and straight to Uncle Bill's open casket.

After the last person filed in his mom pulled him aside. "Don't you think it is a little out of sorts to try to pick up a date at your uncle's funeral."

As if every emotion she'd battled were suddenly loosed Renny shook with anger as tears cascaded down her cheeks.

"Mom, it is nothing like that-."

"Don't make me no fool, Jacob! You've been spending every day over there with her."

Shocked by her sudden explosion Jake tried to guide her to a side room.

"Momma, people are looking out this way."

"Let 'em look." She was now shaking as she spoke.

"Mom, please." Bridget touched mom's arm but she recoiled.

"Really, Mom." Jake kept his voice low and turned his back to the open door.

The funeral director appeared and closed the door. It made a soft bumping noise as it closed followed by a burst of chatter from the mourners on the other side. Thankfully Dreama wouldn't hear a word of it.

"Mom, where is this coming from?" Bridget tried to press.

"Didn't you learn the first time?" His mom burst out then she buried her face in her hands.

***

"Can you top me off?" A gruff voice called from behind Midge. One of the regular truckers held up his white ceramic cup.

"Be right there hon." She stacked the plates one on top of the other and carried them behind the counter and put them in the grey tub. Only days had passed since Bill's funeral and all the muck it had turned up. She struggled to focus on the customers around her and the filling retirement fund but every day just after lunch she remembered.

She walked to the man who was sitting in Bill's usual spot and filled his cup. He thanked her by lifting the cup a bit in the air in a toast before taking a sip.

"How 'bout you try less toasting and more tipping?" She mumbled as she slid the pot back on its hot plate. Janice looked at her then back at the salad she was plating up. The two had barely exchanged a word in a week and Janice's sudden secrecy had

Midge worked up too. The girl was up to something, Midge was certain of that. All

the sneaking around after the diner closed and disappearing for hours at a time for no

reason had started up a couple of weeks ago and this morning Janice had been late.

Midge reckoned in herself that she'd need to sit Janice down soon and have a talk

about things.

"Won't you look at who's here?" Janice said. Midge looked out the front of the

diner as Jake pointed a young lady to the door. She'd recognized the young lady at the

funeral as a river rat. When she'd said hi to the young lady at the funeral she hadn't

even given the least bit of courtesy.

"Jake's a good boy. No need dragging him through nothing today. Boy's in

mourning."

"I'd hardly call him a good boy." Janice said.

"Now don't go stirring the pot. Least not today."

"Yes Midge. Don't got to be sweet as sugar though." Janice said as she smoothed

down her outfit and walked to her section. That was the problem with everyone here

lately. No onle wanted to give the least courtesy due.

Midge turned to look back at Hank working the stove. He'd been better this last

day or two which at least gave her some relief. He wasn't fully himself but he also wasn't as grumpy as he'd been over the last month or two since she said she didn't want to leave town. She looked around the place they'd built together and wondered how Hank could toss aside their memories so easily. Some of her best chats had taken place right along this counter. She grabbed a damp dishrag and wiped the counter down. The gold flecks in the white counter was the exact same as when they opened the shop more than thirty years ago.

Jake walked in the door with the young lady smiling beside him. She tucked a bit of hair behind her ear and only looked at him in fleeting glances. Midge had seen that mating dance countless times through these years. And Jake was doing his part too. He'd gently touch her arm and put his hand across the table as they spoke. Midge didn't need some fancy degree to understand human behavior. She could tell when people were hiding something. She could read the body language when those out of town people thought they were fooling someone with the suntan lines around their ring finger to let the whole diner know they were up to no good.

Most of these people were the same. They came in and drank a cup of coffee, talked about their haul if they were truckers and their plans if they were vacationing. Then they fluttered back out. The anonymous mass and the regular few.

But this was now Midge's legacy. With no kids and no family left the diner and

Hank was all she had. She looked again at Jake and the river rat. She was happy that he was finding love again. She wasn't quite sure it was appropriate this soon after his uncle's passing, but she figured that the poor boy had been in mourning over his last love interest long enough.

***

Charlie checked his tie again and straightened the table settings. Every night since their kiss -the night after Colewick's death- at ten forty-five Janice arrived at his apartment behind the boat rental store. Yesterday he promised her a special dinner and he'd worked since the store closed at eight to get it all ready for her.

It was hard to remember how to do real cooking after living the bachelor's life for so long but it only took a few cooking disasters before he managed to get it back. These dinners had been like a continuous exhale for him. Each time she walked in his apartment a bit of the hurt in his life was sanded smooth. So much of his present problems were tied up in the history Janice and he had created as teens. Time had stood still as he relived over and over every word and gesture. He had relived every act and each mistake. His life had been stuck in a cycle of his senior year. Each fall as the river rats left for their lives outside of the hollow he had time to remember their first meeting, their first kiss and all the promises he'd spoken to her in the park.

"I won't leave you Janice. No matter what, I'll stick beside you."

Of course, at that first opportunity he'd forgotten all his great declarations and noble intentions and he'd acted just like every other selfish boy does when given a freebie. He got out, ran away, left her.

"Hi Chuck." Janice slid in through the back door and her smile instantly washed away the dirt of guilt that he'd been bathing in again. Her hair was pinned up on her head with only the curls in the back hanging down. He walked to her and greeted her with a chaste kiss, resisting the urge to pull the pin from her hair and watch the curls drop in a seductive cascade on to her shoulders.

"You've been on your feet all day. Come on over and sit." He pulled the chair out and she sat down. It was like being on a first date and having dinner with a spouse at the same time. There was tingly newness with every story. However, each memory offered the comfort of an old shoe. They'd spent more than a year together as kids, and he'd spend more than thirty as an adult wishing to have her back. They talked about the mundane things married couples do: town politics, the weather and long term plans.

"Have you looked any more in to expanding your building out that way?" She motioned to the back of the building with her fork.

"I watched it a bit with the storms this spring and I'm not sure that's the best way to go." She nodded in agreement and chewed the pork chops he'd made for dinner.

"It's smart of you to watch but even if there is flooding down that way, isn't there a way to use that to your advantage." Charlie thought on it for a bit but when an answer didn't come he said. "I'll have to think on that."

They talked all through dinner about development of the town, what things were like when they were younger and the chatter around the diner.

"I've decided that I'm not going after Renny's money." Charlie finally said when there was a break in the conversation. True, it was Bill's money now left to Renny...but that meant it was Renny's money.

"Really?" Her eyes were wide as she spoke but then they returned to their normal size and a smile broke out. "Chuck, I knew you were that kind of man." She stood and put her arms around his neck.

"I figure what goes around comes around."

"It sure does and you are going to get everything you deserve for this." She bent down and kissed him.

It wasn't easy watching all the money Bill owed him flutter away like that, but he had a way to keep this place afloat. He'd learned a great deal from talking to Janice.

He'd made stupid business mistakes but he was now on track.

"I don't need his estate." He said his voice becoming thick with emotion. He waited until he knew he could continue. "Getting you back was worth far more than that."

She smiled and pulled him up from his chair. Without a word she pulled his face to hers and kissed him.

For the rest of the night his thoughts didn't drift to the money he was losing, the thirty years he'd lost or even to the uncertainty of his business. His every thought was on Janice and their future together. For the first time since their last time, he connected with a woman. Afterward she laid beside him breathing gently. Her slow breaths and the flow of the river outside created a music greater than any he'd heard in a long time.

For just a moment a whisper of foreboding was carried in on the breeze. Wasn't this the same mistake they'd made as children that ended up tearing them apart? Charlie silenced the fear quickly. They weren't children this time. There was a big difference between seventeen and almost fifty. As he thought of all the women he'd nearly been intimate with he thanked his lucky stars he hadn't. This woman here in his arms was the only one he'd ever loved and the only one he'd ever wanted to sleep soundly beside him.

Let the Reader Discover With You

In the previous section we talked about false clues, now let's talk about real ones. Readers like to discover the story along with the characters in the book. Make sure you're leaving enough information to be discovered SUBTLY [without a character saying, "Oh, looky there!! A clue!"]

Watch throughout the story for clues that point to you a new discovery in the book. Label them.

_____

_____

_____

_____

_____

_____

_____

_____

_____

_____

"Here's your menu hon." Janice appeared out of nowhere and laid the menu

on the table in front of Dreama. "So Jake, awful sad about Bill. Did you know he was

having troubles with his heart?"

Jake shifted in his chair. The small pout mixed with slanted eyes alerted Jake that she was doing more than sharing friendly conversation.

"No." He held her gaze for a moment then returned his attention to Dreama. "I think Dreama will need a minute to decide her order."

"Oh, I don't mind waiting. The place is pretty slow this afternoon." Janice was probing him. He could feel the push of her questions beyond what was being said. He measured each word carefully. Like a game of chess he studied each potential response before making a move. He wasn't a teenager anymore and not as easily intimidated as last time but he knew the ability she had to assemble a few pawns to take out a queen or king.

"We'll take an order of cheese sticks and onion rings for now and figure out the rest while you're getting that." He had her in check. She wrote the order down. He knew her memory. This move was not to place a small order with Hank or even to tally a bill. She was looking at the chessboard herself and trying to see how to move her king out of danger while also making a forward assault on Jake's pieces.

"Well, Jake. I tell you the timing's good far as you're concerned with you wanting to get that business going and all."

Jake leaned back in his chair and crossed his arms. "Having a family member die is never well timed."

Her smile faded. She leaned in, eyes little more than streaks of color and white on a reddening face. "I know that quite well, Jake." Her voice, an accusing whisper. "Just an interesting coincidence is all."

Checkmate.

"Dreama, I think maybe we should go somewhere else to eat." Jake started to stand and Dreama with him. With only a few words Janice had introduced the 'other woman' to dinner. His skin crawled with the dirt of guilt. Not only for Alexa's death but also for thinking of her while sitting here with Dreama.

"Now, now Jake sit yourself on down." Midge scurried across the diner waving away the tendrils of tension that were spawning out from the table. "Janice, go pour some coffee for Tommy and the Chief at the counter. I'll handle this table." She pointed Janice over to the other side of the diner and held her hand on Jake's shoulder. "Don't you pay Janice no mind. She's just something of a busy body." He sat down and Dreama followed.

"Is that what the town's been talking about Midge?"

"Oh now, Jake, people talk. Don't mean you got to listen. I'll get you both something nice." Then over her shoulder she yelled "Hank, give me two of them pulled pork sandwiches and fries." Then back to them. "Hank makes real fine pulled pork.

You'll like those." She smiled and walked back behind the counter.

Jake stirred his coffee again while he worked Alexa's memory back to the place

he housed all the things he tried to forget. "I'm sorry about that."

"No need to apologize." Dreama looked down at the menu. "I guess I don't

need this." She set it aside and leaned forward on the table. Her eyes pulled at the

words he kept trapped inside. While Janice's stare dug in with the same shrill intensity

of a dentist's drill Dreama's gentle concern welcomed his words for the healing

admission they'd be. It was because of her gentle concern that Jake couldn't form the

words that would remove his burden.

"Around here, Dreama, Midge orders your food for you. These menus are just

for show." She smiled at him and turned over the coffee cup in front of her. She rubbed

her arms.

"You cold?"

She smiled and nodded.

"Here take my jacket." He pulled his windbreaker off the back of his chair and

gave it to her. She put it on and rubbed her hands up and down the sleeves.

"So, what are you studying in school?"

She leaned forward and put her chin in her hand, "People".

"Oh you study people?" he laughed. "This town should give you a lot of practice with that."

She shook her head up and down. "I major in sociology."

"Sociology, really? What do you plan to do with that?"

"I'll let you know when I get a job."

Chapter 5

"How is Dreama?" Bridget asked when he walked in the door.

"Good. You should have come with us."

"I don't know." She shrugged and turned the page of a large textbook.

"Which class?" He said motioning to the book.

"Government." She paused. "Again."

He nodded sympathetically. "One more month." There was no reason this

school district hadn't recognized Bridget's classes when they transferred.

"Until I have to take it again in college." She smiled, just a little, and Jake had

to laugh at the irony of her predicament. She hated government and she had to take it

twice because of problems with her classes transferring. That meant she had to give up

the art class she really wanted to take.

"Maybe Mom will convince them you shouldn't have to take it a third time."

"Yeah, that'll happen." Her voice was deep with frustration. Jake laughed, not at

his sister's predicament but rather what it represented.

The house groaned under the assault of years of gravity. Looking at Bridget's

school books Jake remembered back to his years of high school in the hollow. Mr.

Armstrong had taught physics. "The force of gravity is the product of mass times acceleration due to gravity, or F=mg, and is expressed in Newtons per kg."

Inwardly Jake felt that same weight but rather than being expressed in the units of gravity, Jake's weight was expressed in days since dad's death and multiplied by days since arriving in the hollow. The equation resulted in a deep pressure that settled in his stomach and squeezed the hope out.

"Hi hon." Jake turned to see his mom standing in the doorway between the kitchen and the hall. Jake had once been startled by her appearance but she now seemed to wear the tattered robe, tangled ponytail and bloodshot eyes like a uniform. She was not quite fifty and while he'd heard that forty was the new thirty, his mom had not.

Daily her beauty regiment consisted of smoothing on the lotion of sadness and bathing in the shower of guilt. When she did speak the conversation consisted of a questions that started with "What if I had.." or "Do you think he...".

"Would you mind running to the diner and picking us up something for supper?" She said, breaking in to his mental wanderings.

"No need mom. I'll make something." Three meals in as many days from the diner was about as much abuse as his stomach could take. There was a reason those places were called greasy spoons. He turned back to the freezer and started rummaging around.

"That'd be sweet hon. Thanks." She turned and shuffled back in the other room.

"Any requests?" Jake said to Bridget without looking away from the freezer.

"Having my mom back would be nice."

"It's been a lot for her to take in. She lost her brother and husband in a year."

"And I lost my dad and uncle." Bridget snapped back. "Are you ever going to stop making excuses for her?"

"You see her act like this when Dad died?" Bridget's voice waivered and Jake turned to face here. She was stading, two fists balled at the end of straight arms. She stubbornly held back the tears that pooled in her eyes.

"No." He conceded. "But I think it is the cumulative-."

"Whatever, Jake. Always got an excuse for what she does." She snatched up her book from the table. Her footsteps thudded down the short hall then disappeared behind a slammed door.

He closed the freezer and leaned back against the refrigerator. Surely it was tough for mom coming off of dad's death a year and a half ago. But his cancer held on for over a year before he went. They all had time to get ready with the hospice and grief counselors. Mom didn't have that this time.

"Remember, God ain't the one out to getcha. He's the one who helps defeat the one out to getcha." His dad had told him. Two days later, he died. His dad was never angry at God for the cancer or what it did to his body. His concern was always "You take care of your momma when I'm gone. Don't worry bout me none. The Lord's got me covered."

Jake wiped a tear from his eye.

What good was he honestly doing here in the Hollow? He'd promised dad to stay with her to help her adjust to life without him. He'd told Uncle Bill that he would stay with her until he'd convinced her to leave the Hollow so it couldn't destroy her. It seemed the venom was already in and even now it was coursing through her system destroying the mother he'd known.

But Jake was now reluctant to leave. There was a deeper pull within the Hollow. It had been small at first but it was now undeniable.

Did Dreama feel the same pull?

***

It was late, well after dark, when Dreama reentered the Hollow. Weeks had already passed since she'd first arrived, and as she came down the streets houses were dotted with lit window and open doors where a few days before there'd been only black. The random spots of light gave the houses a skeletal look that chilled Dreama.

Her trip back to Columbus had been successful. The audiologist had her hearing aids repaired. She hadn't told anyone, not even Jake or Bridget, that she was leaving town to retrieve them. She didn't want to field questions about her trip. She'd simply told them that she was going to be gone for the day.

As she turned on her parents' driveway her headlights splashed on Mr. Colewick's house. The light caught on the picture window across the front of the house and shined back at her. Its brightness sent a shiver through her body. Much like walking next to a cemetery after dark, she was passing a place where someone had been dead.

It was creepy.

She hadn't wanted to admit it but living these last couple of weeks without her hearing aids had heightened her fears along with the other senses. As if pulling old records off the shelf, her mind played various noises. Twice she shot up in bed convinced that she'd heard a door slam or a footstep, only to realize that there was no physical way for her to have heard such a small sound. Nothing short of a jet engine revving outside her bedroom window would have been able to rouse her without hearing aids.

But now she heard the crunch of gravel under her tires and she crept up one curve, then another. It was nearly 11pm when she pulled up in front of the house.

And a light inside clicked off.

She froze for a moment, the icy hands of fear and the hot hands of adrenaline alternately massaging her heart. Had she actually seen a light click off or was it the reflection like she'd seen at Mr. Colewick's? She replayed the light in her mind. It had looked like a light clicking off in the kitchen. She'd seen that exact thing before when her mom would click off the kitchen light at night when Dreama and her brother were outside talking. The glow through the archway was unmistakable.

She held the brake pedal in and considered what she should do. Was there someone in the house? She scanned the shadows around the house for signs of movement but found none. The memories of a figure in the darkness whispered in her mind. It dared her to turn around and see if the watcher was still there, at the edge of the woods.

She glanced in the rearview mirror but saw nothing. It bolstered her confidence enough to turn slightly. There was no one there. No one was parked in the driveway. There was no reason for anyone to be in the house.

She put the car in park and stepped out. The back door was closed, but was it locked? The screen door opened with a screech. Any intruder would know she was here for sure and would be planning a means of escape. She reached for the knob.

Locked.

She exhaled and stuck the key in the lock, turned, and pushed the back door open. It pushed in effortlessly and she walked through the kitchen, watching for shadows and listening for an intruder.

As she scanned for signs of a break-in she noticed a small lamp sitting along the archway that separated the kitchen and dining room. It was on a timer.

The last bits of fear washed down her body and out of the bottoms of her feet. What she'd seen was the lamp click off with the timer. It only made her feel more ridiculous for creeping around and letting random thoughts control her. She walked in the living room turning lights on as she went. Her own footsteps across the hardwood floor echoed through the empty house. She focused on their rhythmic thud. A splattering of unread magazines sat on the table and she picked one up. She opened it to an article titled "Does he want more than friendship." and leaned back and read through the survey.

"Don't worry. She's deaf." She heard a woman say in a stage whisper in the den directly over her shoulder.

Dreama froze. They didn't know she could hear them. Her heart beat in her ears nearly muffling her reacquired hearing.

"Are you sure?" A man said. She didn't recognize the voice, but it was clearly a man in his 20s or 30s.

"Wait for her to go to bed."

What is your impression of the character?
What is that impression based on?

On the lines below, write some of your impressions [positive and negative] of a few of the characters in the story. List both primary characters and minor characters because all of them are meant to influence the story and the way you perceive it. All of them add flavor to the story. Sometimes secondary characters serve to reflect the qualities of the primary character. How well is that working? Write your notes in the book and below.

_____

_____

_____

_____

_____

_____

_____

_____

_____

_____

_____

"Finally, she's getting up." The voice from the den said. Dreama walked around the small table in the center of the living room and to the steps. Could they see her straining to make out shapes the in the darkness? She sat waited on the couch hoping they'd say something to tell her who they were and what they were doing. She recognized the woman's voice but couldn't place it.

Nothing.

She took even step up the staircase and listened for their conversation to pick up again. Her hearing aids were turned up as loud as she could make them and the microphones at the top were picking up the slightest flutter of air. Digitals may have improved sound quality but it was the hearing aids, not Dreama, who decided what sounds needed amplification.

"See if she is going to bed." She heard a voice through the drone of the hallway fan above her. Frustrated she walked with heavy steps back and forth through the hall. From her bedroom to the main bath, she made it sound like she was getting ready for a shower. She was stalling, trying to consider any way to hear them without-

She stopped. She knew exactly how to listen to them without them ever knowing. She could lie in her bed pretending to sleep and hear every word spoken.

She hurried back to her bedroom and began digging through the box of things she'd packed up from college.

Please be in here.

***

Midged walked up the wooden steps behind the diner to Janice's second floor apartment. The girl had been acting funny over these last days and she was getting a bit concerned that there wasn't something serious with her Aunt and Uncle.

"Land sakes, I don't know how she does these in the rain." Midge groaned halfway up the smooth pieces of wood that were only three-quarters as wide as her feet were long. "Hank needs to put some grippers on you. Someone's liable to slip and break a hip."

The steps creaked back at her.

Finally, she reached the top. The only window she could see clearly from the landing outside Janice's door held a small lamp with a beige shade. It threw off a faint glow, but the room around her looked otherwise dark. Just the same, she knocked.

No answer.

She turned back. The floodlight case a glassy light over the smoothed wood of the step.

"Oh, I'm for sure going to break a hip going down these things." If it weren't for her worry over Janice she'd never have come out this time of night anyhow. Hank seemed to be doing somewhat better. Not himself, but better. Now Janice was out all times of the night, rolling in to work late with dark circles under her eyes.

She made it down the steps and to the house.

"Hank, she's just so secretive bout where she's going and with whom." Midge said as she slid in to her housecoat and slippers.

"Well, she's a grown woman. Ain't no cause for you to fuss in her business." Hank said with about half of his usual gruffness.

"What if things aren't well with her aunt and uncle. Shouldn't we-."

"Nose out? Yes, that's exactly what we should do. You know Janice is a secretive type."

Midge squeezed a bit of lotion in her hands, rubbed them quickly together and massaged her elbows. She'd done the same thing every night since the months leading up to wedding with Hank. She looked at him. Janice wasn't the only one who was the secretive type. Midge knew there was a secret Hank was holding too. And his sudden 'illness' had started about the same time Janice started acting funny.

***

Dreama almost screamed when she found the FM system. She'd forgotten to return it at the end of the semester. She tested the small lapel microphone that her professors had clippled to their shirts.

Her voice was clear, sent directly in to the processor of her hearing aid. She only needed to go down the steps, hide the system with its microphone pointed to the den and she'd pick up everything they said from the den.

She slid it in the palm of her hand and walked down the steps. Fortunately there was no clear den of the bookshelf from the den. It was the closest piece of furniture to the archway and provided ample cover with plants of all kinds.

"She's coming back down." The man's voice whined. Dreama nearly gave herself away by laughing. She faked a sneeze to cover the smirk that snuck on her lips. When she got to the bookshelf she slid one book off of the shelf, slid the system up behind the plant, clicked it on, then thumbed through a few more books. It wasn't perfect, she still heard the hum of something coming in her hearing aid, but it should work.

She put the first book back and the shelf boomed in her ear. She pulled a book off the shelf and quickly clicked off the light. She couldn't hide her smug smile any longer. She tiptoed up the steps and in to her room.

Now that she knew there was no immediate danger she listened. It only took a minute before the voices began.

"Okay, look around." The woman said.

"How do you even know if they're still here?"

"They are, just look."

Dreama heard grunting and dragging from the den. What was "they" and who would go through her house looking for them? She had been gone all winter. A burglar could have had their run of the place.

She should call Jake. Quietly she shuffled around her room for the phone. It was buried in the bottom of her purse where it had pretty much stayed the last two weeks. She'd sent a few texts to Jake and Bridget but without a QWERTY keyboard it was easier to send them a text asking if they were near a computer to IM.

She flipped it open and checked the bars and battery. Both good.

She'd have Jake come, park at the bottom of the drive and walk up. Then he could be hiding in the dark when the people came out. She could have him bring the police too. She didn't think that she could text 911 for help.

She opened the phone and scrolled to his name.

"Jake 911 emergency u there?" She pushed the send.

***

"What do you think? Did the office smell more like a gym locker room or the top floor of a university library?" Jake laughed as he backed out of the lawyer's office.

Renny turned to him and smiled but her insides were on fire. Everything that had gone on in that office froze her with panic so intense that her muscles ached from the effort she exerted to keep them steady. News like she'd heard inside should make a person relieved, heck, gleeful. But Renny knew what it all meant. And that reality brought with it a fresh wash of bile.

"Jakey, what am I going to do with all of that?" She asked to pull the weight of carrying the conversation back off of her.

"From what the lawyer says all that rental property will give you enough money to pay all your bills every year." He smiled and thumped the steering wheel with the palm of his hand. "Why don't you use the life insurance to pay for a house for you and Bridget and then use the other money to pay your bills?"

"No. That just don't seem right." She tapped her thumbnail against her teeth. What business did a poor country girl have in owning all that property? She now owned over a million dollars in rental properties and had a two-hundred thousand dollar insurance policy on top of it.

"Mom, what isn't right about it? It was Uncle Bill's and he wanted you to have it."

Renny knew what happened when one member of a group got too high. She'd seen something similar when she was growing up with a couple of wild cats had staked a claim to the slop pile at the edge of her yard.

She'd taken a special interest in one small cat that never had enough. The small tiger would try to get food but would be pushed away by the larger tom cats.

That night, as a child, she was throwing out a pile of meat bones and some skin. She had held back part of a wing for her special kitten. She'd set it on the ground close and then stepped back to toss the other scraps on the slop pile. The big toms came out right away and began to tear in to the bones and skin on the big pile. There, on the side, was her special kitty.

Slowly it inched over to the piece of wing Renny had reserved. It grabbed the meat in its teeth and ran to the edge of the meadow where the cats hid. It growled as it chewed and Renny felt a strong sense of helping the underdog.

The other three cats, attracted to the growls of their usually meek companion, stopped their chewing and turned to the little one with the wing. They came in slowly and her kitten put her ears back, guarding her prize. Suddenly her little cat ran in the meadow and the three ran quickly after.

There were screeches and screams from the tall grass but she couldn't see beyond the moving tops. The bushes covered in burrs kept her from running in the field. There was hissing, growling and the sound of cats fighting. She hoped for her little cat, but didn't expect much.

"Mom?"

Jakes voice broke in her memory. "Yeah, hon."

"You want to go to the diner and get something to eat?"

"Yes." She flipped down the visor mirror to check her make-up. Her face was ashen and there were dark circles under her eyes. She brushed her bangs back and forth on her forehead. How long had it been since she'd had a hair cut? Her usually shoulder-length brown hair and trimmed bangs now hung in an unhealthy pile on her head. She flipped the visor back up and looked out the window.

Now she was that little kitten and before too long the big slop-pile-cats would find out about the piece of meat her brother tossed her way. They still held the grudge against Jake so he'd be no shield for her. Bridget was too young and innocent in the ways of the Hollow to be pulled in to the mess.

And she knew she was too weak to handle any of this on her own.

Physiology and Feelings

How do you feel when you're nervous? What does your body do? When you hear a noise that startles you, what is your body's response?

_____
_____
_____
_____
_____
_____
_____
_____
_____
_____
_____
_____
_____
_____

The response from your body is your physiology. We have all read about people having their heartbeat thunder in their ears or their face burn with embarrassment, but what are some other ways we can show a range of emotions based on our body's involuntary response to a situation?

_____
_____
_____
_____
_____
_____
_____
_____

Watch for these things in the story [and note them]. Also, write down on the lines below some ways physiology and biology are tied together. Include these in your own writing.

_____

_____

_____

_____

_____

_____

_____

_____

_____

_____

_____

_____

_____

_____

_____

_____

_____

_____

Renny looked over at Janice, the sting of guilt clinging to her body like the tentacles of a jellyfish. Each one plunged its stinger in with a fresh surge of pain that then lingered as the memory went back out to sea.

Janice, for her part, meandered through the diner with the occasional glance timed perfectly to catch Renny's eyes.

Jake sat over at the next booth with the latest object of his affection. Renny knew in some forgotten cavern of her heart that she should feel happy for Jake. That he was moving on from his loss and finding love again. But why here? Why now? Why publically?

The timing couldn't be worse and the selected lady only aroused the suspicions of various chatters in town. Renny tucked her hair behind her ear then, feeling somewhat exposed, pulled the hair back over her cheek. From her spot at the diner's counter she could ignore each person who walked in the door. She could hunch over her plate and lose herself in a meal of fried heart attacks and batter covered clogged arteries.

"How are things, hon?"

Renny looked up to see Midge's bright smile. Among the Blue Hollow inhabitants Renny had always known Midge to have the loudest mouth and the biggest heart. She was the only one who didn't take sides after Jake's accident and the only one to truly welcome Renny and the kids back after Dale died.

"You know, Midge." Renny began. She glanced quickly around the diner and, seeing Janice at a safe distance, continued to speak. "It just seems that all the good things are turning sour on me lately."

"It's this place." Midge said, scanning her eyes around the diner and pausing for a moment at something across the room. The closest thing Renny had ever seen to hate flashed across Midge's eyes, then softened as they completed their circle and landed on

Renny. "It ain't you."She repeated, quieter. "It's this place. Too many secrets."

Renny felt the overwhelming urge to reach out and take Midge's hand and

comfort her old friend, but before she could get up the resolve Midge's voice was bright

again.

"Don't you worry none, Renny. Things turn around here. You just take care of

yourself and things have a way of working around for you."

Renny nodded and Midge left. The temporary insight in to Midge was

unnerving. In the almost forty years this diner had been around Renny had never seen

anything like that. She started to think again about that little cat hiding in the tall grass,

holding the small morsel of chicken as the others began to circle.

***

"I'm glad we ran in to each other." Jake said as he pulled in the parking lot at

the center of town. "I have wanted to see you but I dropped my cell in a mop bucket

and I'm waiting on a replacement."

"I'm parked just over there." Dreama pointed to her car about three rows over.

She had enjoyed lunch with Jake. She hated to admit how happy she'd been when she

saw him come through town. It was even worse that she had made sure her face, hair and clothes were perfect should such an encounter occur.

"Yeah. I dropped my phone so I couldn't call and I didn't want to just show up."

She nodded. The explanation over the phone, the second explanation unsettled her. Since she'd sent the text and heard the chirp through her FM system she'd struggled to compare Jakes voice to the one she'd heard the previous night. They didn't sound very similar at all but how could a deaf woman listening to whispers through an FM system be certain of anything?

The parking spot next to her car was empty and Jake pulled in and put the car in park.

"It was great to see you." His eyes lingered on her.

And she was glad they did.

She dug around in her mind looking for a piece of unfinished conversation to fill the thickening air. Something that wouldn't involve talk of his athletic ability, wonderful sense of humor or charm.

Nothing came. She simply sat staring at him.

Was she waiting? If so, for what?

Was he waiting?

Her fingers tingled and she wondered what it would feel like to hold his hand.

The feelings were there again, dangerous and enticing. She remembered the hurt of the last time she allowed herself to have this ache in her heart. Without thinking she reached up and touched her hearing aid. The little computers that helped her straddle the two worlds but never let her truly become a member of either.

How she'd missed them.

And how she'd hated them.

***

Midge poured hot water in to her foot soaker and slid her tired feet in the water. After more than twelve hours standing behind the counter and walking around the diner her feet resembled swollen sausages.

She was getting older, not old by any means, but older. She was tiptoeing in to her sixties and each night her body groaned at the abuse it had to endure. Across the room Hank had taken his usual evening position on the couch. His ankles were propped up on the arm of the couch, something she'd given up commenting about, and his head was on a small pillow.

She'd hoped that Janice would be her saving grace. When the young girl came back to town a year ago it felt like the beginning of a community healing. She'd been so broken after her cousin's death and it hurt Midge's heart so much. So when Janice walked in asking for a job and her old lodging Midge was thrilled.

"Folks'll be getting back to town in the next week or two." Hank said without ever taking his eyes from the TV. "About time we got to thinking about bringing in more help."

"We can bring in a high school kid or two to bus tables." Midge replied. The betrayal she felt was simmering deep inside but a confrontation, well, Midge wasn't one to confront. She didn't like a fuss. That was likely how she'd been able to float above the problems in Blue Hollow over the years. No one ever felt that Midge had taken the opposing position. She'd mastered the doublespeak necessary to sound like a gossip without being seen as the enemy.

"We need more than just a few kids picking up dishes." He turned now to face her.

"Now don't get on this again." Was it the heat from the hot water soothing her feet or a surge of anger laced adrenaline that pushed her on. "I ain't about to move."

Hank brought his feet off the side of the couch and lumbered to a sitting position. "Midge, I'm not talking about moving. I'm talking about getting help running the diner we already have."

"I've run that place for years." She leaned forward a bit as if preparing to stand. Pain climbed from the bottoms of her feet and made it almost to her knees before she leaned back again.

"Sure. And I'm watching you soak your feet every night now. There ain't no cause you putting yourself through all of this."

"And how will we afford to pay all of this new help." She looked around at their house. It was comfortable but not plush. The wallpaper, couches and carpet had been beautiful in their day. Their day had been about two decades ago. "Hiring anyone else would cut so far in to what little we're making. I'm not sure how we're going to manage."

Hank recoiled as if struck with a physical blow. She studied him for a moment, then continued. "We need to be paying off the house or putting money in retirement."

"Midge, we got plenty of money."

"Do we now?" She lifted her feet from the water and shook them off. She was ready to storm off. She felt the pull of the front door. Escape from all the anger that was settling deep in her. She felt the insane pull and even as frustration bubbled deep her rational side still whispered questions at her.

"Don't you worry about what we've got or don't got. I told you we can hire and

I think we should."

"You hiding money from me?" She stood from her chair.

"Hiding? Midge, since when are you interested in the books?"

"Since things started getting a bit weird out there." She felt her words pulling

at her to last out and tell him all she knew. The suspicions in her mind chanted like

cicadas, like players at a baseball game. Sec-rets, Sec-rets. She wanted to swat them away

but the force was too strong.

She stood like a batter waiting on the pitch.

"I'll show them to you. I've got nothing to hide." Hanks face was red and the

musty smell of grease and sweat began to fill the room.

Sec-rets, Sec-rets, Sec-rets. Midge tried to shake the droning from her mind but

it didn't clear.

"Maybe not with books." She said, suddenly feeling empowered. "I'd like to see

them now."

Something flashed in Hank's eyes for an instant, only long enough to notice,

not long enough to interpret. "What do you mean not with books?" He said, his voice

thick and gruff.

***

"All I'm saying is it would be nice to know these things." Dreama's mom said. At least she was only speaking slowly rather than yelling. Despite her preparations for this conversation Dreama had not expected her mom to get so irate over the hearing aid repair.

"Mom, I covered the co-pay. I handled the problem."

"So you see nothing wrong with lying to your parents." Her mom's voice scaled up to yelling again. Obviously she'd called Dreama as soon as the letter came in the mail from the insurance company.

"Mom, I'm an adult." Dreama said. She looked around the cabin. How adult was she? She had no job, no apartment and owned nothing but her car. She knew all this because her mom had pointed it out to her shortly after the conversation began.

"Dreama, you don't listen to reason."

"What reason? I did nothing wrong." Dreama paced faster from one room to the next but it was frustration, not exertion, which forced her heart to beat faster and faster.

"You knew we'd tell you to come home if we knew."

"Yes, and I didn't need to." She ran up the steps to her room and began to pull things from her dresser.

"You should have been here. You couldn't hear anything for almost two weeks."

"So what!" One suitcase was full with crumpled clothes. She grabbed the next.

"So, wha-. Dreama, do you have any sense about you at all?"

***

Hank turned down one familiar road, then another. Droplets of sweat gathered along his hairline and clustered then crept along his skin like ants crawling on a morsel of bread.

Like a piece of bread he was being eaten alive by what he knew of Colewick's death. He had seen the figure up the road that night when he went to confront Bill, but he didn't think he'd been seen. But Midge's words told him that the truth was coming out.

And it would be soon.

He stopped first at the diner. There had been a few times over the course of their marriage when Hand had been so angry with Midge that he could find no other place to cool off than at the diner. He walked in the backdoor and flipped on the light in the kitchen. The room was silent except for the low hum of the industrial freezers and the incandescent light.

He pulled a large silver milkshake cup off of the shelf and loaded it with vanilla bean ice cream, strawberries and milk. He whipped it up until it was almost smooth then he added two scoops of malt and blended it up the rest of the way.

With milkshake in hand he walked through the swinging door in to the dark side of the diner. His shoes squeaked a bit on the tiles. He admired the large black and white checkered floor. When the time came to fix the place up two years ago he was the one who lined each of these up and put them in place. It wasn't often he got out here to see this side of the diner and enjoy all the work he'd put in to it.

He was tired.

As if the simple act of allowing that thought entry had tapped his full reservoir of strength, Hank sat down in the nearest chair with a solid thud.

How long would he be able to enjoy this town? The large windows showed a two lane road that separated the diner from the rest of the town. The parking lot was more dirt than blacktop and the town square was about three miles west as the crow flies. Nearly his entire adult life had been spent in this town.

In this diner.

And for the last couple of years he'd wanted to get out. His back was hunched from years over a grill and his stomach was huge from fried lunches.

And milkshakes.

He laughed and swallowed down another mouthful of his treat. He held it in his mouth and let it go from freezing cold to melted and warm. How long would he be able to enjoy these simple luxuries?

How had Midge learned about his connection to Bill's death? And why had she pretended that she didn't know.

Then he knew. He had never thought Midge to be an evil woman, never a person to be spiteful. Then a new pain drove through his heart deeper than the fear that had preceded it.

***

The tears filling in Dreama's eyes turned her once comforting room in to nothing more than a swirling world of colors and shapes. They stretched and morphed in a puddle of tears, then cleared in the blink of an eye only to immediately begin morphing again.

She remembered looking at a book of famous paintings once as a child. There was one called "The Scream" where a twisted ghostlike figure of a person stood before a swirling background of color. That painting could have been her in this moment. A ghostly figure standing in the midst of confusion silently crying out for answers as everything around her is stretched and distorted. There were no words to articulate everything inside of her. She felt abandoned. She was insulted. She was-

She stopped and examined her room for a moment. Clothes were jammed in to bags and boxes. Her dresser stood bare with only a few half-open drawers to indicate it had ever been used. The closet was open and two paper covered wire hangers hung on the rod. A third hanger was tossed half in the closet half out.

The room was like her insides: empty with little evidence that anything had once filled her. She walked to the nightstand and scooped up her Bible. It had been a sweet sixteen gift from her parents. A picture fluttered out and landed on the carpet next to her pile of shoes. She knew who was in the photo even before lifting it up. She let Evan's eyes bore in to her again.

It was a posed picture from high school. His chiseled features reminded her of stone statues she'd seen in that same art book. His stare that had once seemed so warm and protective now seemed cold and accusative. The smile was more a sneer than a demonstration of any sort of joy.

This photo represented liberation for her. Standing up to Evan, and her parents, had been the first step in this long road of self-determination. She put the photo back in her Bible and tossed it on top of the boxes and piles of stuff to pack in her car. It landed with a thud and she looked at the mess in front of her.

She blinked away the swirling colors again and with clear eyes took in all she was seeing, feeling. This time the colors did not swirl again. The frustration of stifled screams no longer twisted at her insides. She realized the true meaning of all of this. It was at once liberating and terrifying. She spoke to give voice to all she was feeling even though it was only the walls that would hear her announcement.

"And all of this represents my second step."

***

Dreama scooted her food around her plate with her fork as if the words she needed were hiding somewhere below a pile of home fries and scrambled eggs.

"You not hungry?" Jake asked.

She didn't look up right away. She was fighting back the emotion that was trying to force its way in to the conversation. The monotony of a breakfast in the diner and the cleansing of a good night's sleep had given her a sentimental outlook on the Hollow. She'd come to a realization the previous evening as she looked at her things piled up in a heap on her bed. She wanted to stay.

Originally she'd come to run away from things. There had been the pain of Evan's rejection and then the news of her coming deafness. She didn't fear her hearing loss but rather what that would mean for her place in the family. Coming down here was supposed to help her to get a handle on the emotions bombarding her. She looked up and tried a smile but the effort released the tears she'd been holding back.

This trip had been nothing she expected. Nothing it was supposed to be, so there was no reason for this attachment. She'd lost her hearing aids for two weeks, seen an old friend die and learned how to handle it on her own. She was becoming a woman emotionally. She had been forced to take a few steps down the path of independence, forced down really, and she'd found that she didn't collapse under the pressure. She wanted to keep growing, but she couldn't do that at her parent's house.

And there was the strange pull she was feeling whenever she saw Jake. He stirred up in her kinds of feelings she'd come to the hollow to escape. Not the bad ones where she felt she'd never measure up or the ones where she felt in some way defective.

He stirred up in her the other set of womanly emotions that she'd been too self-conscious to admit she had already. She noticed his protective nature and kind eyes. If she were a few years younger she'd practice writing out her name with his...just to see how it looked.

She'd seen the way Jake looked at her and sensed an attraction from him as well. He could be wondering what it'd be like to date a deaf girl-she'd played to that role a few times-but she hoped it was more than curiosity that caused his eyes to linger on her a bit longer or his smile to take on the nervous edge of growing affection.

And braided in to the strands of these feelings were the lingering questions she couldn't answer. The stolen bits of conversation she'd collected when others didn't realize she was paying attention. Janice's irrational hate. Renny's irrational fear. The sense that there was a dance being played out all around her and, while she was standing in the middle, the others were spinning around her too quickly to follow.

"Dreama?"

She zipped from the spinning thoughts and locked in on Jakes eyes. "What?"

"You were staring at your eggs. Is everything okay?" There was more humor than concern in her voice. She took the opening and ran with it.

"Didn't sleep much last night." She smiled and jammed a forkful of cold eggs in her mouth.

"It's going around." Midge said from behind her. Dreama turned to see her smiling with a pot of fresh coffee in her hand. "Top you off?"

"Yes." Then seizing on the opportunity to blurt out what she had to say with the least amount of emotional investment she added. "I have a long drive back to Columbus today."

"Columbus?" Jake asked. His voice probed but, not realizing the full implication of what she was saying, he didn't go much further.

She darted her eyes to him then quickly back at Midge. It was far easier to break this painful news to her. Right now she couldn't handle either Jake's disappointment, or possibly his apathy, to her leaving.

"My parent's and I have a differing of opinion." She started, hoping that not all of this would get back to them. "I need to get out on my own so I'm going back to the city to find a job. I have a friend I can stay with for a few days-then we'll see what happens."

Midge's eyes widened with the look of a woman who just witnessed a miracle. Dreama tried to smile but was certain the expression came across more perplexed.

"Dreama, you just looking for some work?"

"Yes."

"Well you are just an angel sent straight from heaven." Midge said. She produced a small dish towel, set it on the table and placed the pot of coffee on top. Her hands now free to participate in the conversation too Midge started in earnest.

"I was just telling Hank how I'd like to bring someone on to help me around here. You'd be just the kind of person I'd love to have."

"Me?" Dreama asked. It was more self-deprecating than either Midge or Jake realized. It wasn't often she'd heard of a deaf person being the answer to a prayer to someone.

"Absolutely you." Midge said. Her eyes ran up and down Dreama's frame. "You must be about the same size as Janice." She turned to Jake and said, "So I know I've got some uniforms that'll fit." Then back to Dreama, "And you're a college girl. You'd be more mature than these 16 and 17 year olds who come in here during the summer to pick up work."

It sounded good to Dreama. Not only did she have work but she'd be able to stay in the Hollow. Maybe it would patch things up for her parents to see her in action.

"Can I let you know later today?" Dreama asked. Hope already perking in her mind.

"Sure thing. I'll have your uniforms waiting." Midge winked at her, picked her pot of coffee up and headed back across the diner. Dreama turned back to Jake who was now smiling.

"And I know where you can stay." He smiled.

"Really? Where?" She could hardly believe how things were falling in to place. The shroud of uncertainty lifted and she embraced her independence.

"Don't worry a bit." Jake said. He reached across the table and rubbed the back of her hand with his fingertips.

As if connected to an outlet, tingles surged from the point of contact throughout her body in the time it took her to suck in a breath. Jake drew his fingers back quickly and grabbed his coffee mug.

"I'm so sorry." He stammered.

"No, it is fine."

"I just-"

"Really, it's-"

Jake got up from the table and tossed ten dollars next to his plate. "Breakfast in on me." He glanced at her, then looked away. "I'll call you in an hour or so about the place I know about."

Dreama watched him walk out the door and get in his car. The heat she'd felt dissolved to the cold of loneliness. She reached over and rubbed the spot he'd touched her as if somehow she could relive the moment-regenerate it through her own effort.

***

Jake sat on the park bench. The morning sun was above the trees and burning off the last bits of dew from the grass. Behind him a spider web stretched between the bars of a long forgotten merry-go-round. The spider crawled across it like a single black pearl among a string of diamonds.

Jake scanned the familiar landscape much like an angler does his fly. He tossed a glance to the slide that his little sister played on as a child, then jerked it back. Next, he threw a look to the pavilion where his dad finally laid out all he knew about girls, then jerked it back. He tapped the water of his memory until his eyes landed on the parking lot. Here he settled a bit and allowed his thoughts to drift along the surface of the water ready to rip the line of consciousness back up if a bad memory grabbed hold too tight.

Today his mind was almost too distracted with the thoughts of the moment to be tortured by the sins of the past.

Almost.

He pulled back on the memory just a bit. Thoughts of Alexa and their last moments here a decade ago blended guilt and betrayal in to a long forgotten heartache. The line was pulling too hard again so he dropped his memory to his car. He thought about all that his mom wasn't saying. She was like an abused wife returning again to her husband hoping that this time he'd really keep his promise. Mom now knew that she'd been lied to again, but she couldn't escape. She didn't have the strength.

He didn't have the strength either. The tug of his eyes to the parking lot, to the road, forced him to follow the memories where they'd lead. When he'd found Alexa up here eleven years ago it had been confirmation that God had chosen her for his wife.

Of course, he was much older now and realized that God didn't always give those kinds of billboard signs, but he didn't know that then.

Alexa had stood next to him, her hands squeezing his arm. He rubbed the spot now as if he'd still feel her fingers there.

"I told you to end this thing." Janice had screamed at Alexa. No, it had been more of a shriek than a scream and her voice ripped through the park and echoed off the side of the mountain, through the trees and surged through the night.

"I want to be with Jake." Alexa had shouted back.

"Your parents put you in my care and I said you're not getting mixed up in the Colewick bunch.

"What's wrong with our family?" Jake had jumped in, offended that it was his family specifically, and not simply his gender, that had riled such hatred in Janice.

Alexa had been angry. She'd run through the parking lot and down the winding road that twisted from this park down to the Hollow. Janice had followed her.

No.

He ripped himself out of the memory before he could think about jumping in his car and going after Alexa.

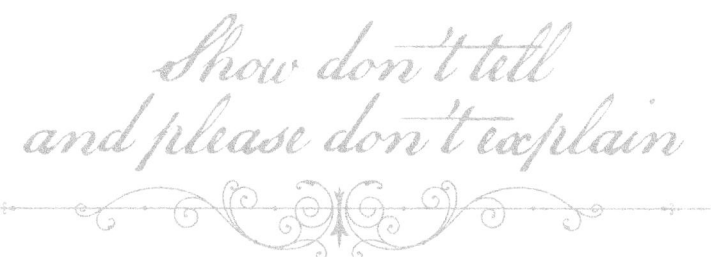

Show don't tell and please don't explain

Every writer who has been writing for long will hear "Show don't Tell!!" chanted at them again and again. A common example is anger. You can say a person is angry or you can show them acting out that anger. Watching someone throw something is far more intense and emotional than hearing that a person was upset.

Whenever possible you need to show the emotions of a character rather than simply saying how they feel. I say, "whenever possible" because sometimes it just doesn't make sense to show and for the sake of pacing you need to just say something.

But when does telling become explaining? That is when a person is TRYING to show but instead of building in emotions, subtle indications and little clues they use adverbs, adjectives, similes and metaphors all together to try to explain what is going on in the scene. Look for examples of that happening as you read then try to rewrite that section to show what is happening.

***

"Everything alright?" Midge asked. Her eyebrows squeezed in a look of concern.

"Yes, fine." Dreama managed to say. She watched the last bit of dust from Jake's exit drift away before she turned back to Midge. "He's got an idea of a place for me to live."

"So you'll take the job?"

Dreama nodded and continued to rub the back of her left hand.

"That is wonderful. You come by later this afternoon." Midge glanced around for a moment. "Say about 3pm when things are slower."

Dreama nodded in reply. "Oh, and this is for the bill plus a tip." She handed

the ten dollar bill Jake had left to Midge. She smiled a reply and tucked it in her apron.

***

It felt like betrayal now that she was here. Rather than leaving home with her

parents carrying in boxes and wishing her well, like they'd done when she moved in the

dorm, Dreama was now sneaking off to a place of her own on the other side of town.

"And you're sure your mom only wants $100 a month for this place." Dreama looked

between Jake and Bridget then back at the loft, her loft, where she'd spend the summer.

"Yes." Jake said. "I don't think you'll be able to afford much more on diner

wages." He laughed but it was hollow.

"Are you ready to move your stuff up?" Bridget said. She stood by the door

and Dreama felt the vicarious liberation Bridget was experiencing through Dreama's

rebellion.

Dreama glanced at Jake. His eyes were focused on the mountain outside her

window. Was he taking in the beauty? She lingered for just a moment but the silent

reflection told her that Jake wasn't living a happy memory.

Feelings had a funny way of appearing when it was least appropriate. She knew the danger of all of the feelings inside her. They were the kind that would trump all logic and had always led to pain. The kind of pain she saw in Jake's eyes now.

She walked down the three small steps to a gravel covered strip of land behind the pharmacy. Here, perched above the downtown shops, Dreama would exercise a bit of freedom.

She had considered the likelihood of running in to her parents with such a prominently located apartment. Then she remembered her only other option was remaining under their room.

"Bridget, is Jake okay?"

Bridget's face dropped, only for a moment. "He's been moody the past day or two." She scanned the buildings that circled them. "Actually, it's been longer than that." She lifted a box and carried it up the steps in to the loft.

Dreama grabbed a larger box and followed Bridget in. Jake met her in the doorway and smiled. Like the haze of sleep had lifted from Rip van Winkle, Jake's eyes were clear and bright. He reached for the box in her arms. "You shouldn't be carrying that." She caught a wink just before the box obscured his face.

Heat surged through her body and she walked back down the steps for the next box. The electricity of the one glance, the confirmation of interest, had ignited a fire in

Dreama's cheeks. Yes, this was really happening.

"You go inside and unpack and I'll haul boxes in." Jake said as he came back out of the house.

"Okay, that should make things faster."

He scanned the trunk. "I'd say we only have two or three more loads. I told Bridget that she can go home if she wants, as long as you can give me a ride home."

"Of course."

She went in the house and told Bridget she could go then began to hang her clothes in the closet and set a few books on the shelf on the left side of the room. The place was usually rented to summer residents so it was fully furnished. Of course, that meant a bed shoved against one wall and a small worn couch on the other. The kitchen was made up of a two burner stove, fridge that was slightly bigger than the one in her dorm at school, a table with two chairs and a splattering of plates, glasses and utensils.

Her pocket vibrated and Dreama reached in to retrieve her cell phone.

"Hi Dad." Her voice quivered a bit behind the cheery façade.

"Hi hon. I wanted to let you know about something your mom just read online." She wondered only for a moment why her mom hadn't called. "It's about a group of CI recipients who are having an informational meeting Tuesday night."

"Okay." She let her voice drop. "Can you email me the information?"

He agreed and hung up. She set her phone down on the mini-table and dropped on the left side of the couch. It was a response to both the fear that overwhelmed her when she thought of telling her parents that she'd moved out, and the frustration that they couldn't allow her the space to make her decision.

"You okay?" Jake said behind her from the door.

"Yeah." She said. Face still buried in her hands. She wanted to shut the world out. Take off her hearing aids and rest in the silence but, with Jake here, she didn't want to isolate herself completely.

"What happened?"

"Parents." Was her one word explanation. She knew at his age that single utterance held in it all the conflicting emotions that raged in her.

She felt the cushion sink down on her right and then Jake's arm wrap around her shoulder. He pulled her close to him and hugged her. He smelled like soap and cologne and the slightest bit of sweat. She kept her face buried in her hands but the anger and fear were fading. In their place was complete comfort.

"Have you told them yet that you've moved over here?"

"No."

"You nervous about it?"

"Yes."

"Chatty today, aren't you?"

"No." Dreama laughed and pulled her hand from her face but kept her cheek

against his chest. He responded by releasing her from the bear hug only enough to

touch her face with his fingertips.

"Dreama, it couldn't possibly be any harder than it was for you to come here in

the first place."

"That was different." She wrapped her arm across the front of Jake.

"How?"

"It just is. I wasn't moving out." She sorted through her emotions trying to

justify her fear while considering that Jake might be right.

"But you were acting independently. Just like you have on that hearing surgery

thing."

"CI" Dreama corrected him.

"Okay, on that CI."

She sat up slightly and faced him. His arm around her feeling as natural as

discussing her problems with him. "But I've never actually given them a final decision on that."

"But you've made your position clear."

"But not firm." She answered. "I always leave the door open to 'maybe' so that I can avoid fighting with them."

Jake looked out the window for a moment then back at her. "But you are being firm now."

"And I'm terrified to tell them."

"Why?"

***

"You've taken a real liking to this young girl, haven't you?" Midge said to Janice as they filled Ketchup bottles.

"No point being rude." She smiled with her southern charm as she spoke.

"Just the same, she seems to be a nice enough girl. And she seems to be good for Jake."

"You mean too good for Jake." The ice reserved for Renny or Jake hissed out. While Midge didn't really approve of the intensity of Janice's hatred for the two remaining Colewick's she knew the pain that had birthed it so she usually didn't fuss over it.

"You been spending a good deal of time with your Aunt and Uncle?" She knew the reason for Janice's frequent trips out over these last few weeks had precious little to do with ailing relatives, but Midge wanted to hear the lie straight from Janice.

"A bit more. My Uncle's ailing a bit these days. I like to do what I can to help Auntie." The southern drawl intensified the more she spoke of family. While Midge had seen it as an endearment in times gone by she now recognized it for the subtle manipulation it was. Midge was learning a great deal these days since Hank and Janice started their sneaking around. Of course, they still saw her as a fat version of Flo from the 80s show "Alice" but this woman wasn't going to tell anyone to Kiss her Grits.

"Did I write this down right?" Dreama came over and handed Midge a green and white order pad.

"That's just fine honey. Now go clip it to that wheel and yell 'Order in'. When it's ready Hank will yell 'Order up' and the table number."

"I'm glad you were able to get more help." Janice said, screwing on a ketchup lid and wiping down the bottle.

"I'm sure you are." The words dribbled out a bit louder than Midge had intended and immediately fear flashed across Janice's face.

"Yes." Janice stammered. "I have felt my loyalties divided and knowing you have."

"Oh, is that what young people call it right now. Divided loyalties?" Warnings flashed in Midges mind but just as an 18-wheeler couldn't stop on a dime when going down the side of a mountain, she couldn't hold her tongue in the face of such bold faced lies.

"And what do you call it?" Janice stopped for a moment then looked between Dreama and Midge.

***

"Janice, stay." Charlie said as her felt her get up from his bed and pull her things around. The beams of moon light mixed with his security light outside to light up the window. Janice's silhouette was dark against its brightness.

"Charlie, you know I can't do that."

"Marry me."

Her silhouette stopped and she turned to him. He would have run to her and knelt before her but residual modesty kept him under the sheet on his bed.

"Charlie..."

"Marry me." His voice was firmer this time. She was considering it. She hadn't said-

"No."

He wouldn't be deflated this time. She was weakening in her resistance. He'd press on, tear down the rampart that circled her wounded heart and rescue her from her own tower of pain. "Janice. I love you."

"Charlie." Pain. There was pain in her voice. He reached down and slid on a pair of pants and walked to her.

"Janice." He smoothed her hair from her face. Empty eyes looked up at him like dark pools of a zombie. If only he could infuse her with his love as he had with his passion. Every night she came over now she had one purpose in mind, and he accommodated her, but he was beginning to feel empty when she left.

"Why can't we leave things like they are."

"I am not looking for a friend with benefits, Janice."

She stepped back at him and pulled her clothes against her. "Is that what this was to you?"

"You know it wasn't." The change in her tone signaled danger. He fought to recover the upper hand. "Janice, I've loved you and hoped for you for thirty years."

"And why was that Charlie?" She yelled. She sniffled in the darkness and he knew she was crying.

"Janice, what I did was wrong."

"You left me, Charlie."

"I know."

"You let the town say whatever they wanted and you just-"

"I know." Frustration brought a near growl to his words. "I've paid for that every

night without you, Janice. Every time-." He paused for a moment to calm the anger that

was setting his muscles in concrete. "Will my love ever be enough for you to forget the

past."

She walked to the side of the bed and sat down. "I'm afraid, Charlie."

"Afraid of what?"

"All of it."

***

The rumbling crackle of potatoes in a vat of grease blotted out the

conversations of the diner. Alone in his little laboratory Hank put together orders for

the various diners.

"Order-up, Burger light on the salt and double order of onion rings."

That order, formerly known as Bill Colewick's Usual, grabbed Hank and flung

him back to the night he'd killed the man.

"Hank?"

He looked up to see the new girl, Dreama, standing in the doorway of the kitchen. Her brown hair was swept up off her neck and small strands laid gently along her cheek. She looked like a little girl, really she was, and her look of concern caused the vice of guilt to tighten around his chest.

"Yes?" He said, clearing his throat and slapping the patty down on the griddle. It made a smacking sound immediately followed by the familiar hiss of cooking beef.

"Midge needs more lettuce for the front." She spoke in a flat voice, her eyes digging deep in to his soul.

He pointed her to the lettuce then returned to the sizzle of the griddle. His breath moved in and out with considerable effort as Bill's final moments played before him. The scene's rolling back and forth in front of him over and over. They rewound back to him at the bowling alley with Midge then ran forward to Bill's final breaths. Then back again to the series of little pranks then forward to the funeral.

Sometimes as he relived it he would imagine if things had played out differently. Of course, they hadn't so he always found himself there again. Puling in to Bill's driveway. Seeing the figure up the road. Knocking on Bill's door and leaving after he died.

And now Bill is buried in the town cemetery and Midge has dug something up.

"Secrets" she'd said. How could a wife, his wife, hold something over his head like this? Of course, he knew how. It was the same thing that had led Hank to Bill's home that night.

If love had driven him over the edge maybe there'd have been something noble in the quest but now that Midge was his, fully his, again Hank had realized that it was nothing more than pride.

The sour taste of the word carried with it bile and sulfur. He had felt ashamed that his wife was making eyes at Colewick. More than the need to keep her love, Hank had wanted to remain her focus. He'd traded his life for a greasy apron and a round belly.

Now escape was impossible. A sudden change in routine could arouse suspicion and but remaining in this town ensured Midge's continued meddling. And since she'd shown him her hand he knew he was fully at her mercy.

***

The coins were in a wooden box behind a loose stone behind a metal door in the basement. Renny was now the only one alive who had that information. She wasn't sure what it was that had suddenly drawn her to Bill's house and then to that memory.

She walked from room to room in her brother's house and admired the simple way he'd lived.

Both of them had masked their wealth in that simplicity. Bill had moved under the radar to keep up his reputation as Blue Hollow's grandpa. The wealthy river rats paid his well to maintain their grounds and winterize their homes. It made them feel charitable to send gifts and money to such a simple person of modest means.

In truth Bill was wealthier than most of the residents he cared for. All of his money was funneled through the various property management companies he owned and tangible assets. Silver, Gold and old coins.

As if ants were running down her spine Renny suddenly shivered. She remembered that cat. She had no one to confide in. If she'd wanted to rid herself of the money and the curse that seemed to follow who would she tell?

She turned on the light at the top of the steps leading to Bill's basement but then stopped. She checked the doors and windows to be sure they were locked, then she went down one step.

She listened.

No sounds of movement below. Only the ragged scratching of her breath and the thudding of her heart. A few more steps and she could the nearly all of the basement. A metal shelf on the left held large plastic storage containers with red lids. Boxes of bulbs and Christmas lights were clearly visible through the sides. The next shelf down held no less than thirty pints of home canned tomatoes.

She came to the bottom step and turned right. The basement was not a fancy living space like many homes were now but Bill had created a respectable area to repair small things down in the basement. The pegboard held screwdrivers, wrenches and a set of vice grips. She walked over to the work bench. Her shoes squeaked as she crossed the silent house. She removed the screwdriver, took down a can of WD-40 and grabbed a blue industrial strength paper towel.

In the far corner she found the metal door. It didn't appear anyone had moved it in years. She sprayed WD-40 on the hinge and pried open one end with the screwdriver. She knew she was alone but the importance of her task surged adrenaline through her. She had to get the coins to safety before someone found out about them or their location.

Remember the cat.

She always remembered the cat.

She worked the hinge back and forth with increased resolve. A sense of approaching danger heightened every sense. The house creaked and shifted as winds drifted outside. The door finally opened enough to reach the brick. She pulled at it and snapped off a fingernail. Pain tore in to her finger and she dropped the brick.

No time. She had to finish what she'd come for. Irrational panic urging her forward and the approach of night reminding her of what was at stake. A shadow darted at the edge of Renny's vision. Someone had been watching through the basement window far over her head. She looked down at the nearly exposed box and back at the windows above her that surrounded the basement. A cuss word slipped from her lips before she realized what she'd said. No time for rational thought, only instinct. She stuck her hand in the hole and grabbed the box.

***

"We were at the wrong house." Janice called Tommy as soon as she got to her car. Her lungs burned from the run and her breaths came out in punctuated wheezes.

"Where were they?"

"Bill's" She said. She pulled around behind the diner and started to unbuckle her seatbelt even before she had the car in park. "I'm just getting home now. I'm going to change and go meet with the investors."

"You have them then?"

"Don't get weak on me now. I told you, I know how to get Renny to give them to me."

"I'm a Lieutenant I can't-."

"I told you it wouldn't be anything illegal."

"I can't think of many legal ways to get someone to give you that much money in coins."

"I don't think she knows their full value."

"Even if they're only worth $80,000, I can't see a person just giving that up."

Janice slid out of her pants and in to a silk pants suit. "Tommy, I have to go. I can't fix my hair and makeup with this wifi thing clipped to my ear."

"Oh, so we're on the Borg phone?" Tommy laughed. Janice clicked the phone off and tossed the earpiece on the bed. Her sapphire suite glistened in the sunlight shining through the windows.

***

Jake walked in the back door and in to the kitchen. Two glasses were in the sink but otherwise the kitchen was completely untouched. He opened the cupboard and pulled out a box of fettuccini and some tomato sauce.

"We need to get out of the hollow, Jake." He turned. His mom stood in the doorway a bag clutched to her chest.

"Mom? What are you talking about?"

She looked left and right before continuing. "We have to leave. Go. Tonight."

She came closer and eyeing the food he'd just set out on the counter continued. "I need you to take me to a hotel. We can come back in a few days but we need to leave. Now."

Without further comment Jake walked back to his room and pulled clothes out of his dresser. "Is Bridget home?" He called as he stuffed another shirt in his bag. He hoisted the bag on his shoulder and hurried to the kitchen. In more rational moments he would have questioned their sudden departure.

***

Dreama walked down the main drag of Blue Hollow. With people coming up for the summer to stay in their various summer homes the city had nearly doubled in size since she arrived a month ago. She'd tried to call Jake and Bridget before she left work but both of their phones rang through to voicemail. People strolled down city streets in groups and looked in the windows of various shops. A few had shopping bags in their hands but most were enjoying the beginning of summer.

These people didn't realize Bill Colewick had died, nor would they care if someone told them. The town was like a person. There was the town that she had always thought was Blue Hollow. That was the town she'd lived in with her parents. It was a smaller version of the big city life. Then there was the town made of people who lived there year round. That was like the inner psyche of a person. Blue Hollow's inner psyche was known only to the people who grew up here.

She remembered the first time her parents took her to a play date for kids with hearing loss. Her parents had been trying to decide whether to put her in the oral program at the school up the street or bus her across town to the mainstreamed school that offered and ASL interpreter. She was six years old at the time but even then she felt the push and pull of the deaf and hearing worlds. She had more hearing than most of the other kids but she was the only one who knew any sign language.

"We don't allow sign language at our play dates." One of the mom's had said. Immediately Dreama's mom had come over, "Dreama, we talked about this. You are not allowed to talk with your hands here. Use your voice."

Dreama had nodded and then returned to playing with the little kids. They played Old Maid and colored pictures.

"It's time to go." Her mother had called and Dreama took her mom's hand and left. "Did you have fun?"

"It was okay." Dreama had answered, trying to show some enthusiasm. In fact there was nothing fun about it at all. All the kids she tried to play with had a hard time understanding her but she wasn't allowed to clarify by talking with her hands. Her mom had told her not to use sign language with the same tone and stern eyes that she'd told her not to track mud in the house or to pick up her room.

Dreama was pulled back to the present by the smell of candles drifting out of an open store door. Just like on that play date she wanted to know the people of this town but she was an outsider. She wouldn't fully be trusted until she was recognized as one of them.

She'd noticed that the grocer always replaced produce as soon as he sold it as if a hole in the pyramid of oranges would imply slothfulness rather than a demand for his product. He smiled warmly but rarely spoke and was always sweeping his store or the sidewalk in front of his store.

She continued down the sidewalk to the diner. A row of cars owned by the usual afternoon customers lined the front sidewalk like dogs waiting for their masters to return. She sat down at the far end of the counter and flipped over her mug. She checked her phone again for a message from Jake but there were no messages-not even from her parents. The dark gloom of loneliness tickled her arms with the coolness of dread. Dreama rubbed them to push down the goose bumps while assuring her mind that there was no truth to glooms opinions.

"You cold?" Midge filled Dreama's mug as she spoke.

"Always." She laughed and opened two mini cups of cream and dumped them in her coffee.

"Well that apartment of yours will keep you plenty warm. No amount of air conditioning can beat windows with southern exposure. Not on the second floor and in the summer."

"I'm sure you're right Miss Midge." Dreama smiled as she brought the mug to her lips and blew across the coffee.

"Now I told you that you're like family now. Ain't no need calling me Miss Midge but I'm impressed with your Blue Hollow language lessons" She squeezed Dreama's arm then turned and set the coffee pot on the hot plate. "What'll you have?"

Dreama smiled, "I'll have this cup of coffee and a bit of conversation if you're not too busy."

Midge patted her hand. "That's what I like to hear. What's eating at you?"

"Lots of things." Dreama stared down at the swirling cream mixing with the coffee. "I actually miss Mr. Colewick quite a bit."

"Me too." Midge whispered. Her the smile on her face falling to a frown and her eyes losing their life to become two white and blue marbles in a piece of taxidermy.

"You know the two of us went to high school together." Midge leaned in really close.

"We were something of sweethearts for a bit in our school days." She straightened.

"Really?" Dreama thought about how torn Midge must feel in grieving over her friend. As if hearing her thoughts Midge continued.

"There's a fine line to walk when grieving an old Beau." She glanced over her shoulder then looked out the front window. "But that was many years, and many pounds, ago." She patted her stomach and smiled. "I met Hank and here we are."

Midge motioned with her arms outstretched to the diner.

"So you broke his heart?" Dreama said trying to be playful. Midge smiled back.

"No, nothing like that. He changed in High School right about the time we'd graduated. He got really bitter." Midge looked off past Dreama. "Honey, been good talking with you but the place is filling up."

How do you feel about the story?

On the lines below write out your impression of the strengths and weaknesses of the story so far. Go back and read all of the question sections to this point and keep an eye out for those issues as we dig deeper in this story. Evaluate this story and the characters that make it up. Go reread the opening and see if your impressions have shifted or if you now identify issues you didn't see before.

Chapter 6

Charlie scanned the semi-annual financial report for his business. Like a sea of red dotted with black boats the numbers were full of missed projections and down revenue. At the bottom was a bold number showing that this month he'd have to dip in to his 401k simply to eat.

Of course, had he pursued the settlement against Bill's estate he could have paid off the mortgage on his boat shop and wiped out the debt from their failed online business venture. He looked at those numbers realizing that he'd have been solidly in the black if he'd done that.

It would have to be an extra large season to make up for the losses from this past fall and winter. The weather hadn't cooperated at all. It wasn't quite cold enough for the ice fishing on the pond in the next town which meant sales of fishing supplies and bait were down. He pointed his pen to the next column. They had a great snowfall as far as the weather man was concerned but the snow wasn't the steady constant snow he needed to make money on snow mobile rentals. Instead they got dumped on a couple of times really good and then nothing. He put a mark next to another red number and moved to the next column.

He looked over the numbers for his utilities then slammed the paper down and tossed the pen on top of it. There was no one to trust these days. In his fifties and he was looking at the prospect of Ramen noodles and social security payment to carry him to the end of his days. What was there to stock up anything for? He remembered when he was little his grandma would tell him stories from the Bible from time to time. She always read to him from Ecclesiastes and Lamentations. To his eight year old mind the horrific ideas of a meaningless life filled with misery and lost opportunities seemed a fate worse than death. It was during one of those Bible readings he'd decided he'd grow up to be rich.

But a person was the sum total of their experiences and as he looked around at the dusty shelves stocked with feathers and weights, fishing poles and bobbers, he wondered if those stories from the Bible hadn't formed him in to a failure. How could a person achieve success when their childhood was full of the assurance that some all-powerful being far above was out to get him?

His phone chirped and he punched the button for the text message.

C U soon. J.

For a fleeting moment he was annoyed that Janice was coming to visit. Since she'd come back in his life every part of him was left wanting. He'd spent thirty years believing that if only he hadn't pulled out of her driveway that summer after graduation that everything would have been better. Every bit of bad luck he'd attributed to some divine karma from that all powerful being his grandma worshipped. Any young man who'd feel relieved that his girlfriend had a stillborn baby surely didn't deserve joy.

He winced again hearing Janice's screams of pain tearing through his ears and down in to every muscle. They were alone and outside of town when she'd felt the final stirrings.

"Charlie, I think this baby is coming." She grabbed the small bump hidden below layers of loose clothing. Despite being 8 ½ months pregnant they remained the only two who knew.

"Just hold on. I know a cabin close by." They'd been on their way to a college visit-or so her parents thought. She'd said they were on their way to find off campus housing in Pennsylvania. Janice had to hide the pregnancy until they had a safe place for just the three of them.

They'd turned up the bumpy road and Janice grabbed hold of his thigh with so much force that his foot slammed down on the accelerator. The engine roared down the dirt hill and Charlie released the steering wheel with his right hand long enough to rip her claws out of his leg.

"You're going to kill us!" He'd screamed, more out of fear than anger.

"It hurts." She wailed. And Charlie instantly softened under his guilt.

"Charlie?"

Suddenly ripped from the past Charlie turned to face Janice who was standing in the doorway. He swatted away a few tears and straightened his back.

"Hi."

"Are you okay?"

"I am now." He said only he realized he was fully lying. The young eyes full of hope now held hardness he hadn't quite noticed before. Janice's mouth had the deep ruts of constant frowning. Every bit of her was mechanical and poised. Even her flirtatious glances held calculation and venom.

"Good." She smiled but it lacked the warmth of the young lady he'd loved all those years ago. There was no flutter of excitement as she brushed past him and the smell of fried food clung to her skin. Like a special meal kept in the refrigerator too long, something about her was stale and impalpable. She brushed his cheek with her fingertips and leaned down to kiss him. He resisted the urge to push her away but when she tried to deepen her kiss he resisted.

"I had garlic for lunch." He offered as a reply to her startled look.

"I appreciate the warning." She smiled and kissed him on the forhead.

What was wrong with him? He pushed the budgeting spreadsheets aside and dug deep for the love that had chained him to her for thirty years and the guilt that had prevented him from ever dating another woman. It was lost, tangled in seaweed in the depths of some warning that he couldn't quite explain.

"I got you something." Janice said in a sultry voice from across the room. She reached in her overnight bag and lifted a small pink bag out. "A new outfit." He didn't need to see the cursive letters spelling Victoria Secret to know that whatever the bag contained was meant to fuel lust.

It was like the beautiful queen of Snowwhite were transforming to the wicked hag with a basket of poison apples. He didn't want to let go but he felt the last 30 years of longing suddenly slipping away.

He looked out the window to the river that had been his livelihood these last 23 years. When he opened this Boat and Bait shop it was the business that was going to make him a rich man. The Hollow should have been called "The Swallow". It took your dreams and swallowed them and left you a shell of your former self.

"I'm going to go try this on." Janice said then she slipped from the room.

Charlie forced a smile.

***

"Mom, you need to calm down." Jake worked to keep his voice steady. His mom hugged a duffle bag close to her.

"Jake, I'm not crazy."

"I never said you were, but you are being a bit irrational."

"Did I ever tell you about a kitten when I was younger?"

"What Kitten?" Bridgett asked.

His mom started to tell the story of a stray cat that disappeared in the tall grass. She lost herself in the story and set the duffle to her side so she could emphasize her point with arm movements and broad gestures. When she finished she lifted the bag up as if everything would now make perfect sense.

"There is more than eighty-thousand dollars worth of gold, silver and antique coins in here."

"What!" Bridget said before Jake could form a word.

"Where did you get that, mom?" He managed to say.

"Your uncle Bill and I used to save up money in a jar. We'd roll it up and go invest in things."

"Invest?" Bridget asked, her eyes fixed on the bag.

"We'd buy stuff." She clarified. "Once we ended up buying something that was worth a good bit of change. We picked it up at a garage sale and took it to an antique shop who gave us a few thousand dollars.

"So how did you‑?" Jake said, still trying to wrap his mind around all of the money his mom had acquired in the month since Uncle Bill died.

"Bill got interested in old coins, and new coins for that matter, and as luck would have it he found he had one of these really valuable ones that something missing on it. He sold it and bought some coins from a dealer." She looked at the bag. "As well as a bit of silver and gold."

Jake thought back about the final conversation with Uncle Bill. It was clear on one level that his mom was much worse off since coming to the Hollow but Jake now wondered if Uncle Bill's concern had been for Mom's mental health or because he wanted to keep this money and these assets hidden from her.

"So that still doesn't explain why we had to get out of town so quickly." He pushed the other thoughts back.

"Someone else knew about the money." She said again lifting the bag on her lap.

"Who?"

"Not sure. I went to get it from your uncle's house and someone was watching me."

"That still doesn't explain what we're doing here."

"We need it in a safety deposit box." She said, her voice both disciplining him for his question and chastising him for his stupidity.

Scene 2

Dreama walked in her parents' house. They wouldn't be to the hollow for a couple more weeks but she felt like a visitor in the home. The fridge was now empty except for a box on baking soda that she'd left to absorb odors. She turned on her laptop and logged on to her email account.

Her dad had sent her three emails since the last time she'd checked her email a day ago. How long would he believe that her lack of online presence was due to jaunts around the town. Hopefully he'd start suspecting a love interest next so she'd have time to tell them that she no longer lived in their house with its wifi access and free lodging.

She sent her replies and scanned her buddy list.

Her sister was online.

"Val, you busy?"

"Nope. U?" Almost instantly her sister was firing back.

Dreama filled Val in on an edited version of her last few weeks in the hollow. She talked about her new friends and told her she was spending a great deal of time around the diner.

"Seems weird being here without Mr. C close by."

Val then caught Dreama up on school and the various antics between her parents and siblings. A hint of longing fluttered in and Dreama again began to question her rash decision to find a place of her own. Like a small butterfly it rested on her computer enticing her to follow it, reconsider, stay. Then just as quickly it was gone from her memory.

"I met a guy." She typed before the longing again landed at her laptop.

"K"

Dreama looked at the response and let it sink in. It had only been a couple of months since Evan broke her heart and she IMed Val making her swear to never allow Dreama to fall in love again. So was it Val fulfilling her charge as guardian of Dreama's heart that caused her to send such a terse reply?

"K?" Dreama sent in reply. Her mind running down one alleyway of logic then stopping at the end and running up the next. Each path required a different response and until she knew which one motivated Val she couldn't respond.

"Is that wise?" Val typed back to Dreama. Her mind, now with a clear sense

of direction took the path that was not defensive but rather informative. She could

persuade her sister that this time it would be different. Jake wasn't someone who saw

her as a project or someone to fix. Jake didn't even pay attention to her hearing loss.

But she couldn't pour all of that in to an IM, Val would have to learn that

herself once she met him. Dreama tried to find a concise explanation for Val. One

that would take her down a congratulatory path so Dreama could gush about all of the

wonderful qualities of her intended Beau.

"Jake is not Evan."

"This the same Jake you mentioned before?"

Dreama sent back an emoticon that formed a smiley face when she clicked send.

The cursor blinked again without a response. The IM window said that Val

was typing-then the message disappeared. Then it said she was typing again-then the

message disappeared. Dreama knew this cycle. Her sister was typing and deleting her

message before she sent it. The pattern didn't bode well for Val's assessment of Jake.

The blinking cursor on a blank screen hadn't been so sinister in her eyes since last

semester when her class required a ten page paper and Dreama realized on page six that

she had run out of things to say.

Then the blinking cursor told her that her work wasn't done. She'd need to return to the library and expand on what she'd already written. This time the blinking cursor dug deep within her. Despite what Dreama hoped Val was always an excellent judge of character. She had no background on Jake to make an assessment but Val knew Dreama intimately. Again Dreama's mind ran up and down alleys of potential responses. One said it was too soon to get involved. Another said she should go for it but not get too emotionally attached. A third-

"I'll reserve judgment." The IM said.

***

Jake picked up his glass and said something to Dreama but she couldn't quite see his lips. He smiled but she only saw what looked like him saying "not in school". She touched the hand he was holding the glass with.

"I couldn't hear you. Your glass was in front of your mouth. Remember, my hearing aids aren't in?"

"Sorry." Jake blushed and sat the glass down. "I said what do you like to do other than school?"

She leaned back on her elbows on the blanket they had put out on the hill near the edge of the river.

"I like to do this."

"What talk?"

"Well yes. I like to spend time with friends and family. I love to read and I love to watch people and nature. I also IM with my friends when I'm on my computer." She sat back up so she could see his answer. She was fairly proficient at lip reading but she understood about half of what he said. She pulled her hearing aids out of her purse and slid them back in. As if breaking through the surface of the water and seeing the world burst alive with color sound exploded in her ears. "We won't be able to swim for a bit but at least I can hear what you're saying." She smiled.

"Sometimes I wish I could turn my ears off like you do." He said through a smile.

"It's not as glamorous as it looks." She fluffed her hair back over her hearing aids effectively disguising her 'handicap' from anyone else who might perceive a precipitous drop in her intelligence because of her little amplifiers. "So, tell me what you like to do."

"I like listening to CDs. I love movies, especially comedies. I also like exploring."

"I love comedies. Did you see Evan Almighty?" She said, excited by something they had in common.

"That was great!" He said and he sat up for emphasis.

Dreama smiled. "When we watched it one scene got my brother Evan laughing so hard that pop shot out of his nose." She started laughing and Jake laughed with her. It was good to remember happy days. It seemed that she was so focused on every negative aspect of her family since arriving in the Hollow that she'd forgotten some of the great ones. It was as if fear of their reaction to her sudden independence had eliminated all the memories of the good times. That perception was amplified by the constant emails questioning her on activities, reminding her about various opportunities to 'explore her options', and expectation of their reaction to her new apartment.

But sitting on the side of the water and talking about some of the things she'd done with her parents, brother and sister Dreama was convicted by her own judgmental attitude.

"Dreama, do you mind if I ask you a personal question." Jake sat twisting a long blade of grass around his finger then unwinding it. The gesture, while likely a nervous fidget, struck Dreama as utterly masculine. Jake was seven years older than her, just recently twenty-six to her nineteen, and he carried on him a confidence that both enticed her and intimidated her. Who was she to think that a handsome man would be interested in a deaf girl?

She knew better, of course. Jake had made his romantic interest in her increasingly clear and this picnic on the beach was only the most recent gesture. Despite this signal she wondered if he was one of those people who dated the girls who came in for the summer then forgot about them when the warm summer breezes took on the crisp chill of fall.

"No, what's on your mind." She responded after she realizing she was staring at the blade of grass rather than answering his question.

"Do you ever miss not being able to hear?" He shifted a bit on the blanket.

"Do you mean when my hearing aids are out?"

He smiled. "Obviously. Like a few weeks ago when they broke. What is it like?"

"Sometimes I wish I didn't have to work so hard to understand what people are saying but I can't say I miss it." That wasn't entirely true. She had missed it a bit more than she'd expected she would. A realization that felt like a betrayal to the deaf side of her.

"Does your whole family use sign language?"

"I wish." The bitterness slipping in her words, just a bit. She recovered her voice a bit and explained so as to smooth the initial reaction.

"My parents and siblings all used to sign but when I got the hearing aids in elementary my mom and dad wanted to promote an oral program rather than total communication. Once I got in high school and could advocate a bit more for myself I was able to enroll in a program that offered a sign language interpreter in my classes which made learning much easier. After a semester my parents saw my grades go up and they no longer objected."

***

"Getcha some more coffee Renny?" Janice asked.

"No thanks hon. I'm doing fine with this. But I could use some of Midge's cobbler if she has any coming out of the oven soon."

"Sure thing. I'll go back and look." Janice tapped her well manicured fingers on the counter and walked back to the kitchen. The diner was nearly empty with only a few summer residents enjoying an late lunch before returning to their vacations.

This had always been a central meeting place but Renny never felt she'd fit in. Although she'd often blamed it on the awkwardness of teenage years the feeling had never left. She pulled her cardigan tighter around her and hunched over her coffee. The coins were safely stored away in a safe deposit box more than an hour from Blue Hollow. She'd even taken the added step up renting a P.O. box one town over and mailing the safe deposit box papers to that address. Now even a robbery wouldn't result

in the mysterious gawker locating the coins.

Janice pushed through the swinging door with a tray loaded down. "Cobbler's

coming. I'll be over in a sec."

"Take your time." Renny waved as she answered then turned back to her drink.

Sunday brunch was lonely without her brother. Jake went to what his church called

a contemporary service on Saturday nights so she could have invited him to join her

but he would try to discuss the message or something like that. So Renny came alone.

Directly across from Renny was a old fashioned shake machine. The long metal arm sat

inside the oversized silver cup. The cup was polished to almost a mirrored shine and she

could see a twisted reflection of her face and a few moving shapes behind her.

Maybe this twisted reflection was the real her and the other Renny was the

creation? She'd spent her life running from the dreams her brother had for her only to

get snarled up in them. She knew what it was to dream big and to excel. She thought

again of the cat.

As a teen she finally realized that it was silly to be paralyzed by what happened

to a kitten when she was a child. So she'd stepped out to.

The coffee in her mug began to quiver in her hand.

***

"All deaf people don't sign?" Jake asked.

She laughed, "Do all hearing people speak English?"

"I guess that was a silly question." He smiled and looked a little embarrassed.

"Show me how to say something in sign language."

"What do you want to say?"

He looked around. "How do you say river?"

She showed him how to cross his fingers on both of his hands and snake them

in front of his body to sign the word river.

"How do you sign Amazon River?"

She smiled "For a lot of words like names you would spell it out with your

fingers. Here like this." She took his wrist and held his hand up, palm facing her. She

wanted to pull his open palm to her face and lay her cheek against it but instead she

curled his fingers down in a fist with his thumb to the side. "That is the letter A. Now

stick your finger under your ring finger and you have the letter M."

Jake moved his fingers slowly and she watched him. His movements were cute,

like a child in preschool using an oversized crayon to form their first written letters. She

showed him how to form the rest of the letters. "Then sign river again."

Jake crossed his fingers and snaked them forward. She showed him how to sign a few other things around them like blanket, tree, leaf and dirt. She could feel him moving closer to her world, the deaf one, and it was both exciting and intimidating. Many men had enjoyed the novelty of dating a woman who was different. They had found a thrill trying to capture the wounded maiden and fix her. Jake was different. Jake was asking to enter her world rather than trying to draw her further in to his.

"But sign language is also different depending on where you live." She said after she'd shown him a few more signs. "For example if you live in a town the local deaf population will often times come up with a sign that is familiar to them but not to other people. You also have name signs so you don't have to fingerspell everyone's name every time."

"Oh that's cool. So is there like a sign for common names or what?"

"Names of places yes, but not people names. Usually people in the same family will all have similar name signs but have different letters. Like in my family my parents, siblings and I all have our first initial tapped below our left shoulder."

"What do you do when you meet someone new?"

"When we introduce ourselves we say "My name is D-R-E-A-M-A, Dreama" she showed him how she would spell out her name then show what her name sign was.

"That way they know what your name is but they can use your name sign from there after. It makes it a lot faster to talk."

"Is it hard to be by yourself, I mean live alone, since you can't hear?"

She laughed. "It's no harder than being a hearing person who is on their own for the first time. I've been alone here for a few weeks and I've managed just fine." She rested her folded arms on her knees and leaned forward to rest her chin on her arms. Maybe her response should have been that it is just as hard to be hard-of-hearing and on your own as it was to be hearing and on your own. Both were equally lonely.

Having him over in the afternoons brightened her day. He gave her something to look forward to each day. For as long as she could remember her mom would smile more about an hour before their dad got home from work. She must have felt the same thing Dreama felt each afternoon watching for Jake's car. Jake touched her shoulder and she turned to face him.

"You want to go up and start the grill?"

"Sure. Let me pick everything up." She started to pick up the snacks on the blanket and put them in the picnic basket. He touched her shoulder again. Oh the pounding in her chest each time he tapped her shoulder. It was as if her heart would burst. She wondered if she'd ever get used to his gentle fingers on her forearm or shoulder.

"I'll do this. You go up to the house and get the meat and charcoal out." She

smiled and nodded and started walking up the hill. When she was halfway up she

turned and looked back down through the trees at him. Every movement seemed like it

was choreographed to point out his qualities. The fluidity of his movements was gentle

but deliberate. He folded the blanket they'd been sitting on in to tight squares with the

precision of a soldier folding a flag. He looked up at her and smiled. She'd been caught.

Embarrassment seared her cheeks and she spun away and climbed up the hill again.

She was moving past mere infatuation. She enjoyed watching him perform

mundane tasks. She found herself imagining what it would be like to talk about the

future rather than always focusing on the past and the present. It was in that instant,

the future, that she wanted to be. Despite their month-long friendship she was looking

to a courtship and what that would mean for both of them. Her chest tightened again.

She was really falling in love with him. It was all too fast, but it was happening

just the same. Reason was being trumped by emotion and physical attraction was

giving way to spiritual connection. She stopped to consider, only for a moment longer,

the implication of all of this. She didn't really know him spiritually. He had never

mentioned his belief in many things. How could she be so attracted to him when she knew so little about him?

It was because he wanted to know about her. He wanted to be a part of her. For once in her life there was someone who saw her as more than a project. Her experience with relationships wasn't extensive but she could still recognize the obvious.

She walked to the grill and started the fire before arranging the food and the condiments. Jake came around the corner a black t-shirt clinging to the bit of river water that remained on him.

"What do you need me to do?" he asked. It was a simple enough question but it grabbed Dreama. He was a man who came along side. He didn't boss. He didn't force.

She was reading too much in to this. It was only a picnic followed by a question. There was no reason to take it this far. No doubt in her mind any more.

She was head-over-heals-throw-her-arms-in-the-sky-scream-thank-you-Lord-in-love.

***

Renny looked down at her hand but the sloshing liquid seemed to be controlled by an outside force. Brown liquid splashed on her hand. She put the mug down with such force that it sloshed over the edge and splashed across the paper placemat. The coffee landed on the white imitation lace mats and widened it to a thick brown river from her mug to the corner. She wiped her hand off.

She too had been that little cat.

And in this diner was one of the bigger cats she needed to confront. As if on cue Janice walked over and placed a double portion of steaming cobbler in front of Renny.

Janice leaned her thin arms on the counter across from Renny. "How are you doing though these days, considering?"

"I'm holding up well but I tell you what. This girl Jakey's making eyes at has me all up in knots." Renny blotted up the coffee with a napkin then set the balled wads to the side.

"How so?" Janice leaned in as she asked.

Renny spun the cup in its saucer. The bigger cat was here and it saw the hunk of meat she had. Renny held on to it a moment knowing that once she released it the other cats would growl, pounce then eventually shred each morsel.

"Maybe I'm just a bit protective. He hasn't dated since the accident." She looked up at Janice. She was the type you'd see somewhere in New York with hands full of handled shopping bags.

"It's alright Renny. You can tell me what's on your mind." Janice prodded. Ten years ago the two of them had shared a cup of coffee in this same diner. Alexa was alive then and Janice was expressing concern about the girl's new mystery beau.

"Well, Janice, you know I'm not a prejudice woman?"

"Surely I do, Miss Renny."

Hanks voice bellowed from the kitchen. "Janice, this order to fly?" Janice walked

over and took the paper out of Hanks hand.

"Eighty-six the fries. They want onion rings then yeah. They called it in about

five minutes ago so you'll want to be quick on it." She was like a chameleon morphing

from soothing confidant to hard-nosed woman but Renny had always seen the burning

passion for more of life in Janice. They'd shared big dreams in their younger days-

Janice's big dreams. Renny's ambition was drowned at that first major swim meet.

"I only got two hands Janice. If you'd like to work your fancy polished ones

then it'd be up faster."

Janice swatted her hand in his direction. Then she turned back to Renny and

took her hand between her own. "I mean it, Renny. You're a real sweetheart. Whole

town thinks it, way you sacrificed the life you had in town to bring your kids back

to Blue Hollow. Not many mommas would do that for their kids." The words were

soothing. Renny wrapped her wounds in them. Janice seemed to be the only one who

was happy she'd come back to this town. It had been more than a year since she'd felt the warmth of acceptance from another person.

"Well that's really sweet of you to say." She took a sip of her coffee. "I tell you, I worry about Jake getting so fond of this Dreama girl. She is just as sweet as the day is long and I don't doubt her sincere feelings towards Jake. I know they're nothing but pure."

She paused. Janice stood ready and eager for Renny to drop the morsel and meat from her lips. In all likelihood the words would be back to Jake before morning. She knew the gossip mill, understood how it works. Even as she selected how best to release this on the town she was considering how to mop the thing up if Jake took it too hard.

"Renny. Tell me." Jake and Janice had never been close. If things went too wrong she could accuse Janice of exaggeration.

"Thing is-" The words stuck on her tongue. As she thought of her true thought about Dreama they sounded awful. She wasn't a bad person, just concerned. She pushed away the needling accusations of her conscience and spoke her mind. "I had to take care of my sweet husband before his passing. Those last few months were so hard. I loved him to death, truly I did, but I was relieved when he passed on." She chocked back a sob. Janice handed her a napkin and Renny held it to her mouth.

Dale's body slowly withering from strength to death as if a movie maker's special effects demonstration.

"He was no longer hurting." Janice comforted.

Renny nodded in agreement. "And all the care giving was over." She wiped back a tear as it slid from the corner of her eye.

"You are a good woman the way you took care of him those final months."

Renny smiled and let a few tears drop to the counter. "It was hard though Janice. We'd had a long life together to remember. That made it easier to keep on, but there were days I wanted to cry from the exhaustion of taking care of him around the clock."

"It'd be hard on anyone."

"I don't want Jakey marrying someone he'll have to take care of his whole life."

It was out.

"I know what you're saying Renny. You want Jake to have a wife who will take care of him the way you took care of his daddy."

"Hopefully never the way I had to care for Dale." Renny was relieved someone understood her. "But if something were to ever happen to my Jakey how would Dreama take care of him? Like she did my brother? Friend of mine let me hear that 911 tape.

She didn't even know if there was someone on the other end. What if that had been Jakey hurt and she doesn't even have the ability to make a phone call?" Suddenly aware that she was almost yelling Renny calmed herself and allowed her mouth to form the balance of her concerns. "And what about grandbabies? Will they be deaf too? How would I talk to deaf grandbabies? If they could hear by some miracle of God how would she hear them cry? What if my grandbaby fell and she couldn't hear them cry?"

Stereotypes

Although stereotypes are frowned upon in society, they can really add to your writing when used the right way. When you turn a stereotype on its ear [a woman who looks like a supermodel who loves hunting and fixing cars] you can create a new dimension to a character. When you use an actual stereotype [like the backwards small town cop] it doesn't always work. That's because many of us reject the idea of being known based on superficial characteristics.

Identify the subtle and blatant stereotypes in this work that are either traditional stereotypes or a play on the standard expectations. List some of them here and then brainstorm how you could have done them better.

_____

_____

_____

_____

_____

_____

_____

Hank watched Renny and Janice through the window separating the kitchen and the grill. The acrid taste of guilt coated his tongue and choked and words of comfort in his throat. Again Hank pushed back the memory of Bill Colewick's final moments. Always those memories were mixed with the fear of discovery in a film reel that played constantly in his mind. His constant caution, now even at home since Midge's confrontation, had stolen sleep from his eyes and as well as his appetite. In times past Midge would have noticed the twelve pound drop but her focus was constant on his guilt. She no longer worried for his heart as she had before and after Bill died.

Clips of conversation floated back to him in the grill. The hushed tones only offering enough words for his mind to wildly construct the full dialog in a way that would most damage him.

He lifted the scrawled order. "Janice, this order to fly?" He left Renny at the counter next to a pile of napkins. Her eyes were red with crying.

"Eighty-six the fries. They want onion rings then yeah. They called it in about five minutes ago so you'll want to be quick on it."

"I only got two hands Janice. If you'd like to work your fancy polished ones then it'd be up faster."

Janice swatted her hand in his direction. The motion was one of sweeping dismissal. He held his anger down for a moment. What respect did he deserve from anyone? He wasn't the successful entrepreneur as he'd always imagined he'd be. He was one step above a teenage fast food grill employee. Only difference was he was less than ten years from retirement age and he made less per hour than most kids at McDonalds.

"I need to talk to you." Hank turned to see Midge standing at the outside door at the back of the kitchen.

"Can it wait?" He said lifting his spatula in explanation. She hesitated for a moment then looked past him to the front of the diner.

"No. It really can't." She said then opened the door a bit wider. He finished up the few things on the grill and called them up before stepping outside. The air was cool against his musty skin. The smell of old grease clung to him and he hoped the breeze would carry it away and bring fresh air from the river in its place. He thought of the summer memories created by so many people here. He was nothing more than a souvenir photo to them. In fact, the sum total of his life were fading memories of hundreds of people over dozens of years. As their memories of summertime drifted away so did the evidence of his accomplishments.

"I can't handle this anymore." Midge said.

Hank continued to focus on the line of conifers that started up the sill less than two hundred feet from the backdoor of his diner. If Midge was about to burst with her

knowledge of his part in Bill's death there wouldn't be many more days to breath in the

sweet smell of pine needles and sap. The crunch of gravel under his worn tennis shoes

would fade and be replaced by the squeak of sneakers on cement.

"What is it you can't handle?" He asked calmly without looking at her.

"All these secrets you think you're keeping from me."

"What do you feel you need to do with those secrets?"

"I don't know yet but-. Well, I tried to ignore it all but ever since you left

bowling early that night." Her monologue was broken by a sudden sob. He wanted to

reach out and comfort her but a comforting feeling of numb was beginning to wash

over him. If she was going to destroy him because of an accident then their love had

died long ago.

"Midge." He said. The blank feeling offering him a wall of protection against

any response she may throw at him. "You go do what you must. I got customers to take

care of inside your diner."

***

Renny walked next to Brenda down the cement steps from their hotel room to

the chain link fence that surrounded the pool. Like a princess entering a ball or maybe even a debutante, Renny Colewick glided in to the crowd of at least a dozen other high schoolers from around the state who were enjoying the pool.

"Go!" someone yelled from the end of the pool and two boys dove in the water. They cracked open the surface with a plume of white water then glided under like two large trout. Part way down they again burst above the surface. Other revelers stepped to the side to allow them passage until a winner was called. Then people resumed small clusters inside and outside the water.

"Wonder if they're here for the meet too?" Brenda said as she opened the fence.

"I'd guess they are." Renny answered. Two folding chairs sat side by side as if expecting Renny and Brenda to come this afternoon. The tubes of plastic stretched against the metal frame like colorful straws. They were soft enough for an evening sit after you got it clicked to the right angle. The trick was not tipping the darn thing when you sat down.

They spread their towels across the chairs and Brenda stuck the room key in her shoe.

"Ready to get in?" Brenda called over her shoulder then dove in.

Renny slid out of her shorts and t-shirt as quickly and discreetly as possible then ran quickly in to the water.

"I think you're such a fast swimmer because you're trying to keep from letting anyone see your body." Brenda said and laughed.

"No." She laughed and splashed Brenda. "I'm fast because the water in the pond at home is freezing. I have to go fast to keep warm."

"This water is nice."

"Stinks like chlorine though."

"Better than pond stink."

"Says who?" Renny smiled but Brenda's eyes were focused over her shoulder. She turned to see a group of three guys walking their way.

"They're coming over here." Brenda said. Her voice held the excitement of a teenager on her first solo drive. It was the transition from forbidden to free. Renny recognized the voice because she'd used the same voice to tell Bill she was on the high school swim team.

One young man sat down. His arms were strong and his chest incredibly well defined for a high school student. She thought of the boy she'd met back home, Dale. Hopefully Brenda would remember that Renny was already taken.

"You boys here for the meet?" Brenda yelled up as the guys reached the edge of the pool.

"Yes. You are too?"

Brenda nodded and bit her bottom lip like the young ladies on magazines did sometimes. Not the nervous type of bite that made your lip bleed. This was clearly a signal Brenda was sending to this group. "This is my friend Renny."

"I'm Joe and this is Mike and Tim." Each boy nodded as Joe said their name. Their flowing swim trunks made them look even thinner than it should have. She nodded in greeting, eager to start swimming laps. She realized from their vantage point she was almost fully exposed. Renny slid down so she was almost up to her chin in the water. One of the boys, she forgot his name, made clear work of letting his eyes focus below the water. His boldness made Renny uneasy but most things about city people bothered her.

"You on your school's girl's team?"

Renny looked around for a restroom. The water was warm but it was cool enough to make her bladder feel over full. She adjusted her swimsuit and tried to look natural.

"I ain't no star." She said. "I just won the race to make the team is all."

Joe turned to the other two. "I love that accent. Are you from Tennessee?"

"No, Ohio." In her part of the state they pronounced it Oh-hiya as opposed to these northerners who made both the Os long. People from this state could tell which part you were from as soon as you said the four letters O-h-i-o.

"That is such a great accent. Where are you from in Ohio?"

"Blue Hollow."

"Where's Blue Holler?"

Brenda and Renny laughed at his attempt at imitating their accent. "Blue Hollow is down in the southeast corner of Ohio. Over near where West Virginia and Kentucky border with Ohio."

"I could sit here and listen to their accent all day, couldn't you?" Mike said. Tim seemed to be the quiet one. Renny noticed him because it was usually her seeking to be invisible in a group.

Renny stopped, no longer the teenager of her memory but a middle-aged woman. She couldn't allow this memory to go any further. It was quiet but it wouldn't stay silent long.

***

Janice was back in her office dressed in slacks and a cashmere sweater. The smooth warmth against her skin her Bath and Body works scented oils, rather than fryer grease, made her feel clean again.

She reached down and pulled off her black pump. The costume she was wearing

in the Hollow had worn blisters on her feet. It had looked like she was nearly done with

Blue Hollow and its cheap shoes, scratchy waitress uniform and constant standing. As

soon as Renny spotted her through the window Janice was all but certain she'd just

bought another few months. She'd stolen the first set of coins just out of high school

and used it to buy her first properties.

"Siemens and Lehrer are in the conference room." A voice said over the PA on

her phone. She slid her foot back in pump and winced as the back of her shoe bit in to

a blister.

Renny had torn the blister off of Janice's heart as well. Every time Janice had

to look at Renny or Jake she remembered Alexa. A twinge of emotion threatened

to overtake her in her office. If she were a positive person she'd see how her niece's

murder had been the thing that not only thrust her from the Hollow but had also

projected her to the success she was today.

Janice looked at the curio cabinet in the corner that held sketches of each of her

properties. Each shelf held a black and white pencil sketch next to a framed dollar and

a single key. They showed her how far she'd come since her days of poverty down in

the Hollow. Each one was a twist of revenge for what that town had done to her family.

While they couldn't know of the level of her own success, she could bask in it privately.

There was only one photograph in her office. It was matted and framed and hung directly across from her desk. It was the front page of the paper the day Jake was acquitted. The headline reads "Local teen not guilty on all counts." The top right side showed a courtroom full of people. Jake's is hugging Renny, a smile plastered on his face. Behind him is his lawyer assembling papers that are on the table before him. In the rows of onlookers are Midge and Hank, Jake's dad and Bill. The photograph filled the entire right side of the paper above the fold. Then, just above the fold and almost lost among an index and weather is a small school photo of Alexa.

The newspaper was yellowing from the decade exposure but Alexa's innocent beauty remained. It was for Alexa's memory that Janice pushed herself. Her opportunity had been stolen and Janice would not squander the days she'd been given.

She picked up a file from her desk that contained proposals for various properties in need of investors. The gentlemen from Siemens and Lehrer were waiting to see what she could offer them. She had an idea for a few investment properties, two of them businesses, that would soon be available in the Hollow. If they were willing to give her suitable terms she'd allow them the opportunity to invest.

***

Renny pushed but the story marched on in her mind. She turned on the TV but the force of the memory wouldn't be denied. She was drawn back to high school, Brenda and swimming memories.

"Renny?"

"Huh?" She looked up at Brenda.

"Do you want to go with them up the street for dinner tonight?"

"Well, I don't know. What kinda food they got there?"

"All kinds."

Her mind was on her bladder now 100%. She wanted them to leave so she could get out of the pool. "Sure, what time were you thinkin'?"

"We usually eat at about six. Does that work for you?"

"What time's it now?"

"A little after three."

"That should work." She took a couple steps away from them in the pool. Maybe if she left the edge of the water they'd say "see ya" and meet up later. If she had to wait much longer she'd have to get out of the pool or risk wetting herself where she stood.

"Where you goin' Renny?"

She took a few steps back toward them. "Just trying to do some swimmin'. I gotta practice if we're goin' to beat them this weekend."

They laughed. "We'll see." They said then they waved and started back to the other end of the pool. Thank God they'd gone, she was certain her bladder was about to go. She walked to the steps in the shallow end and quickly crossed over to their towels.

She reached down in Brenda's shoe. "Where's the key?" She lifted the shoe and shook out each one, then her own. Then she lifted the blankets.

"What you doing Renny?" She turned around and stood. There was Brenda and following behind were the guys.

"I need to use the facilities and I can't find the room key."

Brenda bent down and stuck her hand in her shoe. "Well I put it right here." She felt around under the towel. "You saw me put it right here."

"You girls lose somethin'?" Mike came up behind Brenda.

"Sure did. Our room key is gone."

The guys started walkin' round in a large circle bending down to look under things. "What room's it for?"

"Seventeen."

"You could get one from the desk I'm pretty sure." Tim said.

"Can you hold it that long?"

"Not really?"

"Hold what?" Mike stopped and looked at the two of them.

"I need to use the toilet." Renny tried not to look as uncomfortable as she felt.

"Renny, you can use ours." Mike said. "Brenda can go on up to the front desk to ask about a replacement and what to do. Tim, you stay here and keep looking for their key and make sure to keep an eye on their stuff."

Tim looked at Mike and Joe. She caught something in his eye. He didn't like to be the third wheel. She knew that feeling and empathized with him.

"Fine, I'll stay here." He never broke his stare with Mike.

Surely, Tim wasn't fond at all of being told to baby sit the towels. Renny smiled at him. "You don't have to watch mine. I'm takin' it along."

Tim smiled at her then looked over her shoulder at Mike and Joe.

"You keep looking for their key. We'll be back as soon as she's done."

Brenda started for the front office that was just around the fence and Renny followed Mike.

"How far is your room?" Every footstep on the pavement made the urge even stronger.

"We're the second room on the first floor."

"Thank goodness."

"You're pretty lucky. Seventeen is down a ways isn't it?" Joe turned the key in

the lock and pushed the door open and motioned for her to go in first.

"Yes, we're on the second floor at the end. Thanks again." She turned in the

bathroom and as soon as she had the door closed behind her she stripped her swimsuit

down.

She finished going to the bathroom and there was a puddle on the floor where

her swimsuit had dripped when she had it down.

"I'm going to clean up this puddle in here I made." She yelled through the door

then realized how it sounded. She wasn't too handy with words it seemed. She grabbed

a white hand towel of the sink and cleaned up the water.

She opened the door in to the room. Mike was to her right in the room.

"Thanks again."

"Oh, it's no problem at all." Mike pulled the knob out on the TV. The volume

was up awful high. She turned and closed the bathroom door but standing on the other

side of the door was Joe. And he was blocking her path to the front door.

"Ready to leave already?" He stuck his finger under the strap of her swimsuit then let it snap back to her shoulder. He took a step forward and she took a corresponding step back.

"Yes, I need to get a few laps in before dinner."

"Always got your head in the game. I admire that." Mike said behind her. She took another step back and bumped in to something. She spun around and was nose to nose with Mike.

"We'll see you about seven then?" He stepped back so they weren't so close.

Her thudding heart began to slow down. "Yes." She kept her eyes focused on Mike. His friendly eyes calmed her. He'd tell Joe his little joke wasn't funny.

"Great. Let's meet by the office building." Mike walked to the TV and turned the little volume knob to the right. Renny recognized it as the same soaps her mom watched. The sound was almost deafening. He turned it down a bit but he still had to yell over the television to be heard.

"Sorry about that. Didn't mean for it to be quite so loud." She nodded in reply, put her hands over her ears and turned for the door. Joe stood as a wall directly in front of her. What had looked to be ribs on a skinny boy were now clearly exposed to be muscles.

"You don't need this." Joe said and in one motion grabbed the straps on her swim suit and ripped it down. She tried to reach for it and cover herself. Mike put his hand in the center of her chest and pushed her straight back across the bed and pressed his lips hard against hers. This wasn't happened. She was a cat being locked in a cage. She tried to pull her arms and legs against her to cover her nakedness but he was now pressed hard against her with only his swim trunks separating her from what she feared might be coming. Her feet dangled over the side of the bed and there was nothing to grab to get away.

His lips smashed against her and he tried to force his tongue in her mouth. She could only move her head so she spun it to the side and back. His nose connected with her forehead as she struggled.

"What the-." He yelled an explicative and dabbed his nose with the back of his hand. "You're lucky there's no blood."

"She must like it rough." Joe said leering down at what Mike was doing.

"Good. I do too." Mike spun her on to her stomach. Her swimsuit was now gone and she clawed for the comforter to protect her.

"Hold still you little tease." Mike's mouth was so close to her ear she could feel his breath. "You don't fight and this will be quick but if you want to be feisty we can go that way too." He smashed her face down hard in to the mattress. Air. She needed air but her mouth was full of cloth. She flung her arms around desperate to grab anything. Suddenly he let go of her head. She sucked in the cool air.

"Now, you going to be quiet?" She nodded her head. Tears choked the words in her throat. "Good."

Joe walked around to the other side of the bed and grabbed her wrists and held her arms straight above her head. Mike pressed against her then a flash of pain tore her insides and he forced her body down deep in the mattress with their combined weight.

"Ow." She cried but her words were drowned out by the TV soaps.

"You a virgin there Renny?"

She nodded her head as he pressed against her again. She was splitting in half. Fire burning her insides. She wanted him off.

"Aw man, you always get the virgins." Joe said off to the side.

"You'll get yours." Mike said.

"Yeah, your sloppy seconds."

"You hear that Renny." Mike's breath was hot in her ear again and he pressed against her with painful vigor. "You ain't a virgin no more you little tease. You know you wanted it though."

Tears rolled down her cheek. The television blared. She tried to make out the words. Words of escape, away from here, this room, this.

"Save some for me." Joe looked straight in her eyes as he spoke. "You think you can flirt with guys, follow them to their room then not finish what you start?"

"She...knows...better...now." Mike said with jagged breath. She let her arms go limp. There was no need to fight. They'd already stolen her purity.

Mike finished and she felt him climb off of her. She was naked and didn't want to get up. She wanted to get back what he'd just stolen from her. Joe let go of her wrists.

"My turn."

She pulled the comforter to her face.

He spun her over. "I want you to watch." He snarled the leaned in to her face. Pain ripped at her again. She closed her eyes. She didn't want to remember a single moment.

"You were ready for me weren't you?" Joe said. "Didn't move a bit cause you were waiting on old Joey to make a woman out of you." His breath stunk and she pulled the comforter across her face out of shame and to avoid the smell.

This wasn't happening. She was home in the Hollow sleeping on the couch. Mama's soaps were on the television. She wasn't living this. Joe let out a scream and grabbed her by the hair and ripped her head back.

"You like that don't you tease? You want Joe don't you?" He grabbed her hair down at the roots and slammed her head up and down in a nod.

"That's what I thought. You wanted Big Joe to make you a woman you little tease."

He let out one more yell then slammed her head down in to the mattress and got up. She pulled her legs up and curled up in a little ball in the center of the bed. She didn't want to move. She didn't want to walk out of this room where everyone could see what had happened to her. She heard the volume on the television go down.

"What you think you're spending the night or something?" Mike bellowed at her followed by an explicative. "We're done with you."

Something wet slapped against her face and she lifted her face from the bed and pulled her swimsuit on. She sat up on the bed and faced the men.

"Go get yourself cleaned up and get out of here."

She walked in the bathroom and cleaned up with the same towel she'd used to dry off their floor a few minutes earlier. She slid on her swimsuit and pulled it up. It was cold and damp on her skin. She looked in the mirror at her tossled hair and swollen eyes. She shouldn't have come to this meet. She belonged in the Hollow.

She smoothed her hair back and wrapped the ponytail back up then came out of the bathroom.

"Of course, Renny Colewick." Joe pressed her back to the wall and grabbed her face with his right hand. "You go telling anyone about our time together this afternoon and we'll come down to Blue Holler and teach you a lesson."

She nodded her head.

He jerked the door open. "Now get out of here you tease."

She pulled her towel tight against her and looked in the direction of the pool. Water ran down her leg and she was certain she was wetting herself. She couldn't go back to the pool where everyone could see her. They'd know she was different. No longer pure. They'd sense it. She turned to the right and walked slowly, tenderly to the steps and walked up. Her insides ached and she wanted only to go to bed. Get dressed curl up and go to sleep.

She got to room seventeen and tried the door. It was locked.

"Brenda? You in there?" She tapped on the door.

She sat down next to the door and watched the traffic go up and down the road nearby. How did she get to this place? Life at home, with Dale, it should have been good enough. She knew there wasn't a future in swimming so why waste her summer chasing after fancies?

"Renny you okay?"

She turned and saw Brenda jogging toward her. She stood up gently. "Mike and Joe told me you wasn't feeling well."

"No, I ain't." She whispered. "Can you let me in?"

"Sure thing." Brenda turned the key in the lock and pushed the door open.

"I don't feel much like going out this evening if you don't mind." She reached in her drawer and pulled out a grey jogging suit she'd brought to sleep in.

"Sure thing."

Brenda sat on the side of the bed and watched her.

"Can you stay in with me?"

"Well...I suppose." She was a bit hesitant. "I'll need to go tell the guys I can't come."

Renny nodded. "Just don't do it near their room. Tell them at the pool okay?"

"Why..."

"Please." Tears started down her face.

"Renny, is soemthing wrong?"

We'll come down to Blue Holler Renny Colewick. "No, I just need you to please tell them at the pool you can't come."

"Okay, I'll be right back." Brenda set the key down on the dresser and walked out the door. Renny grabbed it and took it in the bathroom with her. She pulled her swimming suit down and threw it to the side. She couldn't look at the mirror. Her own reflection disgusted her. Filth, that was what she was. The shower steam began to fill the bathroom with white fog and it billowed around the curtain. She stepped in and let the hot water burn her skin. The little soap in the shower wouldn't be enough to wash off her shame. She scrubbed wiping away where they had touched her. She scrubbed her ears desperate to remove any trace of their breath.

Phonetic Dialog

If you ever read Tom Sawyer or Huck Finn in school you may remember how Mark Twain wrote his dialogs: Phonetically.

You may also remember how difficult it was to decipher what was said. In fact, many times I had to read a piece of dialog out loud in order to figure out what the characters were saying to each other.

While having some phonetic writing early on can add flavor to a story, too much is just distracting.

Find places in this manuscript and in your writing where an attempt to show sounds, animals or even the cadence of speech detracted from the story. Now fix them.

_____

_____

_____

_____

_____

_____

_____

_____

_____

_____

_____

_____

_____

_____

_____

_____

Jake slid the Marshmallow on to his stick and put it in the fire. Orange flames jumped up and wrapped around it and changed the bright white to a smoky brown. The best marshmallows were kept out of the flames and put down by the glowing embers. He found a spot to position his marshmallow and turned to Dreama.

"Have you ever made a S'more with a Reese's cup instead of Hershey bar?"

"It's burning." Dreama said.

Jake looked down at his marshmallow. It was now a flaming torch and black as pitch. He jerked the stick up from the fire and blew it out. He took out another marshmallow and tried again.

"I'll need to make it a little less black if I want a decent s'more." He said. The small fire pit in Uncle Bill's backyard glowed in the shadows growing across the lawn. The windows were drawn shut to the house and the lot felt as if the spirit of the place had left it. They'd come here looking for a neutral place to enjoy a cookout but the eerie remembrance of the last picnic here had created a deeper sense of loss than either of them had anticipated.

"Do you know what your mom is going to do with Mr. Colewick's place?" Dreama asked, her eyes focused back up at the house.

"I imagine she'll sell it."

Dreama nodded. She turned her face back to the fire as if her source of comfort was written in the orange glow that wiggled along the logs. His heart hurt for her but her vision of Uncle Bill was build on the illusion of the Hollow. It was an illusion Bill had fostered both to build his reputation with summer residents and to hide his true nature from Blue Hollow natives.

Jake reached back in his memory to piece together broken conversations and unanswered questions between his mom and uncle. He twisted and turned each piece but didn't find a clear picture form. Instead it seemed he had pieces from three or four puzzles all mixed together. The pieces were cut to the same shape but once you built enough of the puzzle to look at it you realized the shape, not the picture, matched.

And then there was the puzzle of him and Dreama. He sat here in the glow of the fire with darkness deepening all around them. It was a scene that he could create in his own mind as he imagined what a fun date with Dreama would be. But Alexa was here. The memories of here were just as strong as if she sat on this bench between them in a physical body. He had closed the door on her death years ago but his growing feelings for Dreama felt like a betrayal.

He looked over at Dreama and she replied with her eyes. They looked up at him quickly then darted away before he could try to read her. That was followed by a hidden smile and a second quick glance to see if he was still watching her.

He put another piece of wood in the fire pit. It hissed and crackled as the flames enveloped it. The flames threw dancing light on Dreama. Her long thin fingers rested against her cheek.

"Mine's done." She said as she lifted a perfectly toasted marshmallow and scraped it on to her cracker.

He looked down his stick and turned his marshmallow. His chest was tight with the thoughts weighing on his heart that he couldn't yet say out loud. Like a runner hunched at the starting line waiting on the pistol his tongue sat perched to form the words "I love you".

Next to him Dreama was crunching in to her S'more. He looked over at her and she smiled and brushed the cracker crumbs off her thighs.

Oh, the effect she had on him. There was nothing she did consciously to control him. It was just who she was. He wanted to see her smile. He wanted to be with her. He liked the way he felt when they were together. Unfortunately he couldn't tell her how he felt. He couldn't fully understand yet why he was wrapped up in her when very few people had even got a second glance. His heart slammed shut with Alexa's coffin lid but Dreama had pried it open with nothing stronger than her friendship.

With Dreama he couldn't pinpoint a moment. She came back over and sat down beside him on the bench. He knew she was different from the moment he met her at Uncle Bill's house. He picked up this piece of the puzzle and looked at the picture he was building in his mind. He twisted and turned it looking for a spot but he didn't know where a relationship would fit in the overall picture. Despite every cry of his heart he set the puzzle piece with Dreama's face back in the box.

It was a piece he could try to fit in later.

***

***

Dreama walked in to the boat shop, Boat and Bait. A bell jingled over here as she closed the door. The place was designed to give it the look of a fishing shack. Maybe one of those things people stayed in when they were ice fishing. Despite the smell of soil and sawdust there didn't appear to be a spot of dust in the place.

The floor was made of wood slats, not pergo, and the five small aisles had shelves neatly arranged with lures of various colors and sizes, weights, feathers and bobbins. As if the weapons of a soldier, metal fishing poles lined the walls. Dreama walked to a cane pole sitting in a corner and picked it up. The top wobbled as exaggerated dance in her hands and she put it down before she broke out a light or knocked something off of a shelf.

She had come to this shop with her dad a few times over the summer but she was always too drawn to the dock behind the store to ever go inside.

"Can I help you, miss?"

Dreama walked up the nearest aisle and admired the bright life jackets with Teenage Mutant Ninja Turtles and various Barbie Princesses on the front as she made her way to the counter

It was split in to three parts. Closest to the door was a glass case with a cash register, an assortment of lures and a small refrigerator. On the refrigerator someone

had scribbled in ink on a post-it note "Grubs and Meal worms $1 small cup, $2 large

cup". The center section was a five foot long glass case with a variety of books neatly

arranged. Dreama looked along the titles and saw most concerned various trees, plants

and bugs native to the area. None of these interested her but the soda shop on the far

left did appeal to her. She absorbed all these details in the three or four steps from the

end of the aisle to the beginning of the counter.

A large built man who looked to be in his late forties came out of a doorway

behind the counter. He wore a white cotton shirt with a collar, jeans and a ball cap that

read "Boats 'n Bait".

"Hi, I'm interested in renting a small boat for a few hours this afternoon."

***

"So what did you think of Charlie? Jake asked as they lifted their paddles and

allowed the current to carry them."

"Kind of creepy." She said. There was nothing she could point to as the source

of her fear but the man in the boat shop watched her as if he thought her to be a petty

thief or a target.

"You tell him you knew my uncle?"

"I told him my parents owned the house behind Mr. Colewick."

"He probably charged you double for this canoe then." Jake laughed and dropped he paddle in the water.

"Why's that?"

"Those two have a history. I don't get all of it but I know Charlie feels my uncle stiffed him out of a good bit of money." Jake lifted the oar and dipped it on the other side. Dreama responded by putting her oar in the opposite side and paddling. The image formed by the people she spoke to in town didn't fit with Mr. Colewick as he was. Increasingly the town of Blue Hollow, even with all its hospitality and charm, didn't hold the warmth she'd always known it to have.

She rowed down the river taking in the sound of the gentle splash of the oars as they broke the surface of the water followed by the churning sound of water as they pushed hard against the oars and glided through the water.

Her parents would be coming to the Hollow tomorrow. She looked at the trees, homes, beaches and cliffs they passed with the splash-slosh of water in the background.

"You're pretty quiet back there." Jake said after one of her longer silences.

"Thinking about tomorrow."

"Want me to come along?"

"Probably would be best if you didn't." She paused for a moment then continued. "I just don't like confrontation." It was the best explanation she'd ever been able to give herself when she'd wonder why she could have such a loving home and yet feel such fear of disappointing them.

"Not many people do." He answered.

She continued to play a variety of possible scenarios in her mind. Sometimes they congratulated her on her independence and in others they all but disowned her.

"That's our exit." Jake said then pointed to the right with his oar.

***

Janice kissed Charlie before she left. His lips were cold and dry, like kissing a shedding snake. She managed to control her impulse to wipe her lips off until she was in her car and driving down the road. It was late but the sun was still up. She hadn't slept with Charlie this time. Mercifully he seemed too tired or distracted the last week to force her to endure that again.

She was distracted too. The meeting with investors had gone well and all that was left was for the properties to come available. She drove down the old part of town with its simple porches and small lawns. She'd bulldoze every single one if she could. Make this place in to a proper town. People would pay top dollar to have a house with a boat slip, pier and private beach behind it. Instead these people lined the river with rusty clothes lines and decaying woodsheds.

The scene of so much wasted potential disgusted her, so she turned up her radio and let the satellite radio scan through her preferred radio stations. She'd only have to endure the town a few more months and then she'd leave. Even if she hadn't yet finished what she started.

Her cell jingled signaling her assistant was calling. She pushed the button to mute her radio and clipped her Bluetooth hands free to her ear.

"What do you need?" She said in greeting.

"Good news on the investors."

"What is it?"

"They're all in."

Janice thought for a minute. She could show her hand and see if the three groups would go in a bidding war to participate. That could pad her margin. Or she could see if she could create other opportunities in the Hollow for investors.

"I'll let you know what to do in a couple of days." She said. Her shack above the diner now coming in to view.

"What should I tell them in the meantime?" Her assistant's voice had the giddy lift of success. The amateur recognized the potential in these deals.

***

At 6:42am Dreama turned off the alarm and got out of bed. Although it wasn't

set until 8am she had slept fitfully through the night and couldn't risk another series of

dreams. She picked up the clothes she'd laid out the night before and quickly dressed.

Her parents weren't supposed to arrive at the summer house until around 9am, but

they told her they'd call when they were on the road and they were notoriously early.

She poured a bowl of cereal and stirred it until it was soggy beyond edibility. She

dumped it out and drove to her parent's summer home.

It was seven in the morning on a Saturday but Blue Hollow was remarkably

awake. A few older people well in to their retirement years walked along the sidewalks

of the town. She drove past the diner and saw the parking lot was full of cars belonging

to the regulars, and a few more besides. She had the day off. She wasn't sure if this

would be an easy break or an ugly one with her parents so she wanted freedom of

movement.

She drove past Mr. Colewick's empty house and up the driveway to her parents'

cottage. Her breathing was shallow and despite looking steady her hands felt as if they

were vibrating from the inside. The trembling stopped suddenly when she saw her mom and dad in their bathrobes drinking coffee on the front porch. Her breath caught in her throat.

She pulled around to the side of the house and parked the car, flipped open her cell phone and scrolled to Jake's number. Seeing them here broke all resolve she had to do this alone and she sent off a quick text asking Jake to please arrive ASAP or faster. She flipped the phone shut and took a deep breath.

Like spaghetti placed in a pot of boiling water her legs softened with each step she took. The invisible heat from that same pot of water was making her face burn and her entire body sweat.

"Dreama." Her dad's cool voice said as she came to the front of the house. Her eyes studying her carefully mulched flowerbeds and weeded sidewalk.

"I thought you weren't coming until tomorrow." She began up the steps, eyes still fixed below her dad's gaze.

"We got off early and decided to drive in."

"You should have called."

"We shouldn't need to." Her mom broke in with a voice as cold and flat as her dad's.

"Where were you?" Dad said, picking the conversation back up.

Tires crunched on the gravel behind her and Dreama turned. A dark car emerged from the sea of green. Jake couldn't have been more welcomed if he'd come in on a white horse in full jousting armor. She turned her back to the house, and her parents, waiting for the strength his gaze would offer her. Jake climbed out of the car, his eyes still puffy from the deep sleep she'd roused him from.

Thank you. She mouthed as he approached. Jake simply smiled and walked to the house. "Sorry I'm late. I didn't think you'd be here already."

Dreama spun suddenly realizing what the sleepless look and the empty bed might mean to them. "Jake is the one who helped me find my apartment."

As if choreographed, her parents shifted their gaze in unison from Jake to Dreama. "What apartment." Dad said.

"The one in town." She relaxed for the first time in weeks now that the worst was past. Like ripping a bandaid it stung for a moment but the pain was gone as soon as it was over.

"Why do you need an apartment?" Mom followed.

Jake turned to Dreama. "Tell them all about it." He smiled as if she were about to let them in on an exciting secret. She dug in for a smile, but it was out of place with the feeling of impending doom coursing through every nerve. "Oh, c'mon. You should be excited!" He coaxed his eyes begging her to follow suit.

She loved him for this attempt to soften the blow, but she was never confrontational. She didn't exactly know how to do this. She didn't know how to be fully independent. What if they threw her out? Told her she couldn't come back? What if she couldn't go to college? What if they-

"And you'd be?" Her dad said, his gaze firmly on Jake. It was no longer neutral but fully engaged. As if turning up the heat on that pot of boiling water Dreama was sitting in, her father took a step off the porch and down to the steps. On the top step her dad was a full foot taller than Jake, maybe more. He looked like a rooster about to lean over and peck.

Jake never broke his smile. "My name's Jake." He extended his hand. "I'm Bill Colewick's nephew." Dreama exhaled a bit. "And Dreama's boyfriend."

Chapter 7

"Your shift isn't for another hour." Janice said as Dreama walked behind the counter.

"Nothing much to eat at my house so I thought I'd eat breakfast here." She replied. A family sat at a booth along the front window and a few other tables. "You don't look very busy today."

"It's been fairly slow." Janice agreed. She poured a cup of coffee for Dreama then looked at a retired couple in matching jogging suits. "I'm going to check on them and I'll be right back. Write your order up and send it on back to Hank.

"Thanks." She wrote an order for a pancake, scrambled egg and sausage links and sent it to Hank on the metal wheel. "Order in." She said.

"That yours?" Hank asked.

"Yes. I'm grabbing a bite before my shift."

He smiled at her but his eyes lacked the sparkled she'd seen other times. Although a gruff man Dreama had quickly learned he was a gentle giant. If he worked in the city rather than chained to the kitchen at Blue Hollow's main diner she figured he'd have been called the Blue Hollow Teddy Bear. "You want fried mush too?"

"I can't eat that. It sounds like mud."

He laughed. "You city people will pay $20 for sliced chicken with fried polenta but you call the stuff mush and I can't sell it for $3.99."

"Then call it polenta and give me two slices." She said, smiled and walked back to her seat.

"Hey Dreama you've been spending a bit of time with Jake lately."

"Yes."

"I was wondering if he mentioned what the family is doing with his uncle's belongings."

"I don't think they've even gone through everything." Dreama sipped at her coffee with an eye to the window to the kitchen.

"Reason I'm asking is there's a clothing drive at my aunt's home church. I was hoping maybe I could get some of Bill's belongings and take them in to town."

"To the best of my knowledge they haven't said what they're going to do with any of his things. I know Renny has gone over there a few times and that she cleaned out his fridge and freezer so nothing would spoil but beyond but I don't know that she has done much of anything." Dreama took a sip of her water.

"Dreama, foods up." Hank yelled from the kitchen. Dreama started to stand but

Janice put up her hand.

"I'm up." Janice said and got the plates. "Hank talked you in to the mush?"

"We're calling it polenta."

Janice laughed. "There here is your fried polenta, eggs and sausage. Should I call your pancake a crêpe?"

"No, pancake is fine." Dreama cut in to her meat

"I know Renny is so tore up about her brother's passing." Janice continued. "She was in here a week or so ago just so sad."

Dreama shook her head as Janice spoke. "It must be tough her needing to make all of those arrangements for her brother's things. I can only imagine when people start asking her about Mr. Colewick's house."

"Who's been asking bout that property?" Janice said.

"My parents asked me about it but I'd be surprised if they made an offer. I'm sure she wants to get it sold before too long, unless of course she just moves over to Mr. Colewick's place and she sells her own."

"Well now, that would work out just fine for her now wouldn't it? She could have one of the finest pieces of property in town and it wouldn't cost her a dime."

Janice stood up and picked up the pot of coffee and glanced around the diner. "Hon, I don't mean to start up anything for you. I just want you to be careful when it comes to

Bill Colewick's affairs."

Dreama felt a need to justify herself. As if she suddenly learned she was a

member of the home team sitting on the visitor bench. Janice's eyes scanned the

diner with each word as if watchful of some unseen danger that would pounce at any

moment. Dreama, caught up in Janice's tone looked around as well. "I haven't really

involved myself in any of the stuff with Mr. Colewick."

Janice continued, her words running over Dreamas. "The Hollow is a beautiful

place but when something happens round here it's like there is a code of silence

instituted. I don't know what's going on but an awful lot of people keep bringing up

Jake's name."

"Jake's name? For what?"

"I don't want you getting in the middle of something you're not ready for."

Janice snapped as if coming from a trance. Her eyes once again held a charming glow.

She turned to Dreama and smiled. "You need to eat that before it's cold. Enjoy your

meal."

***

"Mom, I'm back." Jake yelled as he took off his shoes.

"Hi Jake. Mom's in the back yard." Bridget said as she came out of the kitchen.

"How is she doing today?"

"Alright. Quiet."

"I know. I think I like quiet more than panicked."

"I'm worried Jake. She was nothing like this when dad died."

Jake walked to the window over the kitchen sink. "I know." Uncle Bill's words were coming true before his eyes. While Jake had expected that he would need to protect his mom from the people of Blue Hollow and their destructive chatter, the real enemy was inside. There was a silent danger that lurked in this town. It didn't come out in an unkind word or obscene gestures. It came of silent snubs and failed expectations. It was everywhere in the Hollow from Hank's lost dream of business success to Dreama's shattered hope for acceptance from her family. It even lived in the memory of Alexa's death on that hill.

He looked at his mom and wanted so desperately to deliver her from the danger all around them but without a willingness to turn loose of Blue Hollow and all it stood for in his mom's mind the evil would simply follow. It had lied dormant inside for decades like a malignant cell that suddenly began to multiply and spread. The pain of

rejection from the Hollow had metastasized throughout his mom's entire body and only

she could fight it back.

He pushed out the backdoor and walked to his mom.

"Jakey." She lifted her arms to him. She looked more like a child reaching up

for its parent than a mother reaching out to hug her son. He bent down to hug her and

was startled by the thinness of her frame. She wore the same clothes she'd always worn

but they only masked the fact that she wasn't well.

"Mom. Bridget tells me you're having another rough day." He pushed back from

her and looked down at his mother. She had always been a strong woman. Even when

his dad died she stayed strong and handled everything. She was incredible to watch

then which only made this more difficult to watch now.

"No, I'm having a fine day, honey. I'm just a little tired is all." Her voice was

mousy. "Did you see the peas are coming in nicely already?" She motioned to little

green leaves poking out of the dirt.

"They look great. Mom, why don't you go get dressed and we can go in town

and grab a few things for dinner? Dreama's working tonight. I might be able to snaggle

some extra cobbler for you." He smiled warmed by the idea of seeing Dreama again today.

"No." She answered flatly.

"I could take you to the city and you could get a couple of summer outfits. I'm sure Bridget would enjoy that. I have a few things I need to get anyway."

"No thank you honey. I'll just stay home and rest." Her voice remained flat. Not sad, not happy, not even annoyed. Her voice was completely devoid of emotion. Her eyes were in another place completely. She looked away from him.

"Mom, what's wrong?" He said it gently but tried to have a bit of force behind it too.

"What do you mean Jake?" She looked up at him with hollow eyes.

Could she really be completely oblivious to the way she had been acting these last few weeks? God help me. I need you to step in before I step in it. He dropped his arms in total frustration. "What do I mean? You have never been like this. Get up, do something. Don't just sit around and wait to die or something."

She crossed her arms across her chest "Jake, how dare you speak to me like that." There was a little of the spunk he knew was in her. "I am your mother young man. You will not talk to me like a child."

"Well mom, you've been walking around here for three weeks now acting like the world has ended."

"I just lost my brother."

"And we lost our uncle."

She pointed her finger at him not more than six inches from his face. "Don't even pretend that you're sad at his passing young man."

"I never wanted him dead."

"I didn't say you wished him dead but don't pretend you're near as broke up as I should be because you barely knew the man. Then the two of you were always butting heads."

"I know but you weren't this upset when dad died."

"Well when your dad died I still had you, Bridget and your uncle. I didn't have everyone dying off and leaving me."

"And now you have me and Bridget." He motioned for her to sit down with him on the wooden bench at the edge of her flower garden.

"I most certainly do not. You spend every free second over there at Dreama's house and when you're not doing that you're stirring things up in town so I can't even show my face. And of course before your uncle died you were conspiring with Charlie on something..."

Jake leaned back against the bench. "Mom, what in the world are you talking about? I went to Charlie to see if he wanted to invest in my business. I spend a couple hours every day with Dreama but the rest of the time is spent with you or doing things for you." Like a fly from Charlie's shop Jake could recognize that this was not the real issue, just as the fish must have understood on some instinctive level that bugs weren't attached to strings, but a very real anger stirred inside him in response to this false issue. "This town has a new rumor every month. Give it a couple more days and they'll be bored with what we're doing and it will move on to its next victim."

"Well, I go in to town and I learn that the whole town is buzzing about how you were over at Charlie's a few hours before the cook out at Uncle Bill's. Then later that night he dies. You know how this town likes to talk, especially after the last time. I don't want to have to move again and leave the Hollow. I don't want to endure all the gossip and the funny looks from people when I go through town and I don't like the idea you spending all your time with that girl neither."

From lethargic kitten to enraged lion his mom pounced on him with a ferocity he'd never seen. "Mom." He stuttered to form the words. "Do you think I had something to do with Uncle Bill's dying?"

She looked up at him, then away, then back at him. "Course I don't but it don't much matter what I think. It's what the town thinks. They're going to believe what they want about any given situation."

"And that doesn't mean we have to pay attention to them, mom. If they really thought I did something then I'd have heard it by now." His heart slowed and he began to soften. She had convinced herself that everyone was accusing her of the unspeakable. She must have felt like she couldn't go out. "Why didn't you say anything to me about all this before?"

"I tried but you been gone so much with Dreama that there's never any time to really have a heart to heart."

"Yeah." He paused. " I like her mom. A lot."

"I just don't like you spending all your time with that handicap girl." Her voice was calm as if suddenly rid of the anger she'd held on to.

"She is not handicap, at least not in the way you're trying to make it sound." His mom was still teetering back and forth between exasperation and relaxation and he tried to maintain her calm, but he'd defended Dreama to her parents already and would do it with his mom too.

"Oh no? Have you heard the 911 tapes?" She focused hard on his eyes but didn't give him any time to respond. "I did. Chief Fogg let me listen to them. She didn't even know if anyone was on the other line or not. She kept saying her name and location over and over." She held her fingers to her head as if a telephone. "What if Uncle Bill had tried to contact her and she never heard the phone ring. She could have saved him."

Jake shook his head. "Mom, if Uncle Bill had tried to call anyone it would have been us, not Dreama. And as for her calling 911, that's what anyone would have done."

"She was closer. What if she could have saved him?"

"Mom, he was gone. No one could save him."

"I liked her just fine before you started liking her. She's a sweet and pretty girl but you're not deaf. How are you going to be able to communicate with her?"

"Like we do now. She has hearing aids and I'll try to learn to use sign language a little too."

"What if she expects all of us to do that? I'm too old to learn a whole new language."

"Mom, I really care about her. I thought you'd be happy that I found such a wonderful woman. She is Proverbs 31 as far as I've seen so far. That's what you told me to look for. She is Beautiful on top of that."

His mom rubbed her forehead with her fingertips and looked at the flower garden. "Jake, there are so many beautiful girls out there to choose from. Why do you feel you need to pursue someone you have no future with?"

"Who says we have no future?" He stood up. His real mom was slipping away. Uncle Bill had warned him but he was too late.

She smiled at him "Oh come on now, truly Jacob. How in the world could you two have a future? You want to have deaf babies? You want to have to get up all through the night with them because she don't know they're crying. You want to spend all your days with a woman you'll have to take care of like I had to do for your dad."

Jake had to walk away from his mom so he wouldn't forget himself. "Ok momma. I'll keep what you say in mind. I need to get going." He turned out of the yard and walked back to the car.

***

Dreama looked up at the clock. It was already one o'clock in the afternoon and she was still running around the house in her pajamas. She wanted to get up at a decent time this morning but the pillow didn't want to release its hold on her. Now she was running around the house trying to get things cleaned up before Jake came over at three.

Outside the sun beat down from a cloudless sky and a cool summer breeze washed across the town in regular bursts. She enjoyed the smell of lilacs that blew through her parents' house tangled with the other flowers and river. Her mom planted bushes and bulbs every year so when they would arrive the house would be inviting. Dreama didn't share her mom's love of gardening but she did enjoy the look and smell of her mom's hard work. Here in town, above the pharmacy, she had only the smell of baking cement and tar.

She quickly finished up her bowl of cereal and set it in the sink. She'd spent the morning doing her devotions and picking up but she had allowed herself too much time. "Late as usual." She laughed to herself. She scanned the dishes, laundry and dusting she needed to do. She shouldn't do anything else until she got herself dressed. She was more motivated when she wasn't running around in grey sweats and slippers.

Last night's mascara was coming off and made dark circles under her eyes. She washed her face, threw her hair back in a twist and clipped it in place. She was looking forward to dinner with Jake. She had made a special dessert with lots of chocolate. She figured she could send the leftovers home to his sister and mom.

She liked his family a lot. Renny was quiet since her brother died but she still was full of southern charm. Dreama pictured her sitting on a front porch of some grand southern estate rocking back and forth in a chair sipping on southern sweet tea. Bridget and Jake had quite a bit more city in them than their mom did, but that was fine, so

did Dreama.

Dreama's phone chirped and she flipped it to read the text from her sister.

"Hey Dreama. How are things in Love Hollow?"

"Ha, Ha. Glad you called."

"What's up?"

"Total confusion."

"?" Val typed back.

Dreama smiled "Jake." Dreama hit send and starting putting on her makeup

while she waited for her sister to reply.

"You like him?"

"Yes."

"Well..."

Dreama kept the banter back and forth, more to find reasons in her mind to

push away the stirring inside. They were dating now. She was finally in a relationship

post-Evan and she was looking for reasons to mess it up.

"Ok, Val."

"Did you make Chocolate Mousse Cake?"

"Of course."

"I knew you were falling for him. You don't make that unless you are trying to impress someone. Laugh." She finished the call and went about the house. Every once in a while she stopped at the window facing the mountain. She couldn't see it from her parents' house because of the tall trees that surrounded their house. It seemed to her that it was an appropriate parallel. While in the protective cocoon of her parents' home Dreama had been shielded from the real world but the trade off was that she wasn't fully exposed to the immensity of what was available to her.

Here, in her little studio apartment, Dreama could open her curtains at night and ponder the mountain bathed in moonlight. She could imagine what it would be like to be on that mountain and look down at the town. She could feel the rush of confronting an insurmountable challenge head-on.

Her parents had started out with the same dreams. They faced an unknown future and looked at it as something to be conquered and climbed. She wanted to have that same opportunity. She was not having that opportunity. The first mountain she needed was climbing beyond the safety of their provision. Now she was beyond that she prepared for the second challenge.

   ***

"Dreama do you have a minute?" Jake asked. It was a stupid question, of course she had a minute. They'd planned this afternoon to talk and watch a movie so it would seem reasonable that she could talk now. Jake berated himself as they crossed the small studio to face the mountain to the north of town.

"I love looking at that mountain." Dreama said.

Jake stopped looking out the window for a moment and looked at her. She didn't know that the mountain she admired was the last mountain that prevented him from fully opening up to her. To Dreama it was simply a beautiful piece of God's creation. To Jake it was a tangled mass of memories where the good times spent with family was melted and mixed with the pain of a hot-headed teen.

He realized that he'd fallen completely silent so he turned to face her. "It's part of the reason I came by a bit early."

She nodded. Her eyes held a pained anticipation. While he wasn't going to break her heart he could hardly call this good news. Jake fumbled for a way to start in. He wasn't even entirely sure what he wanted or needed to tell her at this moment.

"The night my uncle died he warned me about this town and its effects on my mom." Jake paused to consider how far he should take it. As if sensing his struggled Dreama reached over and patted his hand. The simple gesture calmed him. He dove in and told her everything about the coins, the odd behavior, the person watching mom in Uncle Bill's basement and the town's reaction to his uncle's death. With each word he felt like a tube of toothpaste being squeezed and emptied. Nothing he said to her could ever be taken back and he battled within himself to determine when he'd said enough, and when he was about to say too much.

As he peeled off layer after layer he felt as if the mountain separating them were also being chiseled away in large chunks. He stopped short of the violation against his mom or telling Dreama about his mom's outburst about their relationship.

"That's quite a bit to take in at a single moment." She said, her eyes focused across the room.

"Uncle Bill was a great businessman who was smart with his money. He wasn't what I'd call greedy. It's more like he didn't want to be wasteful and he viewed passing up an opportunity to make money as wasteful."

"I'd always known him to be frugal but kind." Dreama agreed.

"He made a couple of bad choices as it pertained to Charlie and Charlie saw it as a personal issue. Uncle Bill never saw it that way at all. He was very fond of Charlie as a person until he started smearing Bill's reputation. Then they didn't have much to say to each other."

"What were things like between you and your uncle?"

"We got along in small doses."

"How about your mom? She seems to be pretty broke up by things. Did they have a good relationship?"

"That was why I could only take him in small doses. I guess Uncle Bill felt like he needed to take over mom's life when she moved back to the Hollow. She only wanted to be here to be close to family in the neighborhood where she grew up. He thought she came back because she needed a man to run her life." As soon as he said it he was sorry. He saw the glimpse of the love his uncle held for his mom on that last night his uncle was alive. Ropes of guilt wound around Jake and he paused to consider a retraction.

"I can't imagine him being like that? Shrewd and controlling are not words I would have used to describe him at all."

"No. Not Shrewd. He just seemed to have a way about him. He wasn't evil, just a bit controlling."

Dreama continued to sit quietly.

What was he expecting from her, really? Did he think that she'd be able to give him action steps to solve a problem that was decades in the making. Or was it that he simply needed to have someone to talk to who would listen?

Showing Foreign Languages

In the previous section we talked about writing phonetically, but what do you do when you want to integrate foreign language in to your story? There are a few tips to make the integration of foreign language work:

- Use it periodically and in splashes.
- When someone speaks in a foreign language have the other person respond in English or someone else ask for the translation.
  - Example- "Je veux y aller!" Jean-Jacques screamed.

    "I know you want to go." Sarah replied. "But we can't."
- Give a bit of foreign language and then shift to English. [The Movie: The Hunt for Red October did this incredibly well in the opening in transitioning from Russian to English.]

It can be difficult to determine how much of a foreign language in the scene is interesting and when it gets distracting. Evaluate its use in this book and in your own writing. Then look at other books that did it skillfully and study their technique. Finally, go through this manuscript and rewrite sections that don't work in a way that helps the reader understand the language without pausing the action to explain it.

_____

_____

_____

_____

_____

_____

_____

_____

_____

_____

_____

_____

_____

_____

_____

_____

Midge had had enough with Hank. They hadn't been one of those silly-in-love couples to start out with. Theirs had been a relationship based on mutual respect and goals from the very beginning. She'd realized after her relationship with Bill Colewick in high school that relationships couldn't be all about chasing a handsome young man who made your insides flutter. That kind of love was exhausting and painful.

When they were just kids she had that kind of giddy-love with Bill. Theirs was a secret love. He'd told wild stories about his parents being the need for secrecy but Midge had always suspected that it was more because of Bill's nature. He had always been a private man. Midge remembered with fondness the times they had met in groups and made eyes at each other. The sense of danger invigorated her. Eventually word got out of their romance but only after they'd been sneaking around for a few months and the novelty had worn off. They began to get sloppy in hiding their touches, whispers and winks.

It was shortly after this time that Bill started talking about Renny's desire to join the swim team. While she didn't actually join the team for a few years after, it was something very important to Bill.

"Renny says she doesn't want out of the Hollow, but she needs to." He'd said on many occasions.

"What about you?"

"Aw, I think I'll stay." He'd said then wrapped his arms around her and kissed her forehead.

Bill could sense what it was Midge needed at any moment to smile or feel loved. She always knew, however, that she was second on his list of special ladies. He was protective of Renny as the day was long. She didn't resent Bill for it, at the time. In fact, it was a quality she found very endearing. A man that protective of any woman would surely know how to love and care for his own woman when she made an honest man out of him.

Renny understood and respected that level of care. She never sought to drive a wedge between Midge and Bill. She'd been overly cautious of causing any kind of scuffle between the two of them. Unfortunately, Bill had far less restraint.

Midge had been there the night Bill got the desperate call from Renny. She'd been north of Columbus as some major swim meet. She wouldn't explain at the moment but something horrible had happened. Bill and Midge got in his car and drove hours to go get Renny. During those hours they drove in virtual silence the roads a dark unknown stretching from one small town to the next.

"I'm not sure what happened but she's real shook up." Her hotel roommate had said when they arrived after midnight. Renny had always been diminutive and unopposing but when Midge saw her that night Renny was broken. She sat waiting on the end of the hotel bed. Her clothes were in a duffle next to her feet and her shoulders hunched forward.

"I don't feel well, Bill." She'd said but Midge didn't think it was the flu that had transformed Renny.

"Let's get her to the car." Bill said and he led her out.

The ride home was no less tense. Muffled sobs periodically rose out of Renny but she remained curled up in the backseat.

When Bill told her what had happened Midge was heartsick.

"I think the best thing for her is to take the next step with Dale." Bill had said as if this were the planning session of one of his projects and not the welfare of his little sister.

"How will marrying a boy help with rape? She needs to report them boys." Midge had said.

"She needs protection and to feel wanted. I can't give that to her and my parents refuse to."

"What she needs is to press charges and put those creeps behind bars."

That marked the beginning of the end for Midge and Bill. Not long after their relationship fell apart, she met Hank, Renny got married and moved away. Midge let out a sigh as she remembered getting the news that Renny and Dale were going to have a honeymoon baby. Rumors circulated about the reason for their short courtship but Midge always insisted that Renny had simply been lucky enough to find the right guy. Then Midge would point to her own whirlwind romance with Hank as further evidence that those things happened.

Midge pulled herself to the present to consider that 'romance'. She had been fond of Hank but doubted that she could call it love as she'd heard love described, or like she'd felt with Bill. Perhaps that allowed her to take such a methodical view to this foolery she suspected going on between Janice and Hank. She viewed it as more of a betrayal than heartbreak. Hank belonged to her, not to her heart.

Chapter 8

"Hank, what can I do for you?" Charlie came out from behind the counter and

shook his hand.

"Well I had a couple of things on my mind I need to discuss with you if you

have a moment."

"Sure thing." Charlie said indicating a seat at the counter.

"Do you mind if we go over to the soda counter. I'd really love to have a malt I

don't have to make myself."

Charlie smiled and pointed to the counter. Hank sat on the stool. It creaked

slightly under his weight as he adjusted himself on the too small seat.

"I know things always taste better when someone else makes them. To this day I

don't like Peanut Butter and Jelly sandwiches because they tasted better when my mom

made them." Charlie said as he lifted up a large silver cup. He picked up a large glass.

"What would you like in yours?"

"Anything but Chocolate." Behind him the bell jingled on the door. Charlie

finished up the Malt and poured it in an old fashioned malt glass. The glass began to

sweat and Hank's stomach threatened to growl in expectancy.

"Whipped cream?"

Hank nodded his head. Charlie shook the can and put about five inches of whipped cream on top of the malt and stuck a straw in. A bit of malt sloshed over the side and slid down the class.

"Can I get you anything else?" Charlie asked.

"Go on ahead and tend to your other customer first. I'll enjoy this a spell."

Charlie turned to the customer who had walked in, "Can I help you with something sir?"

"I need to buy some bait."

"Yes, sir." Charlie walked over to the cooler. "Anything else I can get for you?"

"I wanted a small pole for my boy. He's eight and loves cartoon characters."

"Right down here." Charlie walked down the aisle and Hank turned back to his malt.

They were supposed to be out of Blue Hollow already. Seven years ago they'd purchased a lot in a retirement trailer park just south of Orlando. The small lawns, constant sunshine and club house with pool glistened in his mind like a mirage. They'd been offered a really good deal on the place when a friend heard about the property coming up for only $20,000 plus monthly lot rent. The plan all along had been to rent it for five years. During that time they'd charge $150 over expenses and not upgrade their car. At the end of the five years they'd own the place free and clear.

The deadline passed two years ago and Midge had always found a reason to stay in the Hollow. Now was the time to sell. Business was booming and the area was growing. The thing was established, the revenue was good but Midge wasn't interested in selling the business. If they'd have been in Florida rather than the Bowling Alley a couple months back it's very likely Bill Colewick would still be alive.

How's that for irony? Hank knew it was always Bill that kept her tied to this place. He tried not to resent her for it. They had a game the two of them played. Bill and Midge had always pretended that they'd remained good friends over the years but she offered Bill a look she'd never cast Hank's way.

Many men would be jealous over the competition but Hank had always known that Midge didn't love him with the depth of his love for her. He'd been sufficiently pleased to have her for his own in name and in body, even if he'd never fully own her heart.

He stabbed at the malt with his straw before drawing in another long sip. Hank figured he'd finally get her out of Blue Hollow and wanted to play a silly trick on Bill as a send off. Hank looked around him as if his thoughts were being transcribed and projected on a screen over his head. Of course, with Midge carrying the secret with her it was far worse than transcription in a deserted bait shop. Midge had influence and reach that most national networks would envy. If she spoke a thing it might as well be Walter Cronkite.

He looked over at Charlie who was ringing up the man's bait and giraffe fishing pole. The man paid for his purchases and went back out the door.

"How's season treating you?" Hank asked.

"Decent. I'm busy but not much busier than I usually am at this time in the season. How are things at the diner?" Charlie said as he sat on a stool just a little way down from where Hank sat.

"Busy. Real busy. I'm sure things will pick up for you in a month or so when it gets warmer."

"It's possible. Now Hank, what can I do for you?"

"I wanted to talk to you about Colewick's death."

"Yeah, what about it?"

Hank stirred his malt with his straw and sucked up the last little bit. "Charlie, what would you say if I told you that I think maybe I had something to do with the man's death?"

"I'd ask you what in the world you meant by that."

Hank hesitated for a moment. The weight of guilt struggling to purge him of the secret he'd carried for more than a month but self-preservation held his lips tight.

Charlie was the only person he knew in town who wouldn't judge him and who wouldn't go off blabbing to the first person he met. Charlie didn't move and Hank had to elaborate.

"Well, see Janice had heard Midge and Bill talking while back and she said from where she was sitting it sounded as if they were sweet on each other." Hank looked up at Charlie for some read on his first impression. He wasn't looking at Hank though. His eyes were focused on the counter directly in front of him. His face was twisted like a person working through a complex task.

Hank continued "I know it seems silly to go on her authority that Midge was really having any affections on Bill but you know when a man hears something like that his first thoughts ain't always rational." The silence emboldened him and he took a sip of his malt and laid it all out. "Anyway, I tried to talk to Midge about it a bit but I'm about the only person in Blue Hollow she don't talk to. She wouldn't give me two words on the topic. So I asked Janice to find out what she could for me."

"You asked Janice to help you with this?" Charlie's voice was low and measured.

It reminded him of a growl he'd heard coming from a stray dog once.

"Sure I asked Janice." Hank counted on his fingers. "I guess it was about two and a half weeks later she tells me she was good and sure that they were exchanging pleasantries beyond what was customary under the circumstances. Well, Midge ain't perfect but she's what I got and I ain't willing to just let someone come and sweep her away."

"So what did you do Hank?" His voice was scolding in nature and it surprised Hank at first but he continued.

"Oh, just little mischiefs. I wanted him to grow less fond of our diner. I would over salt his food or I'd put soggy fries on his plate. There was nothing dangerous mind you, but I figured if I made our food unpleasant he'd come around a bit less and Midge would find herself some lady to spend her afternoons chatting with."

"And then?" Charlie's voice lightened considerably but his voice was prodding as if this were an introduction to some sinister escalation.

"You stop rushing me, hear? I want to be clear I wasn't doing nothing to hurt the man. I was just trying to encourage him to find another watering hole. The man kept coming though except he stopped coming for dinner. He came in the middle of the afternoon or after the dinner rush and he'd get a piece of pie or ice cream. That meant him and Midge was having even more time to chat about things cause there

wasn't much of a crowd."

"So then what did you do?"

"I'm getting to it Charlie. What you on a deadline for the newspaper?"

"No Hank, you know that everything you tell me never leaves these four walls.

You're just starting to ramble and I know some extra pepper in someone's stew isn't

what worries you."

"I just want you to understand I didn't mean him no harm."

"I understand that. Now what did you do?"

"Well, you see the day he died he came by a little later than usual. Midge had

just run to the house for something so I had Janice wait on him. I walked out and told

him I had some new ice cream and would he like to have a nice chocolate Sunday with

nuts on it. He said he'd be pleased to have it."

"So you gave the man a Sunday. Is he diabetic or allergic to nuts?"

"No, don't be stupid. If he was don't you think he would have turned me

down?"

"Guess so."

"Alright so I go back to warm the fudge and I get an idea. I warm up some of those chocolate laxatives I had in the medicine cabinet. I must have warmed up three or four of those and I poured them over his Sunday with the fudge syrup."

Charlie let out a howl "Oh no you didn't." He laughed until his face turned red. Hank jumped suddenly at the unexpected outburst.

"Charlie, listen to me. I didn't know he had no health problems. I heard one of the people say he had high blood pressure. What if all that salt and such I was putting on his food weakened him and then that final Sunday just did him in."

Charlie let out another howl. "Hank, the man didn't die of stomach aches. He died of a heart attack. I'm sure it was all fine. You didn't kill him although you did just make my day. I imagine about the time he got home that day he was feeling none too good. I know from Jake too that he had the family and Dreama over for a barbeque. He must have been quite a host." Charlie let out another howl. "Don't you worry yourself. You didn't kill him with laxatives. Of that I'm sure."

***

Dreama pulled in to the parking lot in front of the police station. Jake's words rumbled inside her as she thought about the lurking shadow outside her home and then everything that had happened to Renny. The station was a small one-story building that shared a parking lot with a convenience store/gas station on the Eastern edge of town. The two car attached garage was to the back of the building and three steps led to

the security door that opened to the offices inside. She parked in the closest spot to the

door in the empty parking lot and got out. There was a coffee can full of cigarette butts

and sand just outside the door and two Styrofoam cups behind the bushes against the

building. She took a deep breath before walking up to the police station. She pushed

the buzzer and identified herself. Immediately after the door let out a loud buzz and she

pushed in.

Lieutenant Cushings and Chief Fogg were each sitting at a desk behind a

counter. It was like walking in to a 1960s sitcom only Dreama felt strangely intimidated.

It wasn't unlike the horrific knot she felt in her stomach in the split second between

seeing a police car hidden on the highway and realizing she wasn't going to be pulled

over.

The Chief looked up at her, smiled then spit in a Styrofoam cup. She quickly

looked over to Lt. Cushings who was up and walking toward the counter she was

standing at.

"Morning Dreama. How you doing?" the Lieutenant said. He was nearly

shouting.

"Good thanks. You?" She intentionally spoke quietly hoping he'd follow suit but just in case pulled her hair back to show she had her hearing aid.

"Oh." He said. "So are you able to hear now?"

She wanted to point out the obvious. She'd just spoken with them through the intercom and then opened the door when they buzzed it but she decided that sarcasm wasn't appropriate in this time or place. "Yes, I can hear just fine."

"I wanted to know if you couldn't tell me a bit more about Mr. Colewick's passing." She looked over at the Chief. He stood up, adjusted his pants and picked up his spit cup before coming to the counter. Dreama dreaded talking to him. While she didn't have to watch his lips this time she'd have to face him and her eyes would be continually drawn to the black tobacco stuck between his teeth and his mouthful of brown liquid. She wondered why it was even legal for him to use this tobacco while he was on duty.

"What's there to know? The coroner told us that his heart gave out." Lt. Cushings said with his eyes on the chief.

"I am concerned that Mr. Colewick didn't die naturally."

Lt. Cushings straightened up and cocked his head to the side. "What makes you think that young lady?"

"There are a few different things." She said. She laid out some of her suspicions from that day with the house being open. She dabbled a bit in to what Jake told her about someone snooping around the house when Renny was cleaning things out but stopped short of revealing the coins or the more personal matters.

"We understand how upsetting this must-spit- be for you. It is hard for the whole town but we looked-spit-and if we suspected anything amiss we'd be all over it. You have my promise on that." Spit.

"I'm not questioning you officers. I guess I just need to put my own mind at ease."

"We understand that but everything is just fine. Mr. Colewick's passing was sad for the community but there is nothing that would have indicated it was anything but an unfortunate death."Spit.

***

"Would you rather get out of this boat and go for a walk?" Jake asked. Dreama nodded and reeled in her line. The thin fishing line sliced through the water and created small rippled on either side.

"I guess it's good we called it quits." She said as she brought up the wormless like that had caught nothing more edible then algae.

"Well, if you're a vegetarian that would be a good day of fishing."

They took the boat back to the shore and walked up the lane to the edge of the wooded area that surrounded the boat shop.

"Word on the street is I need to watch out for you." Dreama said with a chuckle. Jake stopped unloaded his cooler of food to absorb her laugh. It was soft, not childish enough to be a giggle but also not loud enough to be a full howl. If laughs were like smiles then Dreama's laugh was a smirk.

"Yes. I'm very dangerous." He played along.

"Janice said I should watch you."

Dreama continued to laugh but his sense of humor was gone. He knew Janice didn't make off-hand comments like Midge did. Every word from Janice was a threat and she was persistent enough to take what never was and transform it in to what would be. He felt the familiar sense of frustration that rose up whenever her name was mentioned around him. She had a way of connecting him to things that were better left forgotten. And Janice always did them with intent.

Jake turned to Dreama. "She said what?"

"Janice told me that you were dangerous." Dreama wiggled her fingers at him and spoke in an imitation ghost voice.

"Well, Janice needs to keep her opinions to herself."

Dreama dropped her hands and looked at him. The smile slid down and pulled her forehead with it. Creases deepened between her eyes. He didn't want to delve in to Alexa today, but maybe he should.

"What was she talking about?"

Leave it to Janice to resurrect dead rumors and build innuendo. Of course not answering it at this point would make it larger that it really was. He pulled up the story in his mind, careful to stick to the version like a news report. He couldn't open his mind to face the gruesomeness of that moment.

"When I was 16 I was involved in a nasty car accident. I had just gotten my driver's license which made it even worse because they blamed it on bad driving." He felt the tug of the memory. Like a knock on the door in the middle of the night the image waited as it held him in a terrified purgatory. "I had to go to court and lost my license for a year." He clamped it shut now. He wouldn't dig any deeper.

"After almost a year of it my parents moved us in to the city to get me away from all of the chatter. There were some people upset that my punishment wasn't stiffer."

She reached up and held on to his shoulder. "Jake I am so sorry. What an awful thing to have to go through at such a young age." Dreama reached up and touched his cheek. He reached his arms around her and pulled her close. He hugged her tight against him. She didn't judge him. She wanted to comfort him. That was something that didn't happen too often in the Hollow. He bent down toward her. The moment was right to kiss her. He knew that now. She was in his arms. She had slid her arms around him. He looked down at her.

"Why would Janice bring this up all these years later?" Dreama asked.

The late night knocking now flung the door open. Jake watched in his mind as Janice chased Alexa around the mountain. He didn't want to go here. He didn't want to remember. There was no way for him to stop the memory now. It was charging on. He remembered running to the car. Racing down the mountain to catch up to Alexa and speed her to safety. He had craned the wheel too hard to the right. She was there much closer than she should have been to the road and he was much too close to the shoulder. The sound of tires on gravel as he floored the brakes.

"Jake?" Dreama's voice pulled him out in the instant after Alexa smashed on the hood of his car in his memory. "Jake, you're crying."

***

"Janice, a word please." Jake said as he marched in the diner. Nothing around him was in focus and there could be one patron or a roomful. Jake only saw Janice through his white hot flash of anger.

Janice walked over to him "What can I do for you Jakey-hon?" She smiled and crossed her arms.

"What's with you trying to get Dreama worried about being with me?"

"I did no such thing. I only told her what others around here were saying. They said that you had an awful lot of reason to see your Uncle gone and that it was pretty good timing as far as you're concerned. And if you'll recall I said as much to you that first time you brought Dreama in."

"Yes, I did notice how you mention that to Dreama quite a bit. I don't know what you're trying to do here but you are not going to drive me out of town."

Janice put one hand on her hip, "And why would I want to do that?"

"I don't know why but I'm sure there is something in that head of yours that makes you think that by getting me out of here things will somehow work out better for you."

"No, I just want to tell the poor girl the truth."

"And what is the truth Janice?"

"That there are lots of unanswered questions in the Hollow and most of them seem to revolve around you. I wouldn't be doing my Christian duty if I didn't warn wayward travelers."

"Whatever Janice."

***

Janice climbed the steps up to the apartment that Hank and Midge let her stay in. Bill Colewick's place was a fine one that, when occupied, could bring in about a thousand dollars in positive cash flow per month. That relied on Janice getting a jump on the competition and putting a bid on the place before it hit the market.

She put on a jogging suit and checked her voice mail messages. Her muscles groaned and she stretched long on the couch while a litany of voices and beeps filled her right ear. There was nothing of substance and she realized with some bit of relief, that she'd built her business almost to the point of a freestanding entity. These six months of running things in the Hollow had not hurt her business. She had the small hiccup earlier but they'd recovered fine and, on balance, she could quickly see that a weekly jaunt to the office would be all she needed once she closed up the deals she was working on in the hollow.

She finished listening to her voice mail and tossed her tips in a jar. With the summer residents arriving her tips were getting better. She expected she'd only need another few weeks, a month tops, before she could leave Blue Hollow and return to the city with her aunt and uncle. She imagined taking them on a nice vacation with the tips she'd built up as a waitress. Maybe the three of them would go on a nice cruise and use the tip jar for their spending money. The thoughts of leaving this place soothed her aches just as a massage would at a spa.

As the braids of deception twisted around Blue Hollow, Janice relaxed in her chair feeling the knots of frustration falling away.

***

"Thanks again for helping me pack up Uncle Bills' clothes." Jake folded the box lid and taped it shut. The roll of tape screeched as he dragged it across the full seem and then rubbed it down. Dreama watched him as he took the sum total of his uncle's life and hauled it to the other room where it would be given to downtrodden people.

The image smacked Dreama with her own mortality. This sum total of her life would be one day shoved in cardboard boxes and sold at garage sales or given away. Everything she was working and studying for would simply cease to matter. The four dollar latte or the sixty-nine cent cheeseburger would decompose inside her and return to dirt.

The thought was not only morbid but terrifying. In that instant, with a roll of screeching tape, she'd realized what the writer of Ecclesiastes meant when he said "'Meaningless! Meaningless!' says the Teacher. 'Utterly meaningless! Everything is meaningless.'" One day she'd reach the end of her life and what would be in her box?

"Dreama?" She snapped to the present and looked at Jake. Her jaunt in to philosophy now broken she tried to recover.

"I'm sorry. When did you say your mom and sister would get here?" She pulled pants and shirts off of their hangers and put them in the next box.

"They'll be here in about an hour or two. They only want his clothes and shoes though. They're donating those to charity. The rest of his things are going to be auctioned off."

"Are you going to give them to Janice's parent's church?"

"No, there's a homeless shelter mom heard about. They'll be over later to pick the boxes up that we have packed."

Jake hoisted a box on his shoulder and took it in the living room. He came back in with another empty box and set it down. She had expected being in this house would be hard and that every room would carry with it a painful glimpse of his death. Dreama had found that by cleaning up Mr. Colewick's things she was able to say goodbye to him in a meaningful way. She could see his death bringing hope and blessings to many people who desperately needed them.

"Have you thought much more about what we talked about?" Jake asked. His eyes probed her as if trying to determine if that was the cause of her deeply reflective mood.

She had spent a great deal of time thinking about his car accident and the way he was driven out of town by neighbors and people he'd grown up with. It must have been horrible to feel so rejected by your friends.

"A bit." She answered.

"I'm concerned about what it could mean to my mom and sister. I'm afraid to leave them with all of this going on."

"You're going to leave?" Dreama said. Suddenly the idea of the town without Jake terrified her. What was even more frightening was the fact that, while searching for her independence, she'd come to depend so much on Jake. He was a source of strength for her, not like training wheels but more like a father's steady had would be on a child's bike. Jake ran along side her, encouraging her to do it alone. Then he let go of her and she soared down the road. And just like a father he comforted her when she fell.

But Dreama's feelings for Jake were not those of a child for her dad. Jake held in himself the protection she'd always wished her dad would give her. Her dad had been far too ready to criticize her when she fell down.

Dreama looked up. Jake was leaning against the doorway to Mr. Colewick's room and looking out the front window. They hadn't been talking about the same things. He was worried about the other women in his life, not about himself. Now he was talking about leaving. The idea grabbed her lungs and squeezed out every drop of air. She stood, silent, waiting for his verdict.

"C'mere Dreama, I got you something." He nodded to the living room with his head. She followed silently. He patted the couch next to where he sat. He pulled out a small black box. "Open it." He said.

She opened the box and inside was a small gold band with a key and a cross etched in to the metal. "It's beautiful" she said although she wasn't sure what it was.

"I had it made just for you." He lifted the ring. It looked so small between his fingers. "This is a promise ring. I want you to wear this on your right ring finger so you don't start any rumors." Dreama laughed at his obvious jab at the diner crowd. "I'm giving you this ring because I want you to know that I promise to honor you and respect you." He paused and looked down at the ring. "I will not push you beyond the bounds of purity and I'll respect your future husband, and God, by not attempting to do anything that would violate God's desire for purity."

"Thank you." She said. Tears were filling up in her eyes. She stared at the band of gold between his fingers. It was such an incredible thing to do.

"You're welcome. Here try it on." He slid it down her right ring finger. She had a few friends in college who had promise rings but she had never heard of a man, especially a man in his mid twenties, do something so honorable for a woman. For a moment she wished he was sliding it down the finger on her left hand. Those were the daydreams of a child. She knew that the relationship was far too young for that kind of commitment. Still, the gesture was beautiful.

"See," he continued, "I've asked myself how I'd want a man to treat my sister. I want a person who would love and respect her." He looked at the ring on her finger. "I want to be that kind of man to you." He lifted her knuckles to kiss them and she pulled her hand back toward her shoulder. He stopped and then let go of her hand, lifted her chin and kissed her gently. Dreama felt as if she were floating on a cloud. Was this actually happening? Was she letting her heart have another shot at real love?

Chapter 9

Sometimes Dreama could sense someone was there. She sat up in the darkness

of her studio and picked up her hearing aids from the nightstand. She clicked them on.

As if eyes adjusting from a well-lit room to the darkness of night, her ears scanned the

night air for the slightest hint of sound.

She took shallow breaths and focused on every dark shape in the room. Did it

move? Was it familiar? Was it a lamp behind a chair or an intruder seeking shelter.

Finally satisfied that she was alone she stood up and moved to the window. She

couldn't hear them but she knew something was just beyond her field of vision. Was

the intruder from the woods now outside her apartment lurking behind the shadows of

cars and phone poles?

She looked at the clock. It was nearly eleven. Her parents would only be settling

in for the evening news. It wasn't too late to go over there. She sat down on her bed,

terror pounding on her chest and pushing through her veins.

She had survived far worse the night Mr. Colewick had died. That night she'd

seen the figure outside, tonight it was only the eerie sense that someone was watching

and waiting for her. She had forced herself to remain independent despite the fear and possible danger then and she'd do it again.

But what did she have to prove. The fear inside shook her from the insecurity that told her the only way to prove she was capable was to force herself in to bad situations. This figure she sensed could be no more than the boogey man or it could be a real danger. She'd been stupid before to remain alone in the house.

She decided she'd already proven herself. She fired off a text to her sister saying she was on the way, then drove to her parents' for a sleepover.

***

"I'm going to be leaving town for a little while." Charlie said. He was calling Janice one more time. The truth was he was packed up and leaving Blue Hollow for good but he wasn't certain that Janice would have much of a response to any of that news.

"How long will you be gone?" Her voice was curious, but not pleading.

"Months at least." He paused for a second round of questions.

"Oh. Okay." She replied.

He heard all he needed in her tone. As if demons wielding their pitchforks were jabbing up and down his body Charlie's skin prickled with understanding and regret. If he'd taken the settlement he could have weathered the slow start to this spring. In fact, if he had any ambition to fight on in Blue Hollow he could find a way to make it work, but he was done.

He finished talking to Janice and hauled the last of his belongings in to the camper hitched to the back of his pickup.

"What are you going to do with the place?" Hank asked. It had been good for Charlie that his old friend had come to see him off.

"I'll let the bank come take it." Charlie said.

"You have so much stuff in there." Hank's voice was a mix of condemnation and resignation. Charlie figured the conflicting tone was born from the paradoxical emotions they were both experiencing.

"I've spent my life here." Charlie said. He knew the phrase sounded like one of nostalgia and the bittersweet reflection that comes during times of transition. That was most likely how Hank would interpret the statement. To Charlie, however, the meaning was completely different. Charlie's life was currency and he'd spent the entire wad of money in this town. He was in his sixties and all he had was an empty wallet, in the literal and figurative sense, to show for the time spent here. It was time for him to cut his losses and move on.

Charlie handed the keys to Hank. "You can rent the boats out or sell some of the stuff off if you'd like." Charlie said. His back was to the bait shop. "And help

yourself to the worms in the fridge. You should spend less time on the river and less in

the kitchen."

"You're sure now?" Hank asked. His voice was now more hopeful that Charlie

would reconsider.

"Yes. I'm sure. All the best to you Hank." Charlie stepped out of his truck to

shake Hank's hand then climbed back in. The engine roared to life and then lunged

forward. The tires skidded slightly before grabbing on to enough ground to drag the

weight forward.

The last thought Charlie had as he looked in his rearview mirror at Blue Hollow

for the last time was how much he wished he would have gone fishing with Hank one

last time.

***

Dreama turned north on Main Street and then west on to Maple. It was a

simpler part of town then where her parents lived, or even where she lived now. Oaks

and Maples lined the streets and extended large branches like protective arms over small

ranch homes. Each house, like a series of rolled cookies, was nearly identical except for

the decorations. One house had a flower bed alone the cement porch while another had lined their porch with bushes. There were few parks, no shops except for one convenience store and there was no access to the river.

Dreama looked down at the directions Janice had written out for her. Janice insisted that they not meet at her apartment above the diner. Dreama wasn't sure whose house this was, only that it belonged to someone Janice knew. The secret visit was a little exciting. A great deal had changed in Blue Hollow since Charlie mysteriously closed up his fishing and tackle shop more than two months ago. Hank hadn't been the same. She hadn't realized Hank and Charlie were friends but since he left, things at the diner were tense.

Midge had begun to go on long weekend trips and leave the diner in the care of Hank. For his part, Hank took the opportunity of her absence to train a high school boy on the grill. Now that the boy was trained Dreama could count on Hank fishing when Midge was gone.

Although it was likely these problems were the reason for Janice's secrecy, Dreama suspected more. Like a charcoal sketch, the array of lines, circles, squares and ovals was forming in to a clear picture. This picture was the only reason Dreama had agreed to come.

Dreama pulled in to a gravel driveway and turned off the car. Before she got more than a few steps up the sidewalk leading to the house Janice walked out of the one story ranch and closed the door.

"We're not staying here to talk." Dreama asked.

"No." She replied. "Do you mind giving me a ride to the park? I don't want to talk here."

"Sure, climb in." Dreama got back in her side and moved the directions off of the passenger seat. Janice climbed in. "Where are we going?"

Janice put on her seatbelt then turned to Dreama. "I'll give you directions on the way."

The car ride was silent except for Janice's navigation. Dreama let her mind meander down the streets of her own thoughts. She and Jake had been dating more than three months and they were beginning to have serious talks about a potential future. With only weeks left to the summer season the two of them needed to decide if this would continue when she was at school.

"The next right." Janice's directions broke in to her quandary and Dreama had to smile at the appropriateness of the word choice. It would be dorky to consider the next right as some indication from God that Jake was the right pick, but if she were superstitious she'd likely have settled the matter with that single utterance.

In reality it only confirmed what she knew. Jake was perfect for her.

"Is this it?" Dreama asked pointing to a small park at the end of the road they were on.

"Yes, pull over by the pavilion." The park rested on an unusually flat piece of land in the midst of rolling hills on every side. There were ball diamonds and picnic benches but little else. A group of boys were playing ball on the farthest diamond from the parking lot. They walked to a picnic bench in the shade.

"I've never seen this park before." Dreama looked over at Janice. "It's really nice."

"Yes, this is where the local kids play little league and such. It's not a bad place. There are't too many river rats." Janice said. "Oh sorry." She corrected, "I mean summer residents who get over this way. It's kind of where the local people come to get away from the crowd at the park by the river."

"This reminds me of the little league park by my house."

Janice seemed to trail off to a place only she could see. The firmness in her eyes and cheeks went loose and drooped down to pale curtains hung on windows that were too small to support their length. Her eyes took a mirrored sheen as tears puddle up in the bottom of her eyelids."Well, you remember when I told you to watch getting too close to Jake?" Janice said suddenly.

"Yes." Not only that but she remembered Jake's reaction to that comment. "I remember it vaguely."

Janice smiled a crooked smile as if to say I know you remember it. "Well, if you remember it or not I know you didn't really believe what I was trying to tell you."

"Jake is a great guy. He's never given me a reason to doubt him so I try not to go around pre-judging people because of a little gossip or rumor." She ran her finger back and forth across her promise ring.

Janice paused for a moment before continuing. "You seemed like a lady who wouldn't accept a friendly warning. I was hoping that I wouldn't have to drag all this back out but it seems I'm going to have to for your sake." She looked down at Dreama's hand. If she was hoping for some reaction she wasn't going to get it. She had settled it in her mind to not listen to this town's gossip and rumors. After pausing a few moments longer Janice continued. "Jake has a past that I think you should know about before you get too much more involved with him." Janice's eyes never left the promise ring on Dreama's right hand.

Dreama covered the ring with her left hand. "I don't mean to be rude Janice, really I don't, but I've been in that diner enough to know that gossip gets passed around in there through so many hands that it vaguely resembled any form of truth when it's finished. I really don't want to hear it."

"I know you think I'm some kind of gossip who has nothing better to do than serve of some eggs with a side of smut but I know from first-hand knowledge why Jake was moved from the Hollow all them years back."

Dreama leaned forward "Jake already told me about the car accident."

Janice smiled. "Did he now?"

Dreama nodded.

"Then I guess he told you about the relationship he had with this girl and how he tried to cover up what he did?"

Dreama continued to look at her without a hint of emotion. Janice wasn't going to get a rise out of her easily.

"I knew you wouldn't believe me so I brought this article. After the trial and everything was over his parents pulled their family out of the Hollow and in to town. They only come back cause Renny was in a heap of financial troubles and her brother had a place she could live in rent free."

Dreama knew better from Jake. She'd heard about the money that Bill had hidden as well as what Jake's dad, Dale, had put aside for his family. Renny hadn't been wealthy when she came to the Hollow, but she wasn't destitute.

But how did it benefit Janice to make Dreama believe exactly that? Dreama looked at the headline Local Teen involved in hit and run.. There was a picture of the car, Jake's mug shot and a beautiful girl who would now be forever frozen at sixteen.

Janice twisted the knife. "The girl he killed was my cousin. Her parents were friends of Midge and Hank which is how I got the job at the diner. I had to watch these last ten years while my aunt turned in to a shell of herself. She never recovered from my cousin's murder. My uncle, well, he drinks like a fish and he has a shrine to my cousin. They said Jake was not guilty but my aunt and uncle are still serving time." Janice pulled a couple of pictures out of her pocket and showed them to Dreama. It was a younger Jake, Janice and the girls in the paper.

Janice sat down across from her on the picnic bench. Her southern charm returning now that she had fed her the poison. "I don't want to stir nothing up 'tween you and Jake, honest I don't, but when I heard bout Bill Colewick's passing and then you getting involved with Jake I felt you needed to know who it was you was giving your heart to."

Dreama handed the pictures back to Janice. "I think I should take you back home. I'd really like to be alone now."

"I understand hon but listen to me. You need to leave the Hollow. I don't think you're safe." Janice squeezed Dreama's arm. Her face was soft again.

"What do you mean?" One tear dropped out of her eye. She tried to catch it before Janice saw it.

"Well listen. I know you don't believe Bill Colewick died of natural causes. I also know you been snooping around looking for who did it. Ain't I right?"

"Yes, I am curious."

Janice's lip curled. "Well, I ain't no genius but I can tell you that from what I hear there are three things you need Motive, Means and Opportunity."

"Sure."

"When you look at Jake you got a man who stays late after the whole family left to ask his uncle for money to start up this new business venture. All of Blue Hollow knows now what Jake knew then. Mr. Colewick was one of the richest men in the hollow on account of his real estate holdings."

"He has real estate holdings?"

"Oh yeah, lots of them. They're held in a trust that was willed over to his sister."

"I didn't know that."

"Point is Jake did and he wanted to tap in to his Uncle's pocket to get a business started. He went to Charlie first cause he wasn't too fond of his Uncle." Janice held up

three fingers. "Jake wanted money and his Uncle wouldn't give it to him. That made

him mad. Motive." She bent that finger down. "He was the last one to see Bill Colewick

alive by your own knowledge. Opportunity."

"And his means?"

"That you got to figure yourself." Janice sat up. "I want to tell you again how

sorry I truly am to be the bearer of bad news."

Using All 5 Senses

We learn about the world around us through our Five Senses. At this very moment you're gathering a huge amount of data. As I'm tying this I realize my arms are a bit cold [I should put on a light sweater]. There is sun coming in through the window [which is very nice] and there is a bird chirping. I also feel an itch in my nose [please don't sneeze] and I'm fighting a smidge of a headache. Oh and I heard my stomach growl and can feel that I'm very hungry.

You don't want to give that much information, it will be distracting, but you do want to be sure you're getting enough information to the reader to let them experience the scene.

Go in to the manuscript and select any five pages at random. Look for the senses. Remember they won't always say "smell" or "sight". Try to identify the subtle senses too.

Things were moving ahead quickly between Jake and Dreama. Jake stood up tall and soaked up the August heat. With barely a breeze the temperatures were well in to the nineties. The humidity was low and there wouldn't be many more days like this for the year.

As the final days of summer marched ever closer Jake thought harder about his future with Dreama. He loved her, he was certain, but even with love there was the tug from Alexa that didn't seem to let go. As if his love were a curse Jake hesitated to open his heart fully to Dreama. His family had been driven from family and those they cared for the last time. Alexa had died. So many lives were changed forever.

He wondered if it was worth the fight to maintain a long distance relationship. His mom was no better. The conflicting obligations between his dad, his uncle and his heart pushed and pulled at him. Swimming in the uncertainty of his mind dissolved his defenses and he drifted back to the day that he was supposed to propose to Alexa.

That morning he'd grabbed his baseball jersey, school books, and got in his car. He had made the Varsity cut. He had the car that he and Dad had bought from an ad in the paper. The burst of unusually warm air for the early part of May had invigorated him. He felt invincible. After the game, he'd decided to go for a short drive up the side of one of the rises that overlooked the Hollow. Go to the small pull off area a few miles up and watch the setting sun over his town. Alexa was meeting him there and he had a diamond in his pocket. So he'd mounted this road only an hour ago, trying to remember when there had been a more perfect day.

Nervously he'd kept his hand on the small ring in his pocket. Alexa had been beautiful. The sun radiated through her hair and formed a golden halo of chestnut brown curls. Janice came. The fight ensued. Alexa took off around the corner.

"Alexa!" Janice screamed. Then she turned back to Jake. Hate burned in her eyes. Janice took off down the hill after Alexa. His heart pounded in his ears and his breath pushed out of his mouth in short bursts. He felt like a charging bull, Janice was the waving red cloth.

"You leave her alone." He yelled then jumped in his car. He had to get her to safety and away from Janice. Perhaps they could elope and live with his parents. They'd married young. They'd understand.

Janice and Alexa had taken off on foot and their angry yells echoed up from the blind curves. He got in his car and started around the hill. Janice was quickly in view. She lunged to Alexa and in a flash Alexa jumped away from Janice and in to the path of Jake's car. He slammed the breaks but skidded on the rocks.

Her eyes were wide in the instant before she smashed over the hood of his car and on to the ground behind him.

"No!" he screamed but his cries were drowned out by Janice's.

He wanted to stop remembering, but he couldn't. The images flashed relentlessly.

He had lowered himself to sit on the guardrail along the road. Pain seared through his right hand and he drew back quickly. I sliver of glass dug deep in the fleshy part of his palm. Dried blood, her blood, caked the creases. Now a fresh trickle of his own mixed in. He pulled the offending glass out and wiped his palm on his pants. He tried to wrap his mind around all that was happening. Feet clicked on the blacktop to his left, then crunched in the gravel of the road's shoulder. The person stopped beside him. Jake didn't look up to see who it was.

"So was it worth it?" Chief Fogg's voice was thick with the accent of Blue Hollow.

Jake looked down at the drying blood on his hands and forced out an answer.

"No sir."

The chief remained on Jakes left, close enough for Jake to see the toe of the man's shiny black boot at the edge of his field of vision. What more did the man want him to say? Every word choked in his throat and threatened to bring a flood of bile with it.

"Chief, Coroner's on his way." Someone yelled. The Chief let out a sigh and clicked in the direction of the growing crowd of voices. When his footsteps were barely audible, Jake looked up and to his right. The setting sun that had illuminated his angel now slipped from pink to red on the horizon. The deeper purples were obscured by branches of trees clawing for the last remainders of daylight. The fading light gradually brightened the alternating glare of red strobes, then blue, red, then blue on the trees.

Had it been worth it?

Admitting his part in the carnage around him had done nothing to relieve the guilt that churned inside.

"Jake"

The familiar voice. He looked up in the direction it had come from. Beyond the yellow strip of Police tape, about 3 car lengths to Jake's left, was his dad. For an instant relief swept over him. His dad lifted the yellow banner and stepped under with a smooth motion. Chief Fogg stepped in his path and stopped their reunion with an open palm on his dad's chest. Jake shifted on the guard rail that was now cutting in to the bottom of his thigh. The blood rushed back in with pricks of pain.

His dad and the Chief exchanged a few words, dad's face going limp as the chief stepped back to point the accident scene before them all. Jake followed his dad's gaze until it landed on Alexa's form covered in a white sheet. Jake stood quickly, wanting to

hide his sin, like a child who hides the plate they'd broken in the hopes that it will erase

what they had done.

But there it was. Bile again rose and this time Jake spun away. The drop over

the side was at least fifteen feet. He could jump. He'd escape the pained look in his

father's eyes. A voice inside repeated jump, jump, jump. The cicadas hummed their

agreement, sounding like the chanters at the ball park. Hey bat-ter, bat-ter, bat-ter, jump.

His stomach clenched, invisible hands squeezing hard. He vomited over the guardrail.

Nothing came up but the Gatorade he'd drank all through the game, but his body kept

trying to find something to purge. Deeper and harder the squeezes came until finally

his body realized there was nothing more he could give, and gave up. Jake wiped his

mouth with the back of his hand and sat hard on the edge of the road.

He scanned the scene for something friendly to focus on. His eyes moved from

the trees on his right to the side of the mountain stretching in front of him. Rocks

dangled, and in the daylight, layers of earth were visible. This road was chiseled out of

the side of the mountain that formed the northern edge of Blue Hollow. Workers had

built this road to open a path to I-71.

There, on the ground, covered in a white sheet, was the mountain Jake had created from his own stupidity.

The fact that it was an accident did nothing to asuage his guilt. The gathering mob on his left would see to that. Between him and that mob was his dad.

Dad would defend him-and was at this moment doing just that with Chief Fogg-but his support was more painful than the idle taunts being hurled at him from the Blue Hollow Residents.

Through his sprawled fingers he could see the blury outline of Alexa. Clips of conversations wafted over him. One said he was a dumb kid, another wondered what someone would expect from that woman's son.

"Jake?"

He looked up to see the eyes of the only one here who cared what happened to him.

"Yeah Dad?" He didn't try to mask the tremor in his voice.

"Son, this man over here says they need to put you in the cuffs and take you to the station a bit."

Jake opened his mouth to protest but his dad silenced him with a gentle hand on the shoulder.

"I'm going to follow along behind. Sheriff has promised I can bring you home tonight."

"For your own Safety, Jake." The Sheriff unsnapped a black strip of leather and produced a shiny pair of cuffs. "Best get you out of here fore folks skin you alive."

Jake looked from the cuffs to his dad. A movement of his dad's head-more a twitch than a nod-Jake squared his shoulders and lifted his wrists.

Dried blood covered his palms.

The Sheriff led him to a cruiser.

"NO!"

Jake turned in the direction of the scream. Janice was pushing through the crowd of people.

"Stop her." The Sheriff yelled over his shoulder to a volunteer fireman who was nearest her. Jake was shoved down and to the left. His head crashing against the door frame on the way in. He pulled his feet in and the door slammed shut.

"Janice, you can't be coming over here." The Sheriff ran to intercept Janice less than two feet from the body. Jake brought his hands to his face, stopped when he saw the blood, then buried his hands in his lap.

One common error that I see when editing is people using words like "could" and "heard" and "saw" when we're in the character's point of view. Consider these sentences:

She saw David across the street by the car. Vs. Davis stood on the corner by the car.

In the first sentence, we are being told what "she" saw. In the second, we are actually seeing that through a character's eyes. When we are in a character's point of view then we are to experience everything that they experience. We live thorough them. You don't look outside and think, "I see a bird on that branch." Instead you think, "What a pretty bird."

These are the kinds of subtle techniques that will take your writing to a whole new level and no one will know why. The story will just seem better for some reason.

_____

_____

_____

_____

_____

_____

_____

_____

_____

_____

_____

_____

_____

_____

_____

_____

_____

_____

_____

Jake heard his mom's voice behind him. He put on a smile and turned around. "Mom, you should try to go out and garden today. There won't be many weeks left to the season." Renny had just shuffled in the room with a mug of tea. She looked out the window in the direction of her garden, shrugged her shoulders and took a seat in a chaise near the bay window.

"No mom, really, I think getting out in the sun will be good for you." Jake gave up on the happy voice and sat down in a chair on the other side of the room. She still never went anywhere. Jake and Bridget did all the errands, bought the groceries and did everything else so she could drag herself around under a cloud. Bridget would be leaving for college in less than two weeks and no longer had time to handle all of it.

Jake hated to think the worst but he was fairly certain that she was either suicidal or she was starting to be manipulative.

Bridget walked in the room and straight over to her mom, "Mom, is there anything I can get for you?" Her voice was soothing but was starting to sound maternal. His mom looked up at her and sighed, "No honey, don't worry yourself with me none. I'll be fine."

Jake tried again. "Mom, if you'd like to just sit out in the garden I will do some of the weeding so you can enjoy some fresh air. Then get yourself all cleaned up and we can go in to the diner for lunch."

Renny looked up at Jake, "Well that might be nice Jakey. Would your lady friend be joining us or would this be a family meal?" Her southern drawl could not hide the venom in the statement. Renny looked between the Jake and Bridget then continued gentler "What I mean is will it just be the three of us eating or should we go pick up Dreama on the way?"

Jake wasn't buying this backtrack. "Mom, you're going to have to accept that I care about Dreama."

"Oh, believe me Jacob I do know that. Whole town told me all about you, this girl and a ring showing up on her finger." Bridget looked up at Jake quickly.

"It was a promise ring." He said to Bridget, then to his mom, "And since when is it a big concern of yours what this town thinks of us? And when were you in town to hear about it?"

Renny looked up "I got a phone Jake. A phone that's ringing off the hook these days on account of you."

Jake looked up at Bridget and squinted his face. She shrugged her shoulders back at him. Renny continued

"Promise of what? What exactly are you promising this young lady?"

"No mom, it's not like that." Bridget jumped to his defense, "A promise ring is kind of like exchanging class rings. It just means you're a couple. That's all."

Jake jumped up from his chair and took a few steps toward his mom. "But what if I did want to marry her? What then?" Bridget's shot him a open mouthed looked that was quickly taken over by a little bit of a grin.

"Jake we done talked about this. You want some crippled babies?"

"Mom!" Bridget snapped her head at her mom.

"Is that what this summer's been about? You walking around this house and this town trying to get sympathy to keep me from Dreama?"

"Jake" Bridget snapped her head back at him.

"No. It's been about me missing the men in my life and about you digging up your uncle's grave at every opportunity."

"What are you talking about? I'm not digging up anybody's grave."

"Jacob don't you dare interrupt me. You and I both know wasn't any love lost when my brother passed but you're using his death to try to get with some young lady. I just find that disgusting."

"Mom, you've got to be kidding me. Dreama and I met at Uncle Bill's. What happened after that really had little to do with Uncle Bill."

"Oh really? From the things I'm hearing the whole town's talking about how you snoop about in his stuff, Dreama questioning the entire town about his dealings. Seems to me you both are quite curious about every detail you didn't give a hoot about when he was alive."

"You don't care how he really died?"

"Coroner says it was a heart attack and that's good enough for me."

"Well not for me. Something fishy is going on in this town."

"And Jacob that's why the whole town's going be digging in our garbage, cause you been digging in theirs."

"Yeah, well I've had about enough of this town and its gossip." He folded his arms and leaned against the wall. "Besides, what do you mean I'm digging in everyone's garbage?"

"You are out there asking people questions, sending Dreama around to do the same. It's not going to be too long before someone is going to start bringing up your accident and run us right on out of town again." Renny wiped the tears from her eyes with the sleeve of her sweatshirt and dunked her tea bag in her mug. "Why can't you just leave things alone rather than trying to find sins where sins don't exist?"

"Oh you mean like this precious town of yours did to us?"

"Jake" Bridget whispered.

"No really Bridget. I have never done anything to these people. The one mistake I made has been forgiven by the Lord and that should be enough." He pointed one finger up then raised it to the sky with a jerk. "I paid man's dues, I paid God's dues but people want me on trial all over again. I am not playing their game."

"Jake, do you ever think of anyone other than yourself." Bridget stormed out the door. Jake was quick on her heels.

"Bridget stop. Stop!" Bridget spun around and faced him.

"Bridget you know that I was against us coming back to the Hollow because I was worried that this town hadn't forgotten what happened but you wouldn't hear of it. You and mom thought it would be best if I packed up all and came back to where mom could be with her only surviving kin. Isn't that what you said?"

"Yes but mom needed to get out of that house with all of those memories of dad and the cancer."

"Which we did." Jake motioned for the bench and Bridget followed him and plopped down. "Then Bridget you know that I'm not doing anything I'm doing to hurt mom."

Bridget wouldn't look straight at him. She stared at the porch. "Jake, I know mom's not herself but I think she's had too much hit her all at once. She just needs to have some time to herself. She's probably scared she'll have to up and move again and where will she go. You and I are at the age where we'll be moving in to our own lives."

"But this isn't a shock. I'm twenty-six. You're seventeen. This has been a"

"Eighteen."

"What?"

Bridget smiled, "I'm eighteen Jake."

"No you're not. Your birthday isn't for another month and a half."

"Close enough." She smiled bigger.

Bridget wanted to lighten the mood and he let her. He took a deep breath and put his face in his hands. "Okay Bridget. I'll will try to keep my mouth shut and give mom a little more time to get over all this, but I have to tell you, she needs to let up on Dreama."

Bridget was looking at the house. Jake patted her shoulder as he stood. "I tell you what Bridget. Let's go back in the house with mom and make a nice supper for her. Then we can all go in to the city to that old fashioned ice cream place. We'll have a family night."

"Okay."

They walked up to the house. Jake was sure Dreama wouldn't be upset that he wasn't coming over. They didn't have any plans for the evening. He'd call to let her know he wasn't coming by in a few minutes. His chest ached just a little knowing that he wouldn't see her beautiful face this evening. He didn't know if distance made the heart grow fonder or not. It seemed distance made the heart miserable was a more apt line.

Jake let Bridget go in the house first, whispered a small prayer for strength, and pulled open the door. "Hey mom. Listen…"

"No Jacob you listen to me." His mom stood quickly from her chair. Her face was red and she walked briskly from her chair to Jake. "I was thinking while you were outside and I honestly don't like much how you been acting these days."

Lord, help me. Jake remained calm and braced for whatever his mom was about to say.

"I don't know what's gotten in you boy but I surely don't like it. You're never round when we need you. You snoop in everyone's mess down at the diner and you speak to me in a tone I am not accustomed to from you. Now, I had a hard time figuring what's gotten in to you but there's only one thing I can figure." She looked over at Bridget and back at Jake. She was leaning toward him like she did when he was a boy and had busted a window.

"Mom, I..."

"Jacob, see that's what I'm talking bout. I'm not through talking yet."

"Okay...mom." He spoke very deliberately being conscious of the promise he

had just made to his sister.

"Well, the only thing I can figure is this young lady you've been spending so

much time with has not been the best influence on you."

"Mom."

She held up her hand to him and he stopped. "Now I know Uncle Bill was

quite fond of her and her family and from all I hear she's a fine young lady."

She paused and looked between Jake and Bridget. "Whole town knows of this

young lady and all the trips you take to her house. Going on long walks along the trails

and the like. Now it's bad enough hearing the kind of chat I am subjected to with all

the speculating about what you do at her house all hours of the night."

"Mom, there is nothing."

"Jacob." Her face was bright red and vein on her forehead pulsated. "You

making this family look improper front of all Blue Hollow. Not to mention she's a

cripple."

"And there you go. Bridget I'm sorry I tried. I really tried but..." He looked over at Bridget whose face showed she was as shocked at her mom as Jake was.

"Young man you interrupt me one more time." She squeezeed her lips tight, "I've decided y'ain't to see her any more. It's not proper."

"It's not proper?" What in the world do you mean? Besides, I will see her."

"No Jake, you won't."

Jake walked to the door. At this moment there was only one person in the world he wanted to see and she wasn't here.

"Jacob!"

He spun around to face his mother. "Young man, you walk out that door then I promise you there ain't a place waiting for you here."

He pushed the storm door almost closed and folded his arms across his chest.

"If you can't live by the rules I have for this house this ain't your home any more."

***

Jake slammed his car door and pulled out of the driveway. He had an overnight bag with him and little else. His jaw was clenched and tears welled up in his eyes. This woman was not the mother he loved. That woman died with his uncle. Just as Uncle

Bill had warned, this town was killing her slowly. He pressed the gas down and the car roared to the end of the road.

He looked down at his speedometer. "Just let Lt. Tommy stop me today." Jake said out loud. He had only one place he wanted to be and that was with Dreama. He would go to her and tell her that he was going to the city for a little bit.

He tried to remember where the nice hotels in town were. He'd only need one long enough to locate an apartment. He could ask her parents if he could rent the guest room in their basement.

Jake flipped on the radio to calm down before he got to Dreama's. One great song came on, then another and just as the third started he turned in behind Dreama's apartment. All the anger flowed out of him as he wound back closer and closer to her house. It was a place of refreshing right now. He was about to hug Dreama tight and listen to her laugh. Then he could handle this insanity.

***

Just as Jake thought, sitting quietly with Dreama had calmed him considerably.

"What got her so worked up?" Dreama asked.

Dreama knew about his mom's odd behavior. Unfortunately she assumed this was 'just the way she was' and so didn't find it odd. Jake longed for Dreama to know his mom the way she had always been. What she resembled now was reminiscent of the horror stories she had told Jake about her parents.

"Don't worry about it." He finally answered. The thought of it already was beginning to erase the calm of Dreama's presence.

"You're worried, so I am worried." She said. She turned on the couch to face him squarely. "I can't help you if I don't know what is hurting you."

Jake hesitated again. He didn't want to repeat her insanity. That would only breathe life in to those words. But Dreama also wanted to help him and he needed to open to her if he was going to deepen their relationship.

"She's concerned about our relationship." He said flatly.

"What about it?"

"That it would move forward." Dreama sat for a minute as if trying to understand what he meant. He was being cryptic. The rusty hinges around his heart were stuck shut and the influence of fear over time had nearly welded them in place. He took a deep breath, grabbed the hinges and prepared to rip them off of his heart. "She is concerned that if we get married and start a family that the kids would be deaf."

Dreama stared at him for a moment then a smirk painted her lips in a thin curved line. "Were the two of you discussing something I should know about?"

He leaned over and kissed her. "No, but should we have been talking about that." Her cheeks flared red with nerves and Jake gave her a second quick kiss.

"I'm not sure." She paused, all humor gone. "But this upset her."

"The way she put it was she didn't want us having crippled babies."

"Crippled?" Dreama faced him. It wasn't anger that twisted her beautiful face into a gaping stare. It looked more like pain or disgust.

"I know deafness isn't the same as being crippled. These days there are surgeries to fix the problem."

Dreama's eyes remained fixed on him but now tears ran down her cheeks. One ran down and before it could drip off of her chin a second was fast behind it. "So, do you want to fix me?" Dreama asked.

"Of course not, honey, I love you." He wiped her cheeks. "You are beautiful just the way you are."

"But you'd want to fix others like me?"

Jake reached his arms out to her and tried to pull her against him. He didn't want to upset her. "No, honey. I'm just saying that if we had kids who were deaf it would be easy enough to fix. Mom shouldn't worry about people thinking there would be something wrong with our kids."

He could see he was digging a deeper hole but he didn't know what was making

her so upset. Wouldn't these be good things to say? How could he make her feel better

if he didn't know what was wrong.

"Can you leave me alone for a little bit?" Dreama asked.

Startled Jake's voice stuck in his throat for a moment. "You want me to leave?"

"I really think you should." She said, her voice broken by sobs.

"Honey, let me-."

"Please, just go." She said. Then she ran in her bathroom and slammed the

door shut behind her.

    ***

She couldn't think clearly. She was frustrated, sad and a little scared. What if

Janice was right? What if she really needed to watch out for Jake? Of course it wasn't for

the reasons Janice wanted to try to portray. Jake wasn't a dangerous killer who killed in

cold blood.

Just the same, Jake did have a firm grip on Dreama's heart which meant, like

today, one word from him was capable of ripping her heart from her chest. She replayed

his words in her head over and over. When he first said it the words had sliced at her

ego. Tears came quickly but she knew it was not what he meant. He didn't see her as a project like Evan had, nor did he see her as handicap like her parents did. She waited for his explanation.

It hadn't been what she'd hoped.

She stood in the bathroom looking in the mirror until she knew he was gone. As if her heart were attached to his rear bumper the sound of his engine roaring down the road tore out all emotions. What remained was her reflection and a pile of questions.

While it had only been the summer she had felt a connection with Jake she'd never known before. She felt equal. Most people made her feel just a little less than them. It wasn't always intentional. They simply equated hearing loss with slow learning.

Jake had treated her as if he didn't know she was any different than him. She relaxed and with it her shield fell. Now she had to consider that it was all over. This was a difference that was far too fundamental to be dealt with over time.

It seemed that there was no end to the questions or the let downs this summer.

Growing up sucked some days.

***

Midge walked in the diner a few minutes after one. The lunch crowd was on its downward slide but Dreama and Janice were still moving at a steady clip.

"You're not coming in today?" Janice asked looking over Midge's outfit. She was wearing a pink pair of slacks with a cotton top.

"No." Midge answered. Then she moved quickly to the kitchen. Hank was frying up an order of chicken strips on the grill while the young man he'd trained was busy at the fry vats. He looked over at her and put the metal spatula down.

"Quite an outfit." His voice was flat. Not a hit of admiration or annoyance.

"Join me out back?"

Hank followed through the kitchen and out to the parking lot behind the diner.

"I have an invitation to visit from a cousin out west. I'm going."

Hank looked in the back door and then back at Midge. There was a twinge of emotion in his voice but she could see him pushing it down. "How long will you be gone?"

She squared her shoulders and pulled up the answer she'd worked on for more than a week. "I think we need to spend some time apart."

"Ah." He said, recognition on his face. He knew she wasn't ever coming back. For a moment her resolve wavered but she held firm. He took to first step away from her.

"I need some space." She said again.

"Take all you need." He turned and opened the door to the diner. "I have to go run your diner."

**

Jake drove to the park at the edge of town. It was about seven in the evening and the summer sun was moving toward the horizon. Little league games were in their fourth or fifth inning and the playground swings were full of kids. He got out of the car and sat down at a picnic bench. At this point he didn't know what to do. He had given up his family and defied his mother to be with a woman who just flipped out. The sting of that made his throat tight. What had he even done wrong? He wanted so much for her to feel for him the way he did for her.

A bat hit a ball with a sharp crack followed by the crowd cheering on the other side of the park. This had started when Janice got involved. What made Dreama listen to her? He swatted away a swarm of gnats that flew in his face. Janice was like a gnat. Swarming around just to ruin a great thing.

He had been so angry having the memory of the lowest point in his life being shoved in his face in the place he felt safe and loved. God I guess I should have run to you instead of to Dreama. The worst of it all was now that he had the anger out of his system and only the hurt remained. He wanted to see Dreama. He loved her. It didn't matter if it was only a summer. He loved her.

He'd give Dreama the benefit of time to think. She'd either let him know what it was or she'd not worry about it anymore. They could pull through but he couldn't put up with more interruptions. The main one was at the diner now. It was time to go confront Janice.

***

Jake walked in the diner and took the first booth on the right. Janice came right over and flipped his cup over.

"Afternoon Jake." She said coolly. "Hank's making some good Chicken fried steak."

"Why did you do it?" Jake leaned on his elbows.

"Jake I believe in the truth." She replied without missing a beat as if he were asking what came with that chicken fried steak.

"No you don't." He said coolly. "Why did you do it?"

Janice poured his cup of coffee. "Are you going to be ordering something because Hank don't take too kindly to people taking up tables and not ordering."

"Why don't you tell me the specials Janice?"

"Chicken fried steak, Meatloaf and fish and chips."

"I'll have the Meatloaf. What exactly did you say to-"

"I'll put your order back and grab your salad." Janice said and quickly spun around. Jake watched her go to put in the order. Hank looked out through the kitchen window at him and Janice looked over her shoulder. Hank held Jake's gaze for a few moments before he pulled the paper with his order down.

Janice came back with his salad and set it down. "Can I get you anything else?"

"Janice, I want answers."

She looked over her shoulder toward Hank and then back at Jake. "Jake, whole town knows you were involved and why. You'd best just get yourself on out of town." She looked at him with squinted eyes that seethed with rage.

"I didn't do anything Janice and drop the southern belle act." He emphasized the words do and anything. Her jaw dropped wide open and her eyes were now little slits.

"Oh, you didn't kill my cousin?"

"I didn't kill anyone. Why do you keep trying to make me relive Alexa's death?"

"Buddy you ain't got it half as bad as my aunt and uncle. Don't go telling me about how you deserve forgiveness." Her sweet southern draw was all but gone replaced by poor English laced with venom.

"Why should I be remembered for the worst thing I ever did. I've paid my dues Janice."

"Well, I don't know about that Jake. You know, seems to me you could've got some help for her. You could have done something. Instead you let her die there."

"I did not." The tension of the day was building to a firestorm and Jake could feel it ready to burst. He was an expanding balloon and Janice was running around with a straight pin in her hand.

"I got tables to tend to." Janice turned but Jake caught her arm.

"Wait."

Janice looked down at her arm and then glared at Jake. She leaned in close.

"Listen here Jacob. I know what kind of person you are at the core. You may have some people fooled but you're nothing but a killer as far as I'm concerned. I'll grant you that her death may've been an accident but when you drove off and left'er. Well, that's when you become a killer. And the thing about killers is they keep right on killing."

"What is that supposed to mean." Jake let go of her arm but held her with his stare.

"Means you knew your mama's money was in danger so you took care your uncle before he had a chance to change things around."

"Mom's money wasn't in any danger." A laugh slipped out as he answered.

Janice was so full of hate and so totally wrong.

"Oh Jake, I ain't stupid. Your uncle had himself a love interest and was fixing

to leave a good deal of money to her. That's why he wasn't gonna give you nothing for

your business. That's why your mom was about to be written out the will and that's why

you killed him."

"You're an idiot." He laughed and then dug in to his salad. He ate his salad and

waited for his meal. The whole town was going crazy. The town was focused on making

sure no one moved ahead and that everyone's sins were remembered. After about

fifteen minutes Janice came out with Jake's food.

Jake ate quickly and left his tip, two cents. He got in his car and headed to town.

Hopefully one of the decent hotels would have a room for him.

***

"Don't worry Bridget. I've got a room at the hotel in town. I'm sure mom will

cool off soon and I'll come back." Jake opened the curtains in the hotel room as he

spoke. The day was drawing to a close and he was ready. It was as if he'd lived an entire

week in this one day. Every woman in his life had seemed to go off the deep-end all at

once. If only it was possible to blame it on THAT he mused.

"Jake I wish you'd come back." Bridget's voice was near a whisper. She didn't want mom to know she was talking to him, at least that was what she'd said.

"I know, but I need a bit of time to think. A lot has happened." While to any outside observer this would be a clear statement Jake meant it on a deeper level. He'd spent a good deal of time looking at people, his opinions of them and the reality. He realized that his animosity toward his uncle was no better than what Janice had held against Jake all this time.

Really, it was simply a matter of degrees. If given time Jake could have become Janet. The thought scared him and he wanted to escape the kind of environment that would be a catalyst for that. Dreama and Bridget would both leave for school soon and he would have nothing tying him there-except his mom.

"Maybe I should consider leaving the Hollow for good."

"But Jakey, that'd break mom's heart."

"More than I've already done being there?" He let the question hang for a minute then continued. "Hey Bridget, did you hear about Uncle Bill dating one of the River rats?"

"I don't think Bill was dating anyone. Who said he was?"

"Janice accused me of killing Uncle Bill to keep this woman from taking mom's inheritance."

"WHAT?"

"I know. I think Janice has finally lost it."

"I think she lost it a long time ago. Don't worry no one takes her too seriously

any way."

"I wish that was true."

"What do you mean by that?"

"Nothing."

"Jake."

"It's not like he didn't have secrets. I mean look at all that property he owned

that none of us knew anything about. Maybe he was hiding this woman from us too."

"Well I guess it's possible but I don't know that I'm going to put too much stock

in what Janice says about anything."

Jake chuckled. "Point taken. Hey, if you see Dreama find out how she is."

"Don't worry Jake. It'll all work out. I've seen the way she looks at you."

"Good night Bridget."

"Bye."

Despite being in a hotel room in a city about thirty minutes for Blue

Hollow things felt completely different. The anonymity of the hotel comforted him.

Rather than feeling like a bit of cheese on a rat farm, Jake felt like a normal person.

Unimportant and unassuming. The way it had been for years. Jake closed his eyes and

thought of Dreama. Sleep came quickly.

***

Dreama was sick about the way she had treated Jake. She hadn't offered a word

of explanation or the opportunity for him to understand what upset her. Instead she

lashed out at him with every bit of anger and hurt she'd stored up from elementary

school on. It was true, she hadn't yelled but what greater hurt could she have issued

than to throw him out of her house?

She tried his cell but it went straight to voice mail. She didn't know Bridget's

cell and since it was nearly nine she wasn't going to call his house. His mom still stuck

to the rule of no social calls after nine pm. Even if it was earlier, it didn't seem likely

that Renny would chat it up with Dreama.

That bothered her too. All these that she liked and had gotten to know all

seemed to be on the prowl for ways to hurt each other. How was it that such a kind

picturesque town that called weary cityslickers in to its comfortingly simple embrace was

actually more blood-hungry than any city street?

She walked to the fridge. There was nothing that looked remotely edible and it smelled like tomorrow would be the day to dump out leftovers. She pushed the door closed and looked up at the clock. The diner was open until 10 pm tonight. She grabbed her keys walked out to her car.

The roads were empty as she wound down the couple miles to the diner. The smell of backyard fires flew in her open car windows. The sweet smell of barbeque wafted in and her stomach growled in reply.

There were ten cars lined up in front of the diner. She found a spot along the side and went in. Every seat was taken at the counter where she usually sat but on the far side Bridget was sitting alone with a plate of fries and a large malt. Bridget looked up and, as soon as she saw Dreama, enthusiastically waved her over to sit with her. Dreama smiled and joined her at the table. Hopefully Bridget hadn't talked to Jake yet to hear what she had done to him.

"Hi Dreama. Great to see you." Bridget smiled and leaned over the table toward Dreama.

"Yes you too. Have you heard from Jake?"

"Yeah, He's at a hotel in the city." Bridget said as she pulled the straw out of her malt, licked it off then stuck it back in her tall glass.

"A hotel? Why?"

"He told me you had a fight before he could tell you what happened today."

"Oh, you know about that?" She leaned back in her chair and rubbed her hands together. The promise ring gave her comfort but only until the guilt ground itself deeper in to her conscience.

Bridget looked over at Janice and scowled. "Yes. I heard."

"What happened to Jake?"

"Mom kicked him out today."

"What?" What little bit of selfish pride she'd held on to melted. In her indignation over his comment she hadn't listened to the deeper hurt Jake was trying to tell her. She had known the pain of rejection from family but Jake had been quite close to his parents until recently. She yelled at herself inwardly at her own self-centeredness and promised that she'd try to stop assuming Jake was ever on the attack.

Bridget continued. "Actually, she gave him conditions for staying and he chose to leave."

"Conditions? What were the conditions?"

"I really think that's between the two of you." Bridget sipped on her pop.

"Between the two of us?" Dreama tried to catch Bridget's eye. She finally looked up at Dreama and stopped drinking.

"Mom said he couldn't live at the house if he wanted to keep seeing you."

"Why would she say something like that? I thought Renny liked me." She was really starting to wonder if she had any kind of judgment at all any more. She trusted Janice and Renny who both stabbed her in the back but she didn't trust Jake who did nothing but love her.

"I don't know. My mom is acting really weird lately." She bobbed a straw up and down in her chocolate shake. "She and Jake had a huge argument and finally she said he had to leave if he wanted to keep dating you."

***

"Jake, I just don't want you messing anything up. You and Dreama are so cute together and I hate to see you-." Bridget said but Jake jumped in.

"I'm going to go over and talk to her. Don't worry." Jake slid the Gideon Bible he'd been reading back in the drawer in the night stand. He knew when he left the house that this wasn't a relationship ender, it was only a small spat. He wanted to know what it was that he said to hurt her so much, but first he wanted to see Dreama.

***

It had only been a few months but she really loved him. Why else was every thought of him leaving followed by a flood of nausea and tears? She could walk away and leave a gaping hole in her heart. Eventually her heart would mend and she would forget about Jake. Life had a way of doing that. Like the sandcastles you build on the edge of the water. The waves would come in closer and closer pulling little pieces away until the only thing that remained was a mound of sand that showed something had been there.

Or she could decide to give him the benefit of the doubt. She had no proof that Jake had done anything wrong. All she had was Janice's theories which were clearly laced with revenge and something he said but may not have meant. She had nothing else.

***

Jake flipped through the channels in his hotel room. His mom had kicked him out, his past had come back for revenge and Dreama kicked him out all in one day.

His dad used to tell him not to let a temporary situation change his theology. Hopefully this was a temporary situation. Maybe tomorrow he could try to stop by and see Dreama. He couldn't let her go without making one last shot at setting things right.

There were only days remaining for Dreama in the Hollow. Then she'd be back on campus living her life and focusing on her future.

Jake thought about his dad again. "Well, Dad, what would you think of mom right now?" He was pretty certain his dad wouldn't have kicked him out like she did although his dad also would have called Jake on his tone. Dad was first a gentleman and a gentleman didn't scream at a woman-no matter how irrational she was acting.

***

Renny curled up at the head of her bed and stared down at the wall. "Why did you leave me Dale?" She rolled on to her back and looked at her wedding band. She couldn't bear to take it off. "I've made quite a mess of things round here without you. Jakey's gone and Bridget hardly has two words to say to me these days."

She climbed off the bed and pulled out a photo album from her bottom dresser drawer. Every page was so full of memories. The album started with yellowing pictures of her and Dale in their courting days. Then there were some photos of their wedding on up through her pregnancies. Then photos of Jake in diapers. She ran her finger around each picture. She paused on the picture of Jake with his new driver's license. That car accident made them leave Blue Hollow and the home Dale and Renny spent their whole life in together up to that point.

She brushed a tear off the plastic covering the photos. Bridget left the Hollow

when she was seven and never got to know spring with the town coming alive and the

summers humming with people. The fall festivals that marked the end of season and

brought the town back to a small town. Dale had felt it best that they leave the Hollow

and their families and friends behind to make a fresh start in the city. He died in the

cold city without any of the people they'd grown up with. A wonderful Godly man like

Dale deserved better.

Then she came back to the Hollow. It was time to be with family again. She was

certain the rumors had died and that all would be forgotten. She came back in the fall,

just before the festivals were under way. They had spent a wonderful fall, winter and

spring. Then Bill died. Not only that but she was sure he was killed by someone in the

Hollow. She had her suspicions but there was no way she was going to stir anyone up

or she'd be next, of that she was certain. Then Jake got in with Dreama and the two of

them started digging in to the Hollow.

Renny knew then that she had made an awful mistake coming back. Dale

had told her shortly before his passing "Renny, I know you love your brother and the

Hollow but the kids know this place now. It's where they grew up and Jake's got himself

a life here. He'd pick it all up and follow you wherever you wanted cause he's a good boy but let them keep their life outside of the Hollow."

She looked at their wedding picture on her night stand, "Dale, why didn't I listen to you?"

Just a couple of days after she'd gone in the diner with Jake and Dreama Janice had come by. "Renny, Jakes been out trying to nose around with this stuff with Bill. You might want to remind him that people in glass houses...shouldn't attend swim meets." The message was instantly clear. A icy chill flooded her veins and nearly choked her. Janice had forgotten nothing and the years had only made her sneakier.

She had understood immediately that Jake was involving himself where he shouldn't be. If there was a chance that Jake knew something and could prove that someone had killed her brother shouldn't she let him? Shouldn't that person be brought to justice? But then if he really had been murdered why hadn't the police looked in to it further?

So many questions and conflicting ideas. She couldn't tell the kids any of it and she didn't even understand some of it. She wanted Jake to get to the bottom of this but she didn't want his past brought back up. She thought it best to give him some time to try to find out if there was anything to be learned. She stayed away from the town and hoped Jake would learn the truth quickly but she now knew she had made a mistake coming back.

"You were right Dale." She whispered. As much as it hurt and as long as she tried to fight it she had now made up her mind that they had to pack up and leave the Hollow.

***

"Diner's closing" Hank said as Dreama walked in to start her shift.

"Now?" Dreama said looking at the lobby full of customers. Since Midge left on an "extended vacation" as Hank called it Dreama and Janice were working long days to try to keep up. Blue Hollow was growing.

"No, I figure you have three more days on the schedule until you go back to school. Then it will just be Janice and me to run the place." His tired eyes looked around. "As Charlie said when he left town, I've spent my life in this place."

"You could leave someone else to run the place. It could be like retirement money." She suggested. This old diner was as much Blue Hollow as the river.

"That's sweet, but no. I'm ready to wrap up." He looked at her with the same loving eyes Mr. Colewick had. It was like a Grandfather looking at a beloved granddaughter.

Dreama tied her apron on and started out to her tables. Janice was moving along from table to table with barely a glance at Dreama. For Dreama, death was a time of reflection and it seemed everything she'd known in Blue Hollow was dying around her. The times on the river in boats rented from Charlie's place, dinners eaten at this diner and campfires in the company of Mr. Colewick. All of it was fading. Even summers spent with her parents in the summer house were faded.

As if a door closing on a part of her life, Dreama felt as if a transition was taking place. Familiar things of the past were drifting on and new things were coming in to replace them.

***

"This burger is medium, I asked for medium rare." The customer yelled as he held the cheeseburger inches from Dreama's face. "Does that look pinkish-red to you?" He shouted.

Dreama trembled as if the sloppy cheeseburger with its pink meat and dripping condiments were actually a dagger dripping blood.

"I'm very sorry sir, I'd be happy to-."

"Get me the owner." He screamed as he cut her off. Dreama looked at the two small children at his table. Their eyes were focused on the pile of fries on their plate and they ate as if their food were about to be taken. Her jaw clenched as the thought of this man berating his own children over such a meaningless infraction.

One of the beatitudes proclaimed that the peacemakers would be blessed but at this moment that command seemed barely possible. Nonetheless, Dreama knew her role as waitress and she sought to calm him. If this man were screaming like this Hank was liable to hit him with a raw meat patty.

"Sir,-." She began but was immediately cut off.

"Are you deaf, or something? I said get me the owner." The man slammed his half eaten sandwich on to his plate for effect. Fries splattered off the plate and on to the table. The two kids, Dreama guessed the boys to be between seven and ten, began eating a little faster.

"Technically, I am. And I'd rather be deaf than stupid."

Oh it felt good. The years of avoiding conflict ended in that moment. As she saw those small children trying to become invisible while their Dad screamed Dreama realized that there were times where the lamb had to be the lion. With the ferocity of a lioness protecting her litter Dreama blurted out a series of clichés about catching flies with honey rather than vinegar and salt water vs. fresh water.

"And what kind of example are you setting for your boys. You're not teaching them to stand up for themselves like you say. You're teaching them to be terrified." She stormed away from the table and in to the kitchen. "Hank, table six wants to talk to the owner."

She paced in the kitchen thinking about all she'd said to the man. What would she teach her children by her example? It was time to stop running and grow up.

***

Jake woke up early. He had a stale bagel and decent coffee from the hotel's continental breakfast and headed back to Blue Hollow. He hadn't yet decided if he was going to go to his mom's house or not. Bridget let her know he was safe so she wouldn't worry. He still wasn't ready to talk to her about what was going on. There were too many things bouncing in his mind. The first person he wanted to see was Dreama but seven-thirty was a little too early in the morning to call her.

He pulled back down the driveway, through what had once been a car port and back in to the garage. If no one saw his car in the driveway then no one would drop in unwelcomed. He walked through the house lined with boxes of clothes. The charity truck had mixed up the days so all the boxes he had packed up with Dreama were still stacked in the living room until next Thursday.

His mom had scheduled the auction for the last week of August hoping that there would be a number of summer residents who would want to buy things to take home with them. It could be a final spending frenzy to wrap up the summer.

Jake agreed that was probably a smart way to do it. They had until next week to get everything ready for the auction.

The place would make a really nice rental or summer home if they left it furnished. They could easily expect to receive twice what Uncle Bill's mortgage was since he bought it so long ago. That would be a source of income for his mom. She wouldn't have to go back to work and she could pay for Bridget to go to school without loans. As stingy as the man had been in life he was proving very generous in death.

Jake wondered if he'd actually been happy though. He had a clean accumulation of things and a great deal of wealth but what was his legacy? What had his life been? It seemed to Jake it had been little more than a well orchestrated play that had continued for decades. When Uncle Bill had been alone, in the evenings, was he happy.

Uncle Bill didn't collect much but the few things antiques he had were covered in a fine layer of dust. Jake started wiping down the picture frames on the old wooden mantle. As he dusted he considered the memory attached to the photos. An hour later he had dusted the entire living room and bedrooms. Had Uncle Bill walked from room to room soaking in the memories as he cleaned? Was that why everything was so neat in his home?

Uncle Bill had lived in the confines of the persona he'd created. There was

no room for letting people know him with any depth. They weren't interested in that

anyway. Blue Hollow was simply a creation of their imagination superimposed on a

geographical location. The people were merely characters in this creation. And when a

person created a happy place, like Blue Hollow, there wasn't room for reality.

Know The Rules Before You Break Them

When I'm editing for a client or I'm teaching a class at a conference I will
often hear this phrase, "I read [insert best-selling author] and they broke that rule."
My reply is always the same: You must master the rules before you break them. If you
went through this entire book listing all of the authors who have done the opposite of
what I'm suggesting then you didn't get the full benefit of this book.

The purpose was not to list who can break the rules, the goal of this book is
to help you improve your craft. To do that you must identify the things that detract
from your story and improve them.

Now that you've read nearly all of the teaching points in the book, go to some
of the earlier chapters and see if you identify more issues. Even better, see if you can
identify how to correct them.

Then continue reading the final chapters and read the last lessons and start
digging in to your own book.

When she pulled up to Mr. Colewick's house it seemed to be the symbol of

all that had changed for her. The yard was mowed and the flowers he'd planted were

in full bloom but the lines weren't straight, there were branches out of line and the mulch wasn't uniform. All of these things showed a house that was nicely maintained, but not loved the way it was by Mr. Colewick. A Dandelion never stood a chance if Bill Colewick was around. She laughed at how much he prized his well manicured lawn above anything. A splattering of dandelions grew tall along the edge of the yard as if aware that the danger was gone. Soon they'd go to seed and conquer the territory that had so long been unreachable for them. That little difference reminded everyone who knew him that he was still gone.

***

Jake's cell phone chirped. "Hello Bridget."

"Hi, you still at the Hotel?"

"No, I'm at Uncle Bill's place going through a few things."

"Couldn't get up the nerve to go talk to her?"

"That's not it. I got here at seven-thirty. I know how you ladies like to be beautiful before we show up." He laughed. His sister was one to never leave the house until her hair was perfect, makeup was on and she had the perfect outfit. It didn't matter if they were mowing the lawn or going out for ice cream. Bridget had a look for any occasion.

"Whatever. Do you want some help?"

"You bored or something?"

"A little."

"Sure. Come on over. I'm emptying the attic before it gets too much hotter. I figure I'll bring everything down in to Uncle Bill's room."

"Do you want me to bring anything?"

"Anything to eat. That hotel's food is awful."

"K, see you in a bit."

Jake opened the trap door and climbed up the folding stairs to the attic. Uncle Bill had accumulated quite a bit of "Useful Junque" as he often called it. In addition to the baseball cards there were little odds and ends, antiques and books. He took two loads down and was picking up the third box when he heard a noise below.

"Bridget is that you?" He yelled down from the attic. No one answered. He climbed down the ladder and walked through the house.

"No, it's me." Bridget jumped out from behind a wall.

"Bridget, you about made me jump out of my skin." He held on to his chest.

"I know. That was the point." She laughed. "How are things going over here?"

Jake dusted a few webs off of his shirt. "Okay. This job will be a lot easier with two."

"Here's an egg sandwich." Bridget handed him a sandwich wrapped in foil. It was still warm. He put it on the counter and walked to the kitchen to wash his hands.

"So how's mom?"

"She woke up this morning quiet but not moping around like she's been doing. She seems a bit more peaceful."

"Did she say anything about me?"

"Not really. She said she felt bad for bringing us back to the Hollow. I said that I liked it just fine and you seemed to be enjoying and she gave me a bit of a dirty look."

Bridget laughed. "So it looks like she's getting back to her old feisty self."

"That's good." His mom's feistiness was a joke he and Bridget shared. To call her feisty was like calling Einstein an idiot. It usually didn't match reality.

"Hey Jakey, looks like you have some company."

He looked out the back window. Dreama was walking in the back yard over by Uncle Bill's stone barbeque.

***

Dreama had spent so much time with the issues that surrounded, and came after his death, that she hadn't given herself time to grieve his death. She walked out to the back yard and looked at the brick fireplace and the pile of branches that fell in the storm the night he died. They never remembered to call in that burn permit to burn them. The home was becoming more of a connection to Jake than it was to Mr. Colewick now. There were still things that she'd done with Mr. Colewick, but they all seemed to lead up to meeting Jake now.

It felt like a betrayal to a longtime friend to forget him so quickly but nearly four months with Jake had been the one positive to come out of the tragedy.

She felt a hand on her shoulder and turned around.

***

Renny sat in the last pew of the church. She hadn't been back since that last Sunday Bill was alive. There hadn't been a reason to come. There was no one and nothing waiting for her within these walls other than the judgmental stares she'd received from a few of the faithful. Those who didn't stare at her simply ignored her.

This week's message was about the benevolent God who intentionally brought problems to those who loved him. If that was the case Renny must be among the most cherished of this God's creation.

If Dale were here he'd be able to explain this deity in a way that actually did seem kind and loving. If Bill were here he'd have asked her why she kept torturing herself by coming. Neither man was here because the benevolent God had killed them both.

During the service she sat when asked, then stood when asked, spoke when asked and closed her eyes when asked. None of these actions, or the act of obeying these instructions, gave her any of the peace she'd hoped to find. It was all empty.

She wanted answers about Jake. She wanted to know why she was turning in to such a spiteful woman and she wanted to know how to be happy again.

The organ belted out a deep chord and everyone stood for the Benediction.

"And now may the peace and love of our Lord Jesus Christ be ever with you and comfort you, henceforth and always. Amen."

The choir sang a chorus of A-mens while the robed clergy walked briskly down the center aisle. Renny slipped out the side, out the door and away from this God.

***

Now it was just the two of them. Jake wasn't sure what to say or do at this moment. Dreama shifted from one foot to another and looked around. Finally she spoke.

"Bridget tells me that you're staying in a hotel."

"Yes. My mom and I had a disagreement and we thought it best if I left for a couple of days."

"Bridget said it was about me."

"Not entirely." He didn't even fully understand all that was going on in the

mind of his mom.

"But part of it was." Her voice was sweet to his ears but the tone wasn't sweet.

She was cold, maybe he'd call it guarded. But when she looked at him she played with

her hair and covered a small smile. The voice said hurt, the eyes said love.

***

The sun was hot in Florida, ninety degrees before he'd finished breakfast. Hank

took off a straw hat he'd bought himself as a retirement present and fanned off. Day

two of retirement was treating him well. The ghosts of Blue Hollow had followed him.

They were whispering and reminding him that there were witnesses. Someone saw.

Midge knew. And he couldn't hide.

"Can I get you a refill?" The waitress said.

"No, I'm fine." He said then lifted his cup of coffee for effect.   She walked away

and the memories were back. No good deed goes unpunished.

When he'd gone back that night all he wanted to do was see if Bill was okay.

The little bits of mischief were needling at him all through his bowling game with

Midge. The more she talked about Bill's weird behavior to the team they were playing against, the sicker Hank had felt.

He left the bowling alley and went straight to Colewick's house.

"Hi Hank, what can I do for you this time of night?" Bill had greeted him friendly enough but he didn't look good at all.

"You okay Bill?" He wasn't at all. Sweat was beaded around his hair line like a deadly diamond headband.

"I'll be fine. Had some Barbeque tonight that doesn't seem to be agreeing with me. Got a bit of heartburn."

"Let me get you some water Bill, set yourself down." A ball of lead dropped in Hank's stomach in that instant.

"No, I'll be fine. Thank you though." Hank had ignored him and went in to the kitchen.

"Here's your water, Bill." Bill smiled and took it from Hank.

"Thank you Hank."

After some time of talking Hank fessed up to putting the laxative in Bill's food.

"What did you go and do that for?" Bill had rubbed his stomach while he yelled.

"Well, I wanted you to leave Midge alone."

"Hank, I'm not sweet on Midge. She was catching me up on some people we went to High School with who just up and got married after both were widowed."

"Well I believe you. It's just Janice-"

"Janice's a bigger tale spinner than your wife." Bill had said.

Hank would have laughed if he hadn't been so worried about poor Bill. "I know that Bill but please. I'm worried about you now. Let me take you on in to the hospital. I want to be sure nothing is really wrong."

"I'll be fine."

"You're sweating. I think you're having a heart attack."

"I'm not having a heart attack."

"I think you are. Please take one of these." Hank had handed him his Nitro.

"Hank, I'm fine and these Nitro ain't going to do nothing for me anyhow."

"Just take one."

"Fine, give'em here. I'm telling you these ain't going to do nothing for me." Bill had opened them and put one in his mouth.

"No, Bill. They don't work like that. You got to put it under your tongue."

"Fine." Bill took a second pill and stuck it under his tongue. "There, satisfied?"

"You sure you won't let me take you in anyway?"

"No, I'm fine-" Bill stopped abruptly. "Hank?" He had squeaked. Then he dropped to the ground.

Hank slid back to the present. It was pretty unlikely any of them would believe that Bill had been killed with kindness but that was exactly what had happened. If Bill was telling the truth then Bill hadn't held romantic feelings for Midge, but did it go the other way? Had Midge been secretly pining for Bill? And would she use that to hurt Hank?

Hank drank down the last of his coffee, stood up and left his total and a five dollar tip.

***

"How are things Jake?" Jake looked to the voice and saw a girl that resembled Dreama. Val had the same hair and same eyes as Dreama, but his Dreama was much more beautiful.

"They're good." He said, squeezing Dreama's hand with his.

Val looked over at Dreama and touched her chin with two fingers. Dreama hit her.

"What did she say?"

Dreama's dad smiled looked at the two sisters and said "Haven't you learned about these two yet? Either learn sign language or be totally out of the loop." There was a slight smile on his lips, but not complete. Her parents knew with each passing week that what they called "A window of opportunity" was closing. Her indecision, as they called it, was clearly a decision not to have the surgery. Jake knew they were hurt by her rejection but he also knew it was Dreama's decision to make.

The family was having a picnic in the backyard and Jake and Dreama joined them. Val and Dreama signed back and forth and look and periodically they would all stop to watch something Dreama was signing. Then they'd laugh or express surprise and look over at Jake. It was bizarre. For most of the conversation it was as if he wasn't there.

It was a bit isolating feeling he was the only person who was not being included in the conversation but in those moments he saw a different side of Dreama. Rather than the shy beauty, Dreama was transformed in to an expressive powerhouse where her fluttering fingers and moving arms seemed to loosen her inhibitions. Her face twisted in exaggerated expressions that seemed to have something to do with what her hands were saying. She spoke with him but when Dreama signed, Jake felt she truly communicated a part of herself.

They finished their meal and Jake helped her dad carry the picnic table back. Despite the uncomfortable meeting Jake had been welcomed in to the family. Much of that had been a result of his ability to join Dreama back to them by smoothing over tense moments. And some of it must have been the love they saw between Jake and Dreama.

Or they could simply be great fakers.

Dreama walked out and tapped Jake's shoulder. "You want to go down to the river?" She smiled.

"Uh, sure."

He followed her down the hill. When they got to their usual spot Dreama stopped and turned to Jake.

He spoke first. "So does this mean you're not mad at me anymore?"

"I don't know. Are you still mad at me?"

"No."

"Then I guess I'm not mad either." She smiled just a little. "Hurt a little but not mad."

"How did I hurt you?"

She was quiet for a moment as if searching for a perfect word. "I don't want you to fix me, Jake."

"Why would I want to fix you?"

"Why would you want to fix our kids?" Immediately he understood.

"I wouldn't change a thing about you." He said. "We've been having a lot of fun together this summer but today I really watched you. You come alive when you talk with these." He lifted her hands up in front of her face. "I want in that world because you are there." He said.

She started to reply but he stopped her. He needed to let it all out in a gush because that was the way the words were churning inside.

"When I'm not with you I am thinking about when I am with you." He continued. "Every day I look forward to driving over to your house and having dinner with you or going for a walk." "I have thought a lot about when you go back to school. Do you think there is any chance of this continuing when you go back to school?"

Dreama answered slowly "I really hope so."

"So you do see a future for us once you leave the Hollow?" Jake asked as he rubbed her fingers with his thumb.

"I hope so."

"You keep saying 'I hope so' rather than 'Yes'. That's something we'll have to remedy." He rubbed her arm with his palm. She smiled and tipped her head toward his hand.

"What's wrong with saying, 'I hope so.'?" She pushed a piece of hair back from her face. She was still wearing the promise ring he gave her.

"The problem is some questions require a much more definitive answer."

"What?" Her face twisted in confusion but a smile still glittered in her eyes.

"What's your name sign?" He asked.

"What?" She tilted her head when she looked at him and scrunched her face.

"Your name sign. You told me deaf people create a sign in sign language so they don't have to always spell out their name with their fingers. What's yours?"

She made a "d" with the fingers of her right hand and tapped her left shoulder.

Jake repeated the motion. "Is that right?" He asked. She nodded.

He had been practicing this for a couple of days hoping to impress her. He made an "I" by sticking up his pinky finger and brought it back to his chest so his thumb touched his chest. Then he crossed both of his arms across his chest. Next he pointed to Dreama and signed her name sign. She smiled and tears came out of the corners of her eyes.

"I love you too, Jake."

He reached down to the promise ring on her right hand and kissed her knuckles.

"Dreama, what would you think of putting this ring on the other hand?"

Her eyes grew wide. He took a deep breath and slid down on to one knee. She put the fingers of her left hand to her lips. He pulled her left hand down and held both hands in front of him.

"Some questions require a more definitive answer." His heart pounded loud in his ears. He wanted to spend the rest of his life with her. It was all or nothing. He wanted to be with her, forever. He loved her in ways he couldn't understand or articulate. He needed to know she'd always be with him. "Marry me, Dreama."

She nodded her head. "Yes, I'll marry you." She barely choked out.

He jumped up and reached in to his pocket and pulled out a rectangular diamond solitaire. It nearly trembled out of his fingers but he caught it before the shining platinum landed in the mud. He slid it down the ring finger of her left hand then took her face in his hands and kissed her. She put her hands over his. He slid his arms around her and hugged her close. He stroked her hair. She said yes.

***

It felt good to be in her old clothes again. Janice sat in the living room with a pair of designer blue jeans on and a sweater she'd picked up on sale for $80. The Blue Hollow uniform as she'd called those K-mart clothes she'd worn for the last year were sitting in the bottom of a burn barrel or something.

Her aunt and uncle sat quietly enjoying the pie she'd picked up from the bakery on the way home. She still needed to go back to Blue Hollow to close the deal on the bait shop and the diner but she could dress in her normal clothes for that. No one would care that Janice had bought them as short sales after the owners abandoned them-and the payments. Since she knew about them before they hit the market she was able to buy them low and sell to some out of town investors for a tidy sum.

The money she'd made was by no means what she was going to get for the coins, once Renny told her where they were hidden, but it was bringing the balance of her portfolio back up to where she wanted it.

She gazed at the fall colors outside the window of her aunt and uncle's assisted living condo and marveled at the beauty of the trees back dropped with the city skyline. Few things held the beauty of man's creativity like a city sky line on a sunny fall day. She was celebrating her new deals with the only living family she had-and it felt good. Auntie took in a noisy breath and Janice turned to her. Auntie never spoke without a lung full of air.

"Charlie lost his business?" Auntie said.

"Bankrupt." Janice replied

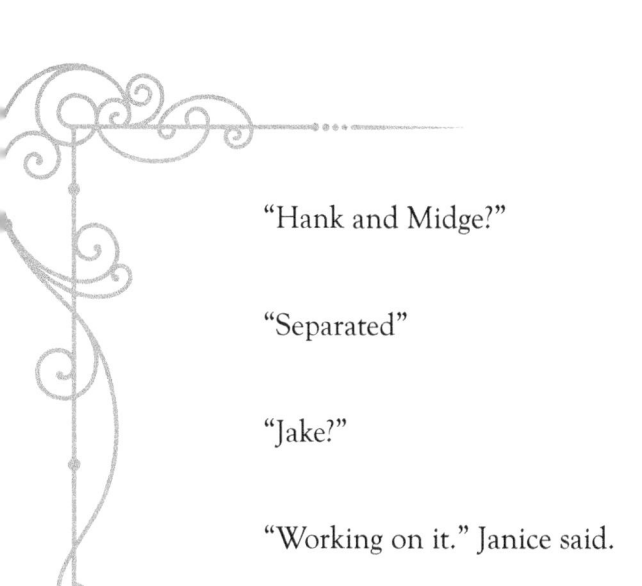

"Hank and Midge?"

"Separated"

"Jake?"

"Working on it." Janice said.

Epilogue

Dreama walked down the aisle arm in arm with her dad. Jake stood at the front of the church looking quite dapper in his black tux. The service began and she watched over Jake's shoulder at the interpreter. Jake had insisted they have one so Dreama's deaf friends could fully participate in the service.

"I, Jake, take you Dreama."

Jake took his right hand and turned her face to him. He let her hands fall and stepped back. He looked over his shoulder to the interpreter then looked back at Dreama. The interpreter walked over behind Dreama. Jake looked at her and began to sign.

"I, Jacob, take you Dreama to be my" he looked up at the interpreter and then continued, "lawfully wedded wife." He signed his complete vows to her. Tears poured down her face. He always thought of her. Always.

"And I, Dreama, take you Jacob to be my lawfully wedded husband." She said. He smiled tenderly as they committed their lives to each other. The over 400 guests who filled the pews of the church didn't matter at all. They were the only two people in the room. It was only her and Jake. That was enough.

The End

Final Thought/Sequels

This book was originally written to be a trilogy. What loose ends were left that could be tied up in a sequel? Even with those few things, did it still feel like the story was complete? Were the characters compelling enough that you wanted to meet them again in another book? Why or Why not?

_____

_____

_____

_____

_____

_____

_____

_____

_____

_____

_____

_____

_____

_____

_____

_____

_____

_____

_____

_____

_____

_____

_____

_____

_____

_____

_____

_____

_____

_____

Synopsis:

In a synopsis you have typically between 1-3 pages to do a bunch of things. You have to:

- Set up the scene
- Introduce the characters
- Tell the main plot points.
- Show the resolution
- And do it in a way that hopefully makes the editor want to read the manuscript.

That can be a daunting task. Thankfully, editors know that and they don't expect the summary to be as exciting as the manuscript itself, but you still need to show you have engaging craft. The example I have here is, again, not an example of everything done right. It is an example of an actual summary. It was done early in my writing career and represents the kind of writing that many editors see. Your goal is to write yours better than mine.

Keeping in mind you only have about 300 words to describe a 60,000 word manuscript, look for ways you'd change this synopsis to better articulate the story and to also get the editors attention.

For added benefit, go through the lessons in this book and find the places where you made changes to the story itself and make those changes to this synopsis. We've included lines on the opposing pages so you can edit on the synopsis and then rewrite next to it.

Finally, we included a few exercises at the end of the synopsis for you to consider for this entry and when you're writing your own. Complete the exercises in a separate notebook, on your hard drive or print out your synopsis and do it next to the workbook exercises to craft a great summary of your work.

Synopsis:

After the death of his father, Jake is forced to return to the town of Blue Hollow with his mom and younger sister. Jake is haunted by an accident in Blue Hollow that killed his girlfriend, Alexa.

Renny, Jake's mom, has brought the family back to Blue Hollow seeking acceptance and to be closer to her brother, Bill Colewick. Her husband, Dale, was an enthusiastic Christ-follower. Renny returns to church hoping for peace but, without Dale's faith to inspire her, the routine of church leaves her empty.

Dreama is also on her way to Blue Hollow but for a very different reason. She has learned that her hearing loss is worsening and soon she'll need to decide whether or not to get a Cochlear Implant [CI]. Dreama has completed her freshman year of college. She is struggling between being a child and being a woman, hearing or Deaf.

Janice, Alexa's aunt, is also back. A shrewd business woman, Janice hopes she can manipulate the relationships she has with long-time residents of Blue Hollow to purchase properties far below market value.

Janice begins to turn individuals against each other. She sows jealousy in Hank's mind. Hank and Midge own a diner in town. Midge's high school beau, Bill Colewick, is a regular at the diner and Janice points out Midge's gives Bill extra attention.

A strong storm blows through the Hollow and during that storm Dreama sees someone watching her house. The next morning while cleaning up debris, Dreama loses her hearing aid. Without a way to make a phone call, Dreama goes to Mr. (Bill) Colewick for help. She finds him dead.

Immediately after this, tensions in Blue Hollow build. Simmering below the surface is the question of Jake's paternity and Renny's fear that her brother told her secret before his death.

The next phase of Janice's plan is ready for execution. She rekindles her relationship with Charlie. She wants revenge on him because he abandoned her 30 years ago, after a miscarriage. She convinces him not to sue Bill Colewick's estate for a large settlement Bill had owed him.

Jake is beginning to have feelings for Dreama but they're colliding with the guilt of Alexa's death. If he loves again it is a betrayal to Alexa. If he doesn't, it is a denial of his feelings. Is it the time to move on?

Renny is increasingly depressed. She makes Jake, and his relationship with Dreama, the focus of her anger. As she cuts off her children and her faith she focuses on her own sins. Memories of a violent rape haunt her.

Dreama still wonders if Bill died of a heart attack or if the person watching her house is really the culprit. This only increases when she finds two intruders searching her house.

Charlie begins to realize that Janice has a dark side. One final encounter with Janice and he knows his heart is no longer in the relationship. He locks his store and leaves town.

Midge too has grown tired with her life in the Hollow. Convinced that Hank's odd behavior is due to a secret affair with Janice, Midge leaves the Hollow.

Jake and Dreama grow closer, but Dreama wonders if he'll accept her for who she is or if he'll try to change her. Jake refers to CI surgery as a way of "fixing deaf people" and she insists he leave.

Hank killed Bill, but it was a complete accident. Hank thought Bill was having a heart attack. He gave Bill nitroglycerine. Bill had a nitrate allergy; the pills killed him.

Dreama has learned to stand up for herself. She hasn't decided on the surgery or not, but she feels confident she can make that decision on her own now. Jake and Dreama reconcile and get engaged.

Janice is visiting with her aunt and uncle, Alexa's parents, and she is sharing with them how she'd exacted revenge on each individual in the hollow. When they get to Jake she says that she's still working on it.

Epilogue: The wedding.

Exercises:

You need to introduce the main characters right at the start. Keeping in mind the character arc, how can you best describe the way the characters start in this book?

_____

_____

_____

_____

_____

_____

_____

_____

What are the key plot points during the course of the story? What is the primary plot? How do all of these things play out in the character arc?

_____

_____

_____

_____

_____

_____

_____

_____

Are there any specific requirements for the publishing house? How can you show that your book meets those requirements?

_____

_____

_____

_____

_____

_____

_____

_____

About The Author

Tiffany Colter is the author of dozens of books, CDs, DVDs, seminars and webinars on topics ranging from writing great novels to business marketing and systems. She also includes personal development books focused on parenting special needs children, reaching your goals during times of trial, and even time management.

As the owner of Writing Career Coach, Tiffany has spent more than 5 years committed to teaching writers "How to make a living at this writing thing." She also teaches businesses, personal developers and trainers how to use words to connect with their target demographic.

Tiffany is the proud mom of 4 girls and is married to her best friend, Chris. They share an old farm house on their hobby farm with 3 large dogs, 8 outside cats, chickens, ducks, and two sheep.

Tiffany is available to speak to groups or to coach individuals. Details are available by contacting Writing Career Coach. www.WritingCareerCoach.com